UNHOLY CITY

ALSO AVAILABLE BY CARRIE SMITH:

Forgotten City

Silent City

UNHOLY CITY

A Claire Codella Mystery

Carrie Smith

CROOKED
LANE

NEW YORK

Copyright © 2017 by Carrie Smith.

Published in the United States by Crooked Lane Books, an imprint of The Quick Brown Fox & Company LLC.

Crooked Lane Books and its logo are trademarks of The Quick Brown Fox & Company LLC.

Library of Congress Catalog-in-Publication data available upon request.

ISBN (hardcover): 978-1-68331-329-8
ISBN (ePub): 978-1-68331-330-4
ISBN (ePDF): 978-1-68331-332-8

Cover design by Andy Ruggirello
Book design by Jennifer Canzone

Printed in the United States.

www.crookedlanebooks.com

Crooked Lane Books
34 West 27th St., 10th Floor
New York, NY 10001

First Edition: November 2017

10 9 8 7 6 5 4 3 2 1

To Cammie and Mattie:
May you always dream

Everyone is a moon, and has a dark side which he never shows to anybody.

—Mark Twain

WEDNESDAY

CHAPTER 1

Anna kicked off her shoes in the spacious foyer of the brownstone that served as St. Paul's rectory. She climbed the stairs and went straight to Christopher's room. He was sleeping soundly, his small body curled on the mattress. She stroked his soft hair and tiptoed out of the room. In the doorway of the master bedroom, she paused while her vision adjusted to the darkness. Todd lay on his side facing his edge of the mattress. He didn't move as she approached the bed. Was he asleep, or simply pretending to be?

She slipped off her slacks, then unbuttoned her blouse and hung it on the doorknob of the closet. In the bathroom, she brushed her teeth and washed her face. Then she crawled into bed. The cool sheets made her shiver. Todd didn't move. She imagined Philip lying beside her instead of Todd. Philip would sense her presence and awaken as soon as she lay next to him. He would stroke her hair and warm her neck with his breath. She would touch his reddish-brown beard, and it would be soft, unlike the scratchy beards of most men. She could almost feel it against her cheek right now as she raised the comforter to her chin and swallowed past the tightness in her throat.

Her mind went to Matthew 5:28: "But I say to you that everyone who looks at a woman with lustful intent has already committed adultery with her in his heart." The same, she supposed, was true of women with "lustful intent." But a thought—a simple fantasy—was hardly *intent*. Intent was the determination to turn a thought into action. Some thoughts—*her* thoughts—were not connected to a plan. They were, in fact, the safeguard *against* a plan. A fantasy could dampen curiosity before it grew into need. She felt no *need*. Her thoughts were innocuous and would pass in due course.

She recalled how her eyes had collided with Philip's across the Blue Lounge at the vestry meeting tonight. Each time their eyes had met, he seemed to be saying, *Stay with me, Anna. Trust me. I told you this would be tough.* Below his reassurance, she'd sensed a deeper message in his eyes as well. A silent confession. *I feel the same thing you do.* Was that true? she wondered now. Did he also feel a little curious? Would he get into his bed tonight and fall soundly to sleep, or would he lie awake and think about her the same way she was thinking about him? Would his body feel half as restless as hers did?

She rolled onto her side, brought her knees up to her chest, and hugged the pillow against her breasts. It was only Wednesday. She wouldn't see him again until Sunday morning—Palm Sunday—when she ascended into the pulpit as she did every week and stared out at him and all the other St. Paul's congregants. But she didn't want to just stare down at him in her vestments. She wanted to be alone with him.

On the high-definition screen in her mind, Anna pictured herself in her office. She imagined Philip stepping through the door and quietly shutting it behind him. She watched him come around her desk and pull her gently to her feet. They stared into each other's eyes, only inches separating them. He was taller than she—her eyes came to the level of his shoulders—and she saw his chest rise and fall as he breathed evenly. They began to breathe as one. Finally she couldn't stand the space between them anymore, and she rested her head on his chest. He wrapped his arms around her waist and pulled her against his body. *I'm willing to pay the price for this*, she heard him whisper. And then he lifted her chin and kissed her mouth, and both of their bodies were alive with the same unholy desire.

Anna couldn't lie still in the bed any longer. She sat up, threw back the comforter, and swung her legs out. It was just a fantasy, she thought. Why not follow it to its conclusion? She tiptoed into the bathroom, shut the door, and locked it. Standing in the dim light, her fingers found the wetness between her legs. She closed her eyes, and then she was kissing Philip again, moving with him in a slow dance of desire until she had to hold her breath to silence the first throb of an orgasm that seemed to splinter every bone in her body.

She exhaled, bending like the branch of a shattered tree. Her front teeth had clenched down hard on her lower lip, but she didn't mind the pain. Urgency drained from her body and was replaced by calm. She stared at her dim reflection in the medicine chest mirror and waited for her breathing to slow.

Then she walked over to the toilet and gave it a flush—just in case Todd was awake. As she washed her hands and dried them, she found herself mouthing the prayer she whispered during the ritual handwashing on the altar at St. Paul's before Holy Communion every Sunday: *Lord, wash away my iniquity; cleanse me from my sin.* But she hadn't sinned. She knew the boundaries and standards she must uphold. She felt no lustful *intent*. She took one last deep breath and returned to bed.

CHAPTER 2

Rose Bartruff sighed when she left the parish house and hit the warm spring air. Why had she let Philip Graves talk her into joining the vestry? This contentious little group of church leaders was worse than a Manhattan co-op board. Tonight's business could have been dispensed with in an hour if the committee members didn't like to hear themselves talk so much. She was almost glad when her babysitter called at ten o'clock to say that her daughter had flushed her asthma inhaler down the toilet. She would have been happy for any excuse to escape that meeting for a while.

Rose had only joined St. Paul's in the hopes of getting to know some nice men. Upper West Side Episcopalians, she'd assumed, wouldn't be all that pious. She had envisioned a spiritual but not very religious group of liberal Democrats who pursued social justice by day and enjoyed their alcohol at night. That had sounded more her speed than Match.com. But so far, she had met no available men, and she was spending way too much time with bombastic vestry members who argued endlessly over stewardship, cemetery improvements, and whether to sell the church's air rights.

She walked down the parish house steps to head home but paused on the stone path that led to the sidewalk beyond the gate. St. Paul's knew how to exploit individual talents for the collective good. While Rose hadn't met the perfect widower in his forties, she had been appointed guardian of the church garden, and it, along with the soothing voices of the choir each Sunday, kept her coming back. She loved this modest plot of land more than any of the outdoor spaces she had designed for wealthy clients with private rooftops high above Manhattan. The little herb garden on the south side of the church could be seen and enjoyed by everyone in the neighborhood, and she had big plans for it.

She decided to check on the bed of Moroccan mint she'd planted last month. She turned right and followed a path that ran along the limestone wall of the parish house. The Romanesque architecture reminded Rose of a medieval castle, and whenever she walked here alone, she sensed the confluence of past and present. The church archives said that two hundred years ago, this Manhattan Valley neighborhood had been a vast stretch of farmland known as Bloomingdale. Wealthy city dwellers from the southern tip of Manhattan had spent their summers on estates overlooking the Hudson River, and those estate owners had built and worshipped at St. Paul's. Who, she wondered now, had tended her garden back then?

Rose reached the southwest corner of the church and paused to breathe in the fragrant night air. Her Moroccan mint was thriving. She could smell it from here. She turned right again and followed the west wall of the building. The lights over the parish house entrance did not reach around this bend, but she knew her way and advanced confidently until her left foot caught under something on the path and her upper body catapulted forward. She instinctively raised her arms in front of her face and braced for bone-breaking impact, but she did not slam down on stone. Instead, her elbows thudded into something solid yet soft. A bag of dirt left by one of the volunteer gardeners was her first thought.

She groped around. No, it wasn't a plastic or burlap bag of topsoil. Her fingers recognized the feel of smooth fabric. As she widened her sphere of tactile exploration, the fabric gave way to the unmistakable texture of skin, and she realized that her hand had followed a sleeve and was now touching another human hand.

Adrenaline surged through her chest, and her racing heart throbbed against her sternum. She scrambled to her feet and stepped back. Her eyes had adjusted to the darkness enough that she could now recognize the dim outline of someone on the ground. Her mind flashed to her husband, Mark, who had collapsed on the kitchen floor of their apartment two years ago, and her daughter, Lily, crying, "Mommy, what's wrong with Daddy?" How would she ever forget that scene? She turned away from that memory and this body and ran as fast as she could back to the parish house.

Inside, she bypassed the vacant Community Room and rushed to the coatrack across from the Blue Lounge where Susan Bentley, the only doctor on the vestry, was speaking with Roger Sturgis. "Come with me," she said, out of breath. "Hurry!"

"What's wrong, Rose?" asked Susan.

Rose couldn't find the words to explain. "Just come with me," she said.

Susan and Roger followed her outside, and Rose led them to the side of the church. "There, on the path." She pointed. "It's a—a body."

Susan kneeled on the hard stones. "I need light."

Roger flicked on his iPhone flashlight and aimed it at the figure in front of them. A man—Rose assumed it was a man from the size of his hands, the cut of his suit, and the style of his black loafers—lay with his back to them.

Susan said, "Jesus Christ. Roger, call an ambulance. Call the police. *Now.*"

Roger managed to hold his small flashlight beam steadily on the body while he dialed 9-1-1 and told the operator to send an ambulance and the police to St. Paul's. As he calmly recited the church address, Rose watched Susan lift the man's limp right arm. "There's no pulse," she said. Then she reached inside his sleeve. "But his skin is still warm to the touch. Tell them he's in cardiac arrest, Roger. They need to get here fast."

"Who is it?" asked Rose. "Can you see who it is?"

Susan didn't answer.

"Is he alive?"

Susan still didn't answer, and Rose realized that she needed to be quiet and let the doctor work. Thank God Susan was a doctor, she thought, and thank God she hadn't already gone home. With one hand gripping the man's shoulder and the other curled around his thigh, Susan pulled hard on the inert body to flip him onto his back. Roger bent down and aimed his small beam of light onto the face of Philip Graves, and all three of them gasped.

One side of Philip's head was bloody, Rose saw. His face was pale, and his lips were bluish. Rose gave voice to the words she imagined they were all thinking. "Oh, my God!"

Rose watched as Susan turned to Roger. She saw Roger's stunned expression. Then Susan looked at her. "Rose, listen to me," she said sternly. "We need the defibrillator. It's in the Community Room."

"By the passage to the kitchen," added Roger.

"Go get it now, Rose. Hurry," Susan ordered as she turned from Rose's gaze and focused on Philip Graves's still body—her patient.

CHAPTER 3

When Rose returned, Roger saw that Peter Linton and Vivian Wakefield had followed her out. He ignored them as he took the defibrillator from Rose and set it on the ground next to Susan.

"What's happened to him?" Peter Linton demanded in his tight lawyerly tone that always grated on Roger.

Roger stared at the bald, thick-waisted man but offered no answer.

"Is that blood on his head? Is he okay, Roger?" Vivian Wakefield's smooth brown skin blended with the night, but he could tell from her voice that the junior churchwarden wore an expression of alarm. He watched as she pressed her palms together in front of her face in a pose of prayer. Why, he wondered with irritation, did people default to magical thinking when there were *real* things to be done?

He turned to Susan. "Tell me what to do."

"Open the lid," she instructed as she performed CPR. "A voice will guide you."

Roger lifted the lid on the bright-yellow defibrillation unit, but no voice broke the silence.

Susan looked over. "Something's wrong. Do you see the green bars on the battery power?"

"No. There's just one bar, and it's red." Roger slammed the lid back down. "Jesus Christ. This thing isn't charged!"

Peter Linton edged closer. "Are you serious? That's a lawsuit waiting to happen."

Roger glared over his shoulder. "Shut the fuck up, Peter!" How many times had he wanted to say that to Linton earlier tonight?

Vivian Wakefield's audible intake of breath told him he had offended her. He turned back to Susan. "You want me to take over for a while?"

"No, I'm fine. I can do this."

And then, for at least three more agonizingly long minutes, no one spoke. They waited and watched as Susan continued to breathe into the mouth and pump the chest. Roger's own ribcage hurt just watching her strong hands press against the torso. It was obvious to him—and surely must be to her too, he thought—that her efforts were futile.

Finally a siren mercifully severed the tense silence. Roger sighed with relief. "I'll go show them the way."

When he reached the front gate, the paramedics were already hauling equipment out of their truck, and an NYPD squad car was rolling up beside it. "What the fuck took you so long?"

Neither EMT acknowledged his question. They probably ignored the same question everywhere they went, he thought. Anybody who read the local news knew EMT response times in this city didn't set any speed records. Roger turned to the cops getting out of their car. He'd been a platoon leader during Desert Shield and Desert Storm, and he knew which one was the sergeant. "We'll need some light back there," he said.

The sergeant looked over at the younger patrolman, who went to the squad car trunk. Roger led the EMTs and the sergeant through the dark garden until the patrolman's powerful flashlight beam caught up with them. When they reached the back of the parish house, the EMTs knelt beside the body across from Susan Bentley. "His airways are clear. Bag him," said Susan, and she continued CPR while one EMT unzipped a defibrillator and took scissors out of a pouch and the other sealed the ventilation mask over Philip Graves's nose and mouth.

The EMT preparing for defibrillation worked quietly and efficiently, Roger noted. He was cutting through the shirt, shaving patches of the hairy chest, positioning white adhesive pads on the shaved skin, and waiting for the defibrillator to analyze the heartbeat. When the digital voice said, "Shock advised," Susan ceased her lifesaving efforts, and the EMT shouted, "Clear!"

The charge sent a spasm through the body. A few seconds later, the defibrillator voice said, "It is safe to touch the patient." The EMT felt for a pulse, shook his head, and the other EMT resumed ventilation and compression with Susan's help.

They gave the body a second shock. Rose Bartruff, Roger observed, was watching the scene with wide, unblinking eyes. Vivian Wakefield's lips were moving—she was praying, he supposed—and Peter Linton had stepped back from the bright flashlight beam and was texting rapidly with both thumbs despite the disapproving glare of the police sergeant. Susan Bentley turned up the collar of her thin blazer and shoved her hands in the pockets as if this cool but pleasant April night was subzero. Roger peeled off his tweed jacket and threw it over her shoulders as the EMTs attempted to revive the body with a third shock. When the shock had been administered and the pulse checked, Roger heard the taller, thicker EMT announce the verdict. "We're done. Call it in."

"Well, that's that," Susan whispered just loud enough for him to hear.

"You did all you could, Susan." He patted her shoulder.

"Thanks, Roger." She removed her hands from her pockets and clasped his right one—in gratitude for his assistance, he supposed—and they stared at each other in silence.

Then the NYPD sergeant stepped forward. "Who found him?"

"I did," acknowledged Rose. "After the vestry meeting. I came back here to check on the mint and—"

"The *what?*"

"The mint. This is an herb garden. I was walking, and I tripped over him in the pathway."

"And he was dead?"

"I don't know," Rose answered.

Rose was such a tentative person, thought Roger as he read the sergeant's name under his shield. Zamora.

"Rose rushed back inside and got me." Susan came to Rose's rescue. "I'm a doctor. Roger and I"—she pointed to him—"came out here with Rose. Philip—he's our senior church warden—was lying here on his side. He had no pulse. We called nine-one-one, and I started CPR immediately."

"And disturbed whatever evidence was here," noted Zamora in a tone that struck Roger as accusatory.

"I was trying to save a life," Susan responded curtly.

Good for her, Roger thought as he slid his right hand into his pants pocket. She was no pushover.

Then Zamora panned the sets of eyes that formed a half circle around the lifeless body. "All right, listen carefully," he said in a crowd-control voice that wasn't necessary. "You're all going to follow Officer O'Donnell into the church." He pointed to his junior partner. "Do not talk. Do not make any phone calls or send any texts. Is that understood?" He gave Peter Linton a hard look. Then he turned to the EMTs. "This body stays right where it is until we get a detective and crime scene unit here. Step back from it now."

CHAPTER 4

Detective Claire Codella reached for her phone. But it wasn't *her* ringtone. The sound she heard was coming from Detective Brian Haggerty's cell phone on the other side of her bed. She shook his shoulder. It wasn't that late—only eleven fifteen—but sex had sent him into a deep sleep, while she lay awake as usual. She shook him again, spoke his name, and finally he groaned, rolled over, and grabbed the phone. "Yeah?"

Codella sat up in the darkness.

"Where?" he asked.

She turned on her bedside lamp.

"How?"

She watched his blond eyebrows furrow, recognizing his look of intense concentration. She knew what it meant, and she wanted to snatch the phone out of his hands. No detective wanted to sit by while another detective caught a case—even if that detective shared your bed.

Haggerty ran his fingers through his curly blond hair. "I'll be there in five minutes." He ended the call, got up, and threw on the jeans and shirt he'd stripped off an hour ago. "There's a body at St. Paul's Episcopal," he told her as he grabbed his shield from the top of her dresser and stuck his arms through his shoulder holster. "Someone cracked him over the head." He grabbed his blazer off her closet doorknob.

Codella pulled on shorts and a T-shirt as he pushed his feet into loafers. She followed him to the front door. She could feel his barely contained excitement. He was a mass set into motion by the unnatural force of death, and now the inertia of a nonstop investigation would keep him in that motion for days, maybe weeks. He opened the door, paused, and turned back to kiss her. "Get some sleep for both of us."

He was trying to be considerate, she thought, but all she felt was envy and irritation. The last body she'd caught had turned out to be an overdosed heroin addict lying under a bench in Strauss Park, and there had been nothing for her to do except wait for the medical examiner and complete a shitload of paper work. "Be careful," she told Haggerty, doing her best to conceal her disappointment until he disappeared down the fire stairs.

She closed the door and went to her living room window. *She* wanted to be down there on Broadway flagging a taxi and speeding to a crime scene. Nothing compared to an all-encompassing homicide investigation. To Codella, it was the ultimate form of self-expression, a pursuit that required the use of all your senses, stamina, and mental powers. You pieced together the solution to a crime like a master builder. Your bricks were forensic evidence; careful chronologies of dates, times, and places; the confirming and contradictory accounts of witnesses; suspects' unintended slips of the tongue. And you arranged these blocks with the stiff mortar of analytical reasoning to erect a solid, impenetrable wall of truth that could withstand the forces of dispute and denial.

Codella hadn't realized how much her work defined her until it was taken away sixteen months ago. That was the day she told her boss, Lieutenant Dennis McGowan, she'd been diagnosed with lymphoma and had to check in to the hospital the next day to begin her treatments.

"Jesus, Codella. So fast? That doesn't sound good."

"It's not," she'd said, unsurprised by his lack of tact. She hadn't expected any sympathy from him—she'd just been promoted to his Manhattan North homicide squad, and he hadn't wanted her there in the first place.

"How long will you be out?"

"I don't know." *Maybe forever,* she was thinking.

He didn't visit her in the hospital. He didn't send a card or flowers. And when she was ready to return to work after six cycles of grueling in-hospital chemotherapy and weeks of rehab, he made her submit to a fitness-for-duty psychological exam in addition to her physical.

"Why?" she asked him as casually as she could because he was one of those insecure and volatile men who didn't like to be questioned, especially by women. "I had cancer. I didn't use excessive force or try to throw myself off the George Washington Bridge."

He crossed his arms over his thick chest and smirked. "You've been out ten months. You want back in, then you sign the informed consent and show up for the exam. That's the deal, Codella."

So she'd shown up, signed the papers, and answered the questions on the Minnesota Multiphasic Personality Inventory-2 as honestly as she could. And she was careful not to display defensiveness during her one-on-one interview with a psychologist who seemed determined to make her acknowledge her vulnerabilities.

"You've got an impressive clearance record, Detective," he began benignly enough.

His short black hair was meticulously gelled into place, and she sensed that his conversation would be equally stiff. "Thank you."

"What do you attribute that to?"

She shrugged. "Persistence, I suppose. Good listening skills. And a little bit of luck, of course."

"You're a classic overachiever?"

The label, she knew, was intended to subtly deflate her accomplishments, but she kept her irritation to herself. "All good detectives are overachievers. We don't like to give up without getting the bad guy." She smiled.

He maintained a stingy poker face. "And you think you still have the mental fortitude for the job?"

"I wouldn't come back if I didn't." She looked him in the eyes. "I know what's at stake."

"But cancer has lasting effects on people."

"That's true," she acknowledged.

"How has it affected you?"

"Well, for one thing, I have a permanent case of dry mouth. Chemo has a funny way of destroying your salivary glands. I don't recommend it."

He didn't appear amused. "You think that's the only way it's affected you?"

"No. There's the nerve damage too. The tips of my fingers and toes tingle pretty much all the time now." She held up her right hand. "But don't worry, I passed my pistol qualification." In the silence, she studied the single painting on the wall of his windowless office. It was the kind of cityscape she'd have expected to see in a guest room at a midtown Marriott, a predictable Manhattan skyline that evoked none of her deep feelings about the city she had fled to at the age of eighteen. She willed herself to be as two-dimensional as that painting. She knew very well the psychologist didn't want to hear about her peripheral neuropathy. He wanted to catch her in a damaging admission of psychological vulnerability. But she had no intention of sharing the thoughts that kept her awake at night after Haggerty was soundly sleeping. Was her lymphoma going to return? Would she ever have to endure another chemo port implanted in her chest? Would she even be alive in another year or two? "I'm fit physically and emotionally," she assured him. "I love my job and I want to get back to it."

He tapped his pen against the thick manila folder on his desk. "I read your background, Detective. Your father murdered a woman when you were a child—just ten years old—and you saw it happen." Then he waited for her reaction.

"That's right," she said matter-of-factly. "Her name was Joanie Carlucci, and my father swung a baseball bat into her body while I watched through a window." Why was this guy bringing up ancient history? Because he'd failed to scare up her emotions about cancer? Had McGowan sent her here knowing full well that this psychologist would do everything in his power to provoke her to anger, guilt, or grief and pronounce her unstable? She recalled the Bible quote a Catholic priest had recited to her when she was thirteen, living with yet another set of foster parents and still having nightmares about the murder: "A child shall not suffer for the iniquity of a parent." What bullshit that was. She'd suffered in so many ways for her father's violent act, and this guy was trying to make her suffer even more, but she wouldn't let him win.

"People describe you as pretty intense on the job."

"I call it hardworking."

"Do you think it's because of what your father did?"

"You mean am I compensating for his crime? Does it matter, so long as I get the job done?"

"Physical and emotional traumas can impact an officer's decision making."

Codella pointed to the manila folder on his desk. "You have fourteen years of my decision making right there," she said. "I don't think my father's crime has affected my ability to put criminals behind bars."

The conversation continued as a long fencing match in which she parried his repeated advances and carefully avoided direct counter attacks that would fuel his hostility. She knew her only option was to wait him out, let him reach the point where he'd exhausted all his energy, used up all his strategies, and finally accepted the fact that their match would end in a draw.

Now Codella turned away from her living room window and walked back to her bedroom. Of course she was compensating for her father's crime. She had to see past Joanie Carlucci's battered body every time she arrived at a new crime scene. But that was no reason to label her unfit. The fact that she'd lived with a homicidal monster and witnessed the brutal death of a terrorized woman was a constant reminder that her work mattered. She wasn't just a really good cop. She was a good cop on a personal mission to right wrongs and fight for those who'd been unfairly silenced.

But tonight wasn't her night to right any wrongs. It was Haggerty's night. So she got back into bed, closed her eyes, and finally sank into sleep.

CHAPTER 5

When Haggerty got to the church, Sergeant Zamora was standing at the south gate, his arms crossed and an everything's-secured-here expression on his face. Haggerty didn't doubt that the sergeant had done his job. Zamora could be irritatingly no nonsense, but he certainly knew how to follow protocol at a crime scene. "I've got five church people in a room, Detective, and Officer O'Donnell is making sure they don't talk to each other."

Haggerty nodded. "What about the body?"

"Around there." The sergeant pointed. "Looks like somebody cracked his skull open."

"Did you find a weapon?"

Zamora shook his head. "Didn't want to disturb the crime scene any more than it already was. I called CSU and the ME. And more uniforms, of course. They should be here within minutes."

"Good. Any first impressions?"

Zamora scratched the back of his neck. "I don't know. When I got here, all those church people were swarmed around the body. One's a doctor. She was trying to revive him before EMS arrived."

"Anybody look suspicious to you?"

"Hard to say. One guy—short and bald—started texting while the EMTs worked. He didn't seem too concerned about what was happening."

"What's his name?"

Zamora removed the notepad tucked in his belt. "Linton. Peter Linton."

"Anyone else?"

"I'll let you be the judge, Detective. It's a pretty odd group." He read off names and descriptions of the vestry members sitting in the church Community Room. Haggerty listened closely. Long ago, he'd discovered he had an uncanny ability to store and recall information without writing it down. Even Claire was impressed by his memory.

Zamora was looking over his shoulder now. "CSU is here."

Haggerty turned and saw the familiar face of Adam Banks, the lead CSU investigator. Banks's team emerged from their van and hauled equipment out of the rear as Banks approached Haggerty. "Show me the way." He grinned as if they were setting off on an adventure.

CHAPTER 6

Anna opened her eyes and sat up. Flashing lights pulsed across the bedroom ceiling. She climbed out of bed and rushed to the window. On the street below, an ambulance, three police cars, and a police van were parked in front of the church. She looked at the clock. It was eleven twenty-five. She had only been home for half an hour. What could have happened in that time?

Todd didn't stir as she threw on clothes and dialed her thoughts back to just before she'd left the church. She'd broken away from Susan Bentley; waved to Rose, who was putting on her coat; and reminded Roger and Peter to lock the parish house doors. But she hadn't seen Vivian. Had something happened to her? The junior churchwarden was, Anna knew, much older than she let on. What if she had collapsed?

Anna hurried downstairs. She found her sneakers in the foyer. But no, she thought as she fumbled with the laces. Three police cars and a van didn't show up just because someone was ill. Something more serious must have happened—a break-in, perhaps, or vandalism, or an incident in the church-run homeless shelter.

She opened the solid front door and closed it behind her. The ten men who slept in the church basement on Monday through Thursday nights had all graduated from substance abuse programs and attended a work-training program during the day. In the three years the shelter had operated, there'd never been an incident. Nevertheless, some parishioners—including Peter Linton on the vestry—didn't like social activism right in their basement, and if a guest had gone berserk, the St. Paul's Weekday Beds program would be in jeopardy.

She almost tripped as she flew down the brownstone front steps. As she ran the hundred feet to the south entrance gate, she heard Peter Linton's voice in her head. *Those people need to be in city-run shelters with guards in place.* Peter listened to her sermons every Sunday, but he still put pragmatism above compassion.

A police officer stood at the gate. "What's going on here?" she asked him.

"Police investigation," he said.

"What sort of investigation?"

The officer was a few inches shorter than she was. She peered over his shoulder at bright light flooding the area at the back of the garden between the parish house and the rectory. "I'm sorry, ma'am. You need to move on."

"But this is my church."

"And you can come back on Sunday."

"You don't understand," she persisted. "I'm the *rector* here. If something has happened, I need to know. Who's in charge? I want to speak to that person right now."

The officer made no move.

"*Now*," she repeated. "I run this church. I have a right to know what's happening here."

Anna didn't know if that was true or not, but the officer turned and walked toward the parish house steps. She watched him point to her as he spoke to an older uniformed officer. That officer headed toward the lights in the back of the garden, and the officer she had spoken to returned to the gate. "Wait here," he said.

She pulled up the collar of her jacket and stuffed her clenched fists into her pockets. The roof lights on the three squad cars flashed at different intervals like strobe lights in a fun house. She stared at the lights until a man in jeans and a blazer came to the gate and stopped beside the uniformed officer. The man was tall and thin with wavy blond hair combed back across his scalp. His eyes were blue. His firm jaw hadn't been shaved in a few days, and the button-down shirt under his blazer was rumpled. "Detective Haggerty," he said. "And you are?"

"Anna Brookes. Mother Brookes." She saw the slight rise of his eyebrows. Was he one of those dogmatic Irish Catholics who objected to women having any church role other than nun? "*Rector* Brookes, if you prefer," she said. "This is my parish. What's happening here?"

"A man has died."

"What man?"

"His name is Philip Graves."

Anna shook her head. "Excuse me? What did you say?"

"Philip Graves," he repeated. "Did you know him?"

Anna was aware that her hands had come out of her pockets, that they were now pressing into her temples. "Did I *know* him? What are you saying? There has to be some mistake."

"I don't think so." The detective spoke gently. "His body has been identified by five church members."

"His *body*?" Anna attempted to push herself between the two men, but they each grabbed an arm and pulled her back.

"I need to see him," she insisted.

"Let's go inside," said the detective.

"*No.*" She returned her hands to her head as she swallowed past a constriction in her throat. She bit her lower lip to silence a cry of anguish the same way she had silenced her pleasure half an hour ago. "I want to see him."

"I'm sorry. You can't. It's a crime scene."

"A *crime* scene? Are you saying he was murdered?"

"No more questions, Rector. Let's go inside with the others."

She clutched his arm. "Please. This is my congregation, Detective. Philip was the senior warden of my church. At least let me pray for him."

The detective stared at her fingers around his arm. "Did you not hear me? It's the scene of a crime."

"Yes, I heard you." Anna let go of his arm. "But it's also the scene of a soul leaving a body." She raised her chin defiantly and held his gaze. Whether he was a good Irish Catholic boy or a lapsed one, he wouldn't deny her the right to bless a soul, would he? "I realize you have a job to do, Detective, but so do I."

She heard him sigh. Then he shrugged in a way that told her he'd relented. He led her in the direction of the lights beaming down at the ground from tripods. Twenty feet in front of the lights, he stopped her, signaled to a police officer, and said, "Get her some booties." They were produced, and the detective told her to put them on. Only then did she notice that he was wearing booties too. She stretched the elastic over her sneakers. Then he led her closer to the lights. When they were ten feet away, he placed a hand on her bicep. "That's as far as you go, Rector. Say your prayer from here. I'll wait."

He stepped back, but she felt his eyes pressing into her shoulder blades. She breathed deeply and exhaled him from her consciousness. And then she looked at Philip's face, bluish under the stark white light. Her eyes caressed the blood-matted beard that her fingers had longed to touch. She stared at the strong hands she'd so desperately wanted to envelop her. She regarded his open mouth that would never press against her lips. She recalled the pleasure of his phantom touch and wished she could lie next to him and feel his real flesh against hers just once. Instead, she kneeled on the stones, folded her hands, lowered her head, and allowed all her unacknowledged intent to streak her face in salty shame. She was not mourning the death of a man, she realized, so much as the death of her own unfulfilled desire. God had punished her, and he had saved her from herself.

She opened her mouth to whisper a prayer for the dead, but the words that came to her lips were a prayer of penance: "May God our Father forgive us our sins and bring us to the fellowship of his table with his saints forever."

CHAPTER 7

Haggerty surveyed the spacious St. Paul's Community Room from the doorway. Ceiling-high windows on the left wall—the south side—faced the street where the squad cars and CSU van were parked. Along the opposite wall, three narrow rectangular tables, set end to end and covered by vinyl tablecloths, formed a makeshift serving line. Haggerty stared at the commercial coffee-maker on the far table and visualized Sunday worshippers filling cups with caffeine to rouse themselves from soporific liturgies.

Between the serving line and the windows were ten round restaurant-style tables. Sergeant Zamora had seated each of the five vestry members at a different table, and now the visibly shocked rector, Anna Brookes, sat down at a sixth.

Haggerty stared at the faces and matched them to the details Sergeant Zamora had given him before the rector's arrival. The blonde woman against the back wall, Susan Bentley, was the doctor who'd performed CPR for a full five minutes. The fact that she looked exhausted hardly surprised him. He'd performed CPR a few times himself and knew how strenuous it was.

The black-haired man sitting by the windows was Roger Sturgis. He was staring intently at the doctor. One of his hands was in his pocket while the thumb and index finger of his other hand smoothed the outer edges of his thick, wide moustache in a slow repetitive motion. He wore a pale-yellow Oxford shirt with the collar open, and his tweed jacket was stylish in a retro sort of way.

The black woman seated near the door—Vivian Wakefield, the junior churchwarden—had a perfectly erect posture, high cheekbones, and a flawless complexion. Her intricately braided salt-and-pepper hair was pulled back tightly and arranged into a bun at the back of her head. When she noticed him staring at her, she smiled. She alone among the gathered vestry members looked relaxed and patient.

In the center of the room, the slim brunette who had tripped over the body—Rose Bartruff, the church gardener—was checking her watch, and one table over from her, Peter Linton, the bald man who, according to Zamora, had texted during the resuscitation efforts, was clicking his pen over and over. Who had he been texting? What had he said? And how willing would he be to share that message when he was questioned?

Were these seemingly upright church members merely innocent bystanders, or were they more? Haggerty had been here only minutes, but that was long enough to know this was not a simple death scene he could process with precinct resources only. If a random crazy guy had cracked open Graves's skull, where was the weapon? If robbery was the motive, why was Graves's wallet still in his pocket? And there was the failed defibrillator Zamora had told him about. Why hadn't it worked? Was that just a coincidence? Everyone sitting in this Community Room was a potential witness and suspect. Every one of them had to be questioned tonight.

He closed his fingers around the phone in his pocket, but before he could pull it out, Officer Milan Kovac appeared at the other end of the corridor. Haggerty turned and walked toward him. Kovac had a bristly crew cut and spoke in a low voice. "Did you know there's a homeless shelter in this church—on the north side of the building?"

"No. Who's in there?"

"Four church volunteers and ten homeless men," said the earnest officer. "A van dropped them off at eight thirty. Supposedly they were all signed in by eight forty-five, and no one left the shelter after that. We're taking statements now."

Haggerty rubbed his fingers across the stubble on his chin. "Okay. Good work. We'll deal with them later. Go help Sergeant Zamora search the rest of the building."

Haggerty pulled the phone out of his pocket, but Officer O'Donnell's voice from inside the Community Room sounded urgent. "I said sit *down*, sir."

Haggerty peered into the room and saw the pen-clicking bald man standing with his hands on his hips. "What's the matter?" the man was saying now. "I can't even stretch my legs?"

Haggerty moved quickly to O'Donnell's side. "What's the problem here?"

"The problem," snapped the angry man, "is that it's almost midnight, Detective. I need to get home."

"You're Mr. Linton?" Haggerty asked.

"That's right. Peter Linton."

"Well, Mr. Linton, I'd appreciate a little patience, and we'll get you out of here as soon as possible."

"And do we have to be treated like prisoners while we're here?" Linton glared at O'Donnell, who had been instructed not to let anyone use their phones or leave the room unescorted.

In Haggerty's early days on the force, a man like Peter Linton might have ignited his own short fuse. But now all he said was, "I'm sorry, but you see, when people send text messages at the scene of a crime, it raises concerns for us."

"What are you implying?"

Haggerty raised his eyebrows in a don't-play-innocent expression.

"Relax, Peter," Roger Sturgis called out.

"Don't patronize me, Roger," Linton turned and snapped.

Haggerty held up his hands and faced the others in the room. "Look, I apologize for the inconvenience. I know this is stressful, but you may be stuck here for a while. Does someone want to make coffee?"

Rose Bartruff raised her hand. "I'll do it." She stood and disappeared through a door behind the serving line.

"Great, now it's coffee hour," grumbled Peter Linton. He combed his fingers through his hair over and over. He was a twitchy man. "I've got a trial starting first thing tomorrow," he announced.

"We've all got things to do in the morning, Peter," Susan Bentley responded with a dash of disgust in her voice. "But someone we knew and cared about has just died." The collar of her tan blazer was turned up, and she seemed to be shivering.

Peter Linton gave her a harsh look and turned away.

Anna Brookes suddenly awakened from her apparent shock. "I think we should all join together in a prayer." She stood, held out her hands, and waited for others to rise and form a circle.

Vivian Wakefield rose calmly from her seat and came to stand beside the rector as if in solidarity. Susan Bentley and Roger Sturgis pushed out their chairs like obedient if not enthusiastic disciples. Peter Linton, already on his feet, sighed loudly as he shuffled over. The rector bowed her head, but Wakefield touched her shoulder. "Wait, Mother Anna. Rose is still in the kitchen. Rose will want to pray too."

Haggerty saw the rector look at him.

"I'll get her," he offered and walked through the same door the gardener had used. He found her in an impressively outfitted commercial kitchen standing in front of a stainless kettle over a gas flame. Her cell phone was pressed to her ear.

When she saw him, she whispered, "I have to go," and hung up.

Haggerty didn't hide his annoyance. "Who was that?"

"My babysitter." Then her eyes filled with tears. "My daughter, Lily, has asthma. She flushed her inhaler down the toilet by accident tonight. I was just checking to make sure the pharmacy delivered the new one." She held out her phone to him. "Here, call her back if you don't believe me."

She met his gaze with a mother's defiance that turned his irritation into grudging sympathy. He pushed the phone back to her even as he told himself, *Claire wouldn't take her at her word. Claire would make that call.* "You're wanted in there."

He followed her back to the Community Room and watched her stand between Roger Sturgis and Susan Bentley. Then the rector closed her eyes. As he ducked quietly out of the room, he heard her begin, "Merciful God, who brought us to birth and in whose arms we die."

The words carried him back to all the masses he'd attended at Queen of Peace Catholic Church on Staten Island when he was a boy. They also brought to mind the battle scenes between his parents every Sunday morning when his mother tried to awaken his father after a night on the bottle. Usually, she failed. "Leave me the fuck alone," he'd grumble until she gave up and dragged Haggerty and his younger brother to mass by herself, and then she'd tell anyone who asked that their father was home in bed with a virus or a migraine headache or a flare-up of sciatica.

"In our grief and shock at Philip's sudden and violent death," he heard the rector saying, "contain and comfort us that we may not be overwhelmed by our great loss." *She* was the only one who seemed overwhelmed by the great loss, he thought. She was the only one who had shed a tear for the victim since he'd arrived.

He had to make the call, he told himself firmly, but something—the pull of his early Catholicism?—compelled him to wait till the end of the prayer. "Grant to Philip eternal rest," he heard the rector say with a fervor that struck him as authentic and touching. "Let light perpetual shine upon him. May his soul and the souls of all the departed, through the mercy of God, rest in peace. Amen."

He turned to see Sergeant Zamora standing beside a woman with blue hair shaved close on one side. Her black-framed glasses, baggy T-shirt, black leggings, and laced high-heel boots made her look more hipster than Upper West Side Episcopalian. As he moved closer, he saw that her fingernails were painted midnight blue and she was carrying a stack of sheet music.

"Found her upstairs playing the piano," said Zamora.

"My name is Stephanie Lund. I'm the interim choir director. I've been practicing a piece for this Sunday. What's going on?"

Things just got more and more complicated here, Haggerty thought. "Put her with the others." He walked out of the building and down the steps as he dialed.

CHAPTER 8

This time the ringtone was hers. She reached through the darkness toward the lighted dial of her iPhone. "Codella."

"Got one for you, Detective," said the dull voice of the desk sergeant at Manhattan North.

Codella sat up and waited.

"Hope you're the religious type. You're going to church."

She switched on her lamp. "What church?" But she knew the answer before it came.

"St. Paul's Episcopal. Detective Haggerty from the one-seven-one is on the scene. Needs homicide support right away. Grab your rosary beads."

She ignored his self-satisfied laughter. *Episcopalians don't count rosary beads, you idiot*, she wanted to say. "Tell him I'll be there in ten minutes."

She ended the call. The clothes she'd worn earlier were lying in a heap on the floor. She threw them on, clipped her shield to her belt, and worked her arms through the straps of her shoulder holster. She stuck her backup gun in its IWB holster inside the back waistband of her slacks and found her leather jacket hanging over a chair in the kitchen. Then she was out the door.

As she stood on the uptown side of Broadway flagging down a cab, she pulled out her phone to speed-dial Haggerty. But as a yellow taxi veered to the curb, she reconsidered. Had he called Manhattan North *because* he knew she was on duty—because he *wanted* her in on his catch of the night—or had he made the call reluctantly because the circumstances left him no choice? As a precinct detective, he knew as well as she did what making that call meant. He had mobilized Manhattan North's central homicide unit. He had handed over control of the case from the one-seven-one to her.

She climbed in the taxi, tucked her phone away again, and stared out the window at the blur of darkened storefronts as the taxi flew uptown. For seven years, she and Haggerty had been partners and best friends at the one-seven-one. Their desks sat side by side in the detectives' squad room, and almost every morning Haggerty arrived with a large latte for her. As a team, they had the most impressive case clearance stats on the Upper West Side. But she had wanted to solve murders, and when their commanding officer at that time, Captain Reilly, let her do some research on a file Manhattan North had set aside, she ended up identifying the killer of Elaine DeFarge, a Columbia Presbyterian nurse who'd disappeared after her shift one morning. In the process, she also solved the cold cases of five other hospital workers killed by the same man—Wainright Blake, an itinerant nurse who'd snipped a lock of hair from each of his victims and kept them in a cigar box under his bed.

Codella's one-woman investigation garnered national news coverage and sent her to Manhattan North Homicide as the only female detective in Lieutenant Dennis McGowan's unit. While she was being interviewed on national television and dubbed the "genius of deductive reasoning" in *New York* magazine, Haggerty remained a precinct detective juggling his caseload of robberies, grand larcenies, felonious assaults, rapes, and only the occasional dead body. He wasn't happy about their new unequal status, of course. She wouldn't have been either. And he was even less happy when he made a drunken proclamation of love one night outside the St. James Pub and she pushed him away.

She should have called him the next day, but she wasn't any better at intimacy than he was then. And cancer happened before either of them figured out how to repair the damage. Restoring their friendship had taken a long time. Becoming lovers had taken far less. But she wasn't sure their relationship was strong enough for whatever this case would demand.

CHAPTER 9

Haggerty waved over the four uniformed officers waiting by their squad cars. They huddled around him outside the church gate. "Here's the deal," he told them. "We've got a dead male in the church garden. Midfifties. Senior warden of the church. He left a meeting tonight sometime between ten thirty and ten forty-five, we think, and from the looks of it, he never made it through this gate. Someone cracked him over the skull."

He paused to stare into each set of eyes, making sure they were paying attention. "This could be an inside job, or we could be dealing with a neighborhood nutcase who has a gripe against God. We need to know if anyone on this block saw someone coming or going from the church. We need a thorough canvass. Two of you on the south side, two on the north. Start in the middle, closest to the church, and move in opposite directions. You know the drill. Get names and take down notes on everyone you speak to. If you get no answer, note that too because we'll have to come back tomorrow. That's it. Any questions?"

"No, sir," came the cops' answers in unison.

"Good. Then get started."

When Haggerty returned to the crime scene, Banks was aiming a plastic spray bottle into a wooden storage chest against the church wall behind Graves's body. In the bright light from an LED, Haggerty saw a fine mist hang in the air over the chest and fall like gentle rain onto the muddy garden tools inside.

As Banks waited to see what the chemicals revealed, Haggerty grabbed a flashlight and aimed the beam over the plants on either side of the stone path. Small engraved markers identified each herb by its common and botanical name. *Creeping thyme (Thymus serpyllum). Wormwood (Artemisia absinthium). Tricolor sage (Salvia officinalis Tricolor). Rosemary (Rosmarinus officinalis).* In the glare of his flashlight, he was struck by the unique beauty of each plant, and he continued to study them until he noticed Banks and another CSU investigator hunched over the chest.

"It's probably a false positive," Banks commented as Haggerty moved closer. "There's a lot of rust on those tools. Still, photo and bag it."

Banks stood and turned to Haggerty. "Don't get your hopes up, Detective. There may be a speck of blood on a garden spade, but if so, it's probably from someone who cut his finger while hacking weeds a year ago. We don't have the murder weapon."

Haggerty pointed to the herb plants. "You'll want to examine those," he said. "Some of them are prickly. Whoever did this might have snagged himself on something."

Banks gave him a look that said, *You do your job and I'll do mine.*

CHAPTER 10

The midnight air had turned brisk, but Codella could smell the humid fragrance of tree buds as she walked between the idle cars lining the curbs. Yellow crime scene tape fluttered against the wrought-iron church gates like ribbon tied on a giant gift box. A crime scene, she thought guiltily, *was* a gift.

She signed in with the recording officer, and he stepped aside to let her through, but a flash of light on the ground in the distance caught her attention. She squinted farther up the dark street. "I'll be right back," she told the officer. Then she followed the light past the parked squad cars and CSU van. A vibrating cell phone was lying face up on the sidewalk near the curb.

She stooped to pick it up, and then she stopped herself. What was it doing here? She peered through the tinted passenger window of a silver Honda minivan parked at the curb. She could just discern the dark mass of something or someone within. She rapped on the minivan roof, but there was no movement inside the vehicle. She pulled her jacket sleeve over her fingers and gingerly lifted the door latch. The car was unlocked, and as she swung the heavy door open, the van's dome light came on.

A woman lay on her left side across the passenger seat. Her straight grayish-brown hair was swept back from her face. Her cheek rested on the empty cup holders molded into the center console, and her open eyes seemed fixed on the dashboard. Codella pressed two fingers against the side of her fleshy neck but felt no pulse. She hadn't expected to find one. It was obvious from the bluish cast of the woman's lips and the unnatural position of her head that no heartbeat pumped blood through her body.

Codella stepped back from the door and shouted to the recording officer. "Get Detective Haggerty out here."

Haggerty arrived a minute later, his hands in the pockets of his blazer. "Claire?" He watched her turn away from the minivan.

"Hey." She smiled.

"Hey." A frown of confusion wrinkled his forehead. "What are you doing here?"

"You called for Homicide. I'm on call. You must have known they'd send me."

"Of course. I mean, what are you doing out *here*?" He gestured to the street and the cars.

"Oh." She sighed with relief—he had expected her.

Then she signaled him to the passenger side of the van. "Look in there. Be careful not to touch anything."

He bent close to the open door and peered in. "Son of a bitch." He pressed his lips together in disgust. "I should have had someone walk this block already. We searched the church, of course, but we just started the canvass—shit! You're here one minute and you find a body I missed."

The words were an undeserved indictment. Just as she had feared, he was letting slip his insecurity—and maybe some of his dormant anger—about their "unequal status." Was he already regretting having made the call he knew would bring her here? Was he afraid to work with her again—afraid she would detect a weakness in his judgment or a lack of thoroughness that would render him less desirable to her? Wasn't it just as possible that working together again would reveal qualities in her that he found unappealing—her intensity, her aggressiveness? If he surrendered to his feelings of inadequacy right now, she knew, they were doomed in more ways than one. And having gone through so much to get where they were now, she didn't want either of them to fuck it up.

She gripped his arm and yanked him into the street, away from the ears of a uniformed officer making his way toward the car. She pointed a finger in front of his face. "Look at me. Remember who I am."

He glanced at her briefly and then down at the pavement.

"I said *look* at me, Brian." She waited until his blue eyes locked onto hers. "I would have missed that body too if I'd been in your shoes. You had a scene to contain. You were alone. You had a church full of possible suspects. The only reason I found her is that her phone is on the sidewalk over there"—she pointed—"and it lighted up while I was signing in."

He gazed to where she was pointing.

"I'm not your enemy," she continued, "but if you don't want to work with me, say it right now, and I'll get someone else over here." She waited.

"No. I'm sorry. It's just—"

"It's all in your mind," she told him. "Whatever you're think-ing, it's yours—not mine. I don't doubt you. You're the only partner I ever wanted to work with, remember?"

He still seemed unconvinced, and the intimacy they'd shared just an hour ago had apparently vanished as well.

"We've got two dead bodies here." She squeezed his arm tightly. "We've got a chance to work together again. Don't spoil it. Reset your head. Right now."

He finally nodded. "Okay."

They turned simultaneously as the footsteps of the uniformed officer approached. "Everything all right, detectives?"

"Call for more backup," ordered Haggerty. "We've got a sec-ond crime scene here." He turned back to her. "I'll go alert the CSU guys that their job is only beginning."

Codella nodded. "Chances are this death is related to the other one. Does anyone in that church have their shit together enough to try to ID her for us?"

"Yeah. I know who can do it."

"Good. Bring him out here."

CHAPTER 11

Roger Sturgis watched Detective Haggerty walk toward him. "Can you please come with me?"

The question wasn't really a request, Roger understood, and he pushed out his chair to stand. His eyes scanned the faces of the other vestry members seated at the Community Room tables. Peter was still clicking his pen, and he kept licking his lips as if he were parched. Vivian was reading her pocket Bible, and Rose had her elbows on the table and her head propped in her hands.

As he passed Susan's table, he caught her narrowed eyes and quickly looked away. He squeezed the ring of keys in his pocket as he followed the detective across the corridor, through the south doors, and down the parish house steps. He had the uncanny feeling that he'd just been taken prisoner, and he flashed to the February morning in 1991 when the armored vehicle he and his men were in broke down in the desert and Iraqi soldiers surrounded them. In the endless five minutes before help arrived, he'd imagined his roadside execution and whispered the SERE mantra: survival, evasion, resistance, escape. He found himself thinking those words now.

On the sidewalk beyond the gate, the detective turned left. Five or six brownstones ahead, bright lights turned darkness into daylight. "What's going on?" Sturgis asked.

Detective Haggerty pointed to a minivan parked in the bath of white light. "There's a body in that car, Mr. Sturgis, and we think it might be someone from the church. We'd like you to have a look."

Roger felt the tension in his shoulders relax slightly. He loosened his grip on the keys in his pocket. "Another body? Another murder, you mean?"

And now all his apprehension dissolved. He wasn't under arrest. The police were not going to interrogate him. They merely needed his help. They had sized him up as the parishioner with the strongest constitution. And that was certainly true. Roger couldn't imagine any of the women vestry members handling the task—except Susan, of course—and he didn't even want to think about how Peter Linton would react to seeing the body. "Whatever I can do to help," he told Haggerty.

As they continued toward the vehicle, Roger wondered if any dead body could shock him. Near the end of Desert Storm, he'd seen the charred remains of an Iraqi soldier who had tried to escape his scorched convoy truck along the Highway of Death. The man's burned fingers still gripped the side of the truck, and his blackened face, with sizzled flesh peeling back from bone, wore a grimace of agony. What could shock Roger more than that?

Haggerty lifted the crime scene tape, and Roger ducked under it. Just inside the tape stood a woman. She was seven or eight inches shorter than Haggerty, and her cobalt-blue eyes demanded appreciation. Her black hair gleamed under the crime scene floodlights. A gold shield hung off her belt. Roger wasn't usually attracted to white women, but he found himself unexpectedly captivated by this one. And she reciprocated his look of interest, he thought.

"I'm Detective Codella," she said. "We need you to look inside the front seat and tell us if you know this woman."

He nodded, his eyes dipping. The detective's breasts were the same size as his wife Kendra's.

"Don't touch anything," she instructed him. "Just look."

He felt her eyes follow him to the minivan. He stuck his head through the open passenger door, and a uniformed officer aimed a strong flashlight beam over his shoulder and onto the figure within. Roger stared at the face for several seconds. She was such a large-boned woman, he reflected, and he'd always found her haircut unflattering. She was one of those St. Paul's women—there were so many of them—who didn't feel the need to conceal their age or compensate for physical imperfections. They let their hair go gray. They eschewed makeup. They came to church wearing casual, outdated clothing. Their shoes were flat and practical.

He stared at her floral blouse. The pattern was strangely delicate for such a large woman. How odd it was, he thought, to see her like this just an hour after watching her ferociously scribble vestry meeting minutes. She'd probably rushed out of the meeting thinking about her next snack—not her imminent death. Just as Philip had likely left the Blue Lounge intending to celebrate his night's victory with an extra dry martini. People who'd never been ill or at war always assumed they'd live on and on.

"Well?" Codella broke his train of thought. "Do you know her?"

He pulled his head back from the minivan's open door. "I'm afraid I do. It's Emily Flounders. She's the vestry secretary and runs the Sunday school program."

CHAPTER 12

Codella stared at Roger Sturgis as a uniformed officer escorted him back to the church. Then she gazed up the block at one of the canvassing cops climbing the front steps of a brownstone. She looked across the street where another officer stood in the glow of a porch light speaking with a man in a bathrobe. A death in the night always woke the living. Most of these Upper West Siders, roused from their sound sleeps, would not have seen or heard anything, but there was always that outside chance an insomniac had looked through a window at just the right moment to see what had happened to Philip Graves or Emily Flounders.

Codella scanned the dark brownstone windows facing the church. Would those canvassers encounter the killer without realizing it? Was the perpetrator peering out from one of those windows right now, watching her and Haggerty, smiling at the scene his actions had brought to life?

Every crime scene was similar in some ways and yet so different in others. Many told a simple, straightforward story that required no inferences or interpretation. Others were like ancient texts that you had to decipher one symbol at a time before you could make meaning. This one did not feel straightforward, and that pleased Codella in a way she would never admit to others, of course. At the beginning of a complicated case, she always felt a secret guilt at the core of her exhilaration.

She felt Haggerty's eyes on her now. "What are you think-ing?" he asked.

"I'm thinking it's going to be a long night, and I better call McGowan before we get started so he doesn't feel left out." She pulled her phone from her pocket and pictured McGowan in a coma-like sleep after one too many shots. Lately the whites of his eyes were road maps in the mornings.

"What do you want me to do?"

"Call Muñoz. We're going to need him." Maybe, she thought, she could manage to run this case without involving McGowan's boys, who would only make her life difficult. "And then we start interviewing those people in the church." She gripped his arm and looked him in the eyes. "Until we determine otherwise, we've got to assume one of them is our killer."

He nodded. Then he leaned in and kissed her lips. "I know that's the last one I'll get for a while."

CHAPTER 13

Detective Eduardo Muñoz rolled onto his side. He watched Michael get up from the mattress, pull on his briefs, and run his fingers through his tousled black hair. Michael's usually pale skin was flushed. "Wait here," he said.

What was he up to now? Muñoz wondered. Michael had a seemingly infinite store of hyperactive energy that wasn't sapped even by sex. He could spend hours glued to his computer, and when he wasn't immersed in his work, he was redesigning the apartment. Did all software engineers rearrange their physical surroundings the same way they manipulated their virtual environments? In the past three months, Michael had spent almost every night with Muñoz, and in that time, he'd completely transformed Muñoz's one-bedroom apartment. The glass vase in the vestibule was now filled with fresh flowers. The bathroom had a new rug. The linen closet had been reorganized so that sheets and towels no longer spilled out whenever Muñoz opened the door. The couch and chairs had been subtly moved. Michael had fixed the loose hinges on the kitchen cupboards, repositioned the contents of the cabinets, and filled the refrigerator with food. He had, Muñoz realized with nothing but pleasure, quietly and confidently altered not only Muñoz's physical world but also the entire emotional landscape of his life.

Now Muñoz heard the refrigerator door open and close. He listened to the rattle of dishes and recognized the sound of the

silverware drawer opening. It occurred to him that if this obviously brilliant man—who had pursued him with calculation
and persistence—were suddenly to disappear from his life, he
wouldn't enjoy his solitude the way he once had.

He slid his palm toward the side of the mattress Michael had
occupied. One year ago, he would never have allowed someone
to share his bed. Back then he was undercover in more ways
than one—as a narcotics officer and as a gay man. He didn't
have relationships. He hooked up, and never at his place. But
now he had his gold shield, and thanks to Marty Blackstone, the
most obnoxious detective at the one-seven-one, the whole precinct knew he was gay. A few detectives still used the nickname
Blackstone had christened him with six months ago—Rainbow
Dick. Hiding was no longer an option, and as difficult as that
was at times, he was glad to finally be himself.

Michael returned to the bedroom with two ceramic bowls
and handed one to Muñoz. Inside each bowl were scoops of coffee ice cream floating in hot fudge. Michael crawled back into
bed, and they sat side by side against the headboard. The hot
fudge was warm, and the ice cream was smooth and rich. The
moment seemed perfect to Muñoz. "Why don't you just move in
with me?" he heard himself say.

Michael's spoon stopped on the way to his mouth. "Is that a
sugar rush talking?"

Muñoz laughed. "You fed me ice cream on our first date,
remember?"

"That wasn't exactly a *date*, but yes, I remember."

"Did you feed everyone ice cream?"

"No one else stayed long enough. But you wanted more. You
just didn't know it."

"Oh, but you did?"

Michael laughed. "I didn't have to be a genius to figure it
out. You didn't stop talking. It was so obvious you were there for
more than a fuck. And I suppose I fell for you right then. Fell in
love with you, I mean."

Muñoz stared at him.

"Uh-oh. I scared the big bad detective."

Muñoz set his bowl on the table by his bed. "What makes you think I'm scared?" He took the bowl out of Michael's fingers and set it next to his. Then he reached his hand around the back of Michael's head and gently pulled the smaller man toward him. "I love you too," he said, and the words felt natural and right. He leaned closer still, and they shared the taste of hot fudge and coffee until the ring of Muñoz's cell phone intruded. He looked at the number on the screen. "Dammit. I have to take this."

CHAPTER 14

Rose followed Detective Haggerty out of the Community Room and down the wide corridor. Detective Codella and a police officer were huddled with Mother Anna in front of the Blue Lounge. As Rose passed them, she thought she heard the woman detective speak Emily Flounders's name, and she distinctly heard the police officer utter the words "next of kin." Haggerty touched Rose's arm and urged her quickly around the corner, past the parish kitchen, and down an alcove into Mother Anna's small office.

"What's happening?" she demanded as he shut the door behind them.

"Have a seat, Mrs. Bartruff." He stepped behind the rector's desk.

"Is Emily all right?"

He frowned.

"I heard them mention her name. Did something happen to her?"

He sat and combed his fingers through his hair. "Emily Flounders is dead."

Rose dropped into her chair. "But—oh, no."

"Was she at the vestry meeting?"

"Of course. Emily *never* misses a meeting. Even when she isn't feeling well."

Rose realized she was clutching her purse so tightly that her fingers hurt. She set the purse on the floor and watched the detective press his elbows onto the rector's desk. "What happened to her?" she asked.

"We don't know yet," he said, "but I need to ask you some questions—while tonight is still fresh in your mind."

Tonight was going to be fresh in her mind for a long time, Rose wanted to tell him. How could she ever forget falling over Philip Graves's body? An unhelpful grief counselor she'd met with once, right after Mark's death, had assured her that the memory of her husband's body on the kitchen floor—an image that still sometimes jarred her awake in the night—would eventually fade from the foreground of her consciousness. "You're focused on your pain right now," he'd told her confidently, "but time will turn the lens of your memory a little to the right or left, and that traumatic image will blur."

Rose had been too polite to tell him his theory of mind was academic and useless to her. She hadn't been looking for facile reassurance that her pain would end. She'd wanted someone strong enough to walk with her into the dense forest of that pain, and Mother Anna had obliged. Rose had never considered herself to be a spiritual person, but Mother Anna's prayers had soothed her. She'd found genuine solace in this little office. But she felt no comfort here now. Would she ever find it here again? "What do you want to know?"

"What time did the meeting begin?"

"We usually start at seven thirty, but tonight we didn't begin until seven forty-five. That's when I arrived. We need to have at least seven members of the vestry for a quorum. I was the seventh. I wasn't going to come tonight—my daughter has a cold—but Philip called to say two other vestry members couldn't make it and he needed me. I had to wait for my babysitter to arrive." She stared above the detective's head at the framed reproduction of Mary Magdalene looking out from her shimmering cloak at

Christ's tomb on Easter morning. Rose had always liked that Mother Anna had this painting in her office.

"And what time did the meeting end?"

Rose twisted her loose watchband around her thin wrist. "Ten thirty or so."

"And Mr. Graves was the first to leave?"

"*Dr.* Graves," Rose corrected. "He has a PhD. He always got annoyed if people called him Mr. Graves."

"I see. And Dr. Graves left first?"

"Yes." Rose nodded.

"At the time he left, was everyone else still in the Blue Lounge?"

"No. Not everyone. Things were breaking up, you see." She closed her eyes and saw those minutes like a movie. "Roger went to the men's room, I think, and Vivian took the tea service back to the kitchen—she always brews tea for the meetings and cleans out the pot when we finish."

Rose looked at her watch. Was it already twelve forty? "Can I please go soon? My daughter—"

"Just a few more questions," the detective said, cutting her off. "Was Peter Linton in the Blue Lounge when Dr. Graves left?"

"He got a phone call, I think. He went somewhere to take it."

"Was Emily Flounders still there?"

"Just for a minute, finishing her meeting notes. She left shortly after Philip. Emily usually helps Vivian with the tea service, but Vivian insisted that she go home right away because Emily's daughter was flying in tonight. Martha. She lives in Seattle now. Oh, my God. Someone has to tell Martha."

Rose watched the detective jot a note in his small spiral notepad.

"And Dr. Bentley?" he asked.

Rose covered her face with her palms, pressed her fingers against her closed eyelids, and wished she were home. She should have told Philip she couldn't make this meeting. Why did she always have so much trouble saying no to people? Waking Lily for school tomorrow would be even more brutal than usual. "Can't we talk in the morning?" she asked.

"This is important, Mrs. Bartruff. Just a few more questions, please. Was Dr. Bentley in the Blue Lounge when Dr. Graves left?"

"I think she walked out with him."

"What time did they walk out?"

"I don't know. I don't check my watch every time someone gets up and leaves the room," Rose snapped uncharacteristically. She regretted the remark immediately. "I'm sorry. You've been very kind to me tonight. I'm just worried about my daughter."

The detective smiled. "Forget the time. But you're sure Dr. Bentley left the room with him?"

"Yes. I heard her say she would walk him to the door. She got up and followed him out of the lounge. I went to the coatrack in the hall as they were heading down the corridor. I saw them turn the corner toward the door. They were talking."

"Did you see the doctor leave the building with him?"

Rose shook her head. "No."

Detective Haggerty squinted at her. "No, you didn't *see* her leave, or no, she *didn't* leave."

"The former," said Rose. "But I don't think she went out."

"Why is that?"

And now Rose considered the purpose behind the detective's questions. The possibility that *any* of her fellow parishioners—people she planted the garden with or kneeled beside at Holy Communion—could be a killer seemed as incomprehensible to her as astrophysics. She pressed her fingers lightly over her mouth. "No. You can't believe that—"

The detective lowered his pen. "Mrs. Bartruff," he said reassuringly, "I'm not drawing any conclusions about anything or anyone right now, and neither should you. These are the standard questions we ask. Please just answer as honestly and thoroughly as you can."

Then Rose began to cry—for Emily, for Philip, for herself. She'd been so negative about the vestry on her way out of the parish house earlier, and she suddenly hated herself for judging the other vestry members and for minimizing St. Paul's importance to her. She reached for a tissue from the box on Mother Anna's desk.

"What makes you think Dr. Bentley didn't go outside with him?" Detective Haggerty asked her again.

Rose pressed the tissue to her eyes. "Because she came right back almost immediately and asked to speak with Mother Anna. I saw them go into the Community Room."

CHAPTER 15

Two rows of framed portraits hung on the wall outside the Blue Lounge. Codella paused to study them before she entered the room. Below each portrait was a plaque bearing the name of a St. Paul's rector and his or her years of service. The oldest was a charcoal drawing of Benjamin Seabury, who had served the congregation from 1793 to 1821. She ran her eyes from left to right across the top row of solemn male faces, noticing the gradual transformation of clerical fashions and facial hair. Anna Brookes's color photograph hung on the far right side of the bottom row. Her straight auburn hair fell to her neck, her green eyes stared out warmly, and her slightly crooked smile made her look vulnerable.

Codella opened the door and stepped into the lounge. The room desperately needed a fresh coat of paint. A long blue couch and matching love seat formed a ninety-degree angle under the window along the back wall. Several straight-backed chairs—also upholstered in blue—were arranged in a semicircle facing the couch and love seat.

Codella visualized the St. Paul's vestry members gathered on those chairs earlier this evening. The fact that they were churchgoers seemed irrelevant now. Beyond their status as leaders of St. Paul's, she doubted they were any more homogenous than the staff of a school, corporation, hospital, or any other microcosm in this vast city. One or more of them might very well hold the answer to what had happened here—and she intended to find out.

As she stepped farther into the room, she thought of Haggerty down the hall in the rector's office with Rose Bartruff, the church gardener who had tripped over the body. *She* wanted to hear that woman's story. She wanted to hear everyone's story for herself—and not because she didn't trust Haggerty to ask the right questions, record the facts meticulously, or accurately judge each person's veracity. He was a skillful interrogator. But dividing the interviews meant that each of them would only hear half the narratives. They could easily fail to draw important connections or detect subtle discrepancies between the account of one witness and another.

She returned to the corridor. She was about to tell Officer Kovac to bring in Roger Sturgis when Detective Eduardo Muñoz appeared at the end of the corridor and called out to her. She waved him into the Blue Lounge and closed the door. At six foot five, he towered over her, and she had to stare up to meet his eyes. "How are you, Eduardo?"

"I'm well, Detective. It's good to see you."

She smiled. "It's good to see you too." There was no time for more. "We've got what looks like a double homicide here. I called you in to be our third on this case."

"Thank you, Detective," he said. "I'm honored."

"Well, you've earned the role."

"Maybe, but I'd never get it from anyone else."

Not from most of his detectives at the one-seven-one, she supposed. He was like her, after all—someone who didn't fit the brotherhood mold—and maybe that's why she'd bonded with him early on. During the Sanchez case six months ago—when she was just back from cancer and he'd been a precinct detective less than a week—he'd chased a fleeing subject down nine flights of stairs when she didn't have the stamina to do it herself. Over lunch an hour later, she'd thanked him for saving her ass, and he'd begged her to keep him on the case. *I don't mean to be presumptuous,* he'd said, *but I imagine being a woman who just got back from a medical leave puts a lot of pressure on you—at least as much as there is on a gay detective who just got outed on his first night drinking with the other precinct detectives. Let me stay on this case with you. Let me help you solve it.* She'd taken a chance on him, and he'd never disappointed her.

"I need you to go give two death notifications," she told him now. "Have you ever done one?"

Muñoz shook his head. "But there's a first time for everything, right?"

"Right. Just be yourself. You know how to say the right things. And listen. Be observant. Find out whatever you can." She patted his shoulder. "There's a female officer working under Zamora. Officer Dunn. Take her with you."

When he was gone, she stood in front of the long blue couch and glanced at the door as Officer Kovac led Roger Sturgis into the lounge. Sturgis's dark-brown eyes held hers as he approached. His black hair, she noticed, was even curlier than Haggerty's. His nose was long and straight, and his moustache obscured his upper lip in a way she supposed some women would find sensuous, but she did not. He stopped behind one of the straight-backed chairs, lowered his eyes to her shoes, and followed the fabric of her tight black slacks to her thighs. She watched his lips curl into a suggestive smile as he studied the shield clipped to her belt. *Don't you look sexy playing the tough detective,* his eyes seemed to say. And then he stared boldly at the contours of her breasts before he returned his gaze to her face.

She gave him a smile, glanced down at his loafers, and ran her eyes up his pant legs to the zipper of his worn khakis. As he watched, she lowered herself onto the couch and patted the arm of the adjacent love seat. "Have a seat. Don't be afraid."

She saw a flash of irritation on his face. He recovered quickly, however, and sat perpendicular to her with his legs spread apart and his hands behind his head as if he were settling in to watch a March Madness game. "You've got your hands full," he observed.

She leaned her elbow on the arm of the couch. "What makes you say that?"

"Well, I'm not a detective, but my math is very good. You've got six suspects right here—myself included, of course." He was staring at her breasts again. "It reminds me of that Agatha Christie movie. You know, *Murder on the Orient Express.*"

"Are you suggesting that everyone here tonight had a hand in whatever has happened?"

"No, of course not. I'm just—never mind."

She smiled. He was just being an asshole, she wanted to tell him as he crossed one leg over the opposite knee and folded his arms so that his thick gold wedding band was prominently displayed. What, she wondered, did his wife possibly see in him? He seemed like the type to do more than objectify the women who threatened him. Was he one of those men who spent time on the most degrading porn sites? Did he cheat on his wife? "What do you do, Mr. Sturgis?"

"I rescue failing businesses." He watched for her response.

She gave him none. "Do you have a theory about what happened here tonight?"

"I can think of several." He shrugged.

She waited.

"I suppose one us could have done it. We're all capable of the unimaginable, aren't we?" He smiled, apparently pleased by his demonstration of psychological insight. "Then again, the church has a basement full of homeless men. And I'm sure every one of them is taking a combination platter of antipsychotic meds. Maybe one of them forgot his dose." Sturgis raised his left eyebrow.

"Maybe."

"And then there's the possibility that a random person on the street ventured through the gate."

She nodded. "That's possible too."

"Three months ago, our rector launched a Christianity-Islam study group, and someone keeps spray-painting over the sign outside that advertises the group."

"Do you have the name of this person?"

"No."

"Can you describe him or her?"

"I don't think anyone actually saw it happen. But clearly somebody in this neighborhood doesn't like our cross-cultural open-mindedness."

Codella leaned closer to him. "What happened at tonight's vestry meeting?"

"The usual boring business." Roger Sturgis rolled his eyes.

"You don't sound all that enthusiastic about your vestry duties, Mr. Sturgis."

"My wife's the religious one. She comes from a long-standing St. Paul's family. It's a point of pride with them."

"So she volunteered you for the vestry?"

"Let's just say she does things for me, and I do things for her." He smoothed his moustache.

Codella found herself pitying the wife. "Tell me about Philip Graves."

Roger sniffled and rubbed his nose. "He's a history professor at Columbia. Divorced. I don't know him all that well. I don't spend time with him outside of church."

"I get the sense you didn't like him."

"Really?" He smirked. "Well, I don't like a lot of people."

Codella didn't like his supercilious grin. "What was the topic of tonight's meeting?"

"There's never just one topic. Each of us heads a committee. We all report on our committee activities. Rose described the flower arrangements for the Palm Sunday service. That went on for twenty minutes. And then Vivian pitched an after-school reading program for children in the Frederick Douglass projects five blocks north. Then Peter gave a cemetery report."

"Were there any arguments or disagreements?"

Roger squinted and shrugged. "Not really. I mean Peter made his usual complaints that we're not investing enough capital improvement funds in our cemetery. He wants us to replace the crematorium furnace and upgrade the chapel. He's a broken record about that. We're all pretty sick of hearing it. But that's nothing new."

"Anything else?"

Codella watched him think for several seconds. "How can I say this delicately, Detective? Most of these vestry people desperately want to have a voice in something. They make *everything* into an issue. We once spent forty minutes on whether or not to serve Starbucks coffee at the social hour."

Codella stared at Roger for several seconds before she spoke. "You can go now, Mr. Sturgis. But I'll probably have more questions for you tomorrow."

CHAPTER 16

Vivian Wakefield lowered herself into a chair on the other side of the rector's desk. Her emphatically erect posture made Haggerty want to sit up straighter. He stared at the large gold hoops that dangled from her earlobes and the intricate salt-and-pepper braids. Was she in her sixties, or was she older? He couldn't tell. The collar of her cream-colored blouse highlighted flawless skin, and it occurred to him for the second time tonight that she was a serene figure.

As he took notes, she named the seven vestry members present at the night's meeting and the order in which they'd arrived. And then, following his lead, she recalled what had happened when the meeting adjourned.

"Philip stood up at ten forty-two. He was putting on his jacket when I began to collect the teacups."

"You're certain of that?"

Vivian smiled. "There are two couches in the Blue Lounge, Detective, and I always sit on the one that faces the wall clock adjacent to the door. I confess I'm a clock watcher."

"Did Emily Flounders get up too?"

Vivian nodded. "She left a couple minutes after Philip. She had to get home. Her daughter was arriving for a visit."

"How long were you in the kitchen?"

"Hmmm." She pressed her thin fingers to her chin. "I'm not sure."

Haggerty observed the junior churchwarden's placid countenance. Was she a little too relaxed? And how was it that she knew the precise timing of everyone's movements except her own? What, if anything, should he conclude from that? "Just give me a rough estimate," he insisted.

"Perhaps five minutes?" she asked rather than stated.

"And when you returned to the lounge, was everyone else still there?"

Vivian's eyes focused on the bright round liturgical calendar on the wall to her right. "I think Peter Linton was there," she said. "Roger might have been in the men's room."

"What about Rose Bartruff?"

"Oh, yes, Rose was there."

"And the rector?"

"She was around but not in the lounge."

"Did you see Susan Bentley?"

Vivian paused. "I don't remember where she was when I came back from the kitchen, but I do recall seeing her in front of the coatrack when Rose came in from the garden and got her."

Haggerty considered the warden's words. If Claire were here, she would be disturbed by the vagueness of Vivian's answers and the many small folds of undocumented time hidden in the chaotic choreography of the night. He knew as well as Claire did that the solution to the night's mystery likely lay in those invisible gaps of time. He massaged the back of his neck. The complete sequence of events would never be reconstructed unless he and Claire could dislodge and piece together all the truths tucked into these multiple minds. He felt Vivian Wakefield's eyes study him. Could she read his suspicion? He switched on a smile. "What happened at your vestry meeting tonight?"

"We always start with a prayer by Mother Anna," said Vivian. "After that, we spend a few moments pouring tea and coffee, and then we get down to business."

"And what exactly was the business tonight?"

"It's always the same. Roger—Roger Sturgis—gives a finance report. That's our reality check." She smiled. "Then there's a report on the church grounds—we had some very expensive boiler issues this winter—and after that, Peter gives a cemetery update, and the other committee chairs have the opportunity to take the floor."

She still hadn't told him what had happened tonight, he thought. "Did Emily Flounders take the floor?"

"Emily doesn't speak very often," Vivian answered. "She's the secretary. She's usually very focused on taking the minutes."

"And you?" Haggerty asked.

"In addition to serving as the junior churchwarden, I also run the outreach committee, and I'm the lay historian."

"I didn't know churches had historians."

"Two-hundred-and-twenty-five-year-old churches often do."

He nodded. "Tell me about the outreach committee."

"We oversee programs that serve our community."

"What kind of programs?"

Vivian narrowed her eyes. "Over the years, Detective, I've launched three programs here at St. Paul's. Saturday Supper feeds about two hundred homeless people a nutritious meal once a week. Weekday Beds shelters ten homeless men in our church basement on Monday through Thursday nights so they can attend a job-training program in Midtown during the day. And the St. Paul's Pantry collects food for the working poor—families who don't earn enough to pay their rent and put food on the table." Vivian paused and stared at him.

Haggerty wondered if she expected him to comment on her good works. "Did you speak on behalf of the outreach committee tonight?" he asked.

She nodded. "I want St. Paul's to do something for the children in this neighborhood, children who are growing up in poverty. The Frederick Douglass projects are only blocks away from our doors. Most of the children who live there leave school every afternoon only to spend long hours alone while their parents work, or look for work, or succumb to drugs and alcohol because they feel so hopeless about their lives. No one helps these children with their homework. No one reads to them, makes them dinner, or even bothers to ask about their day. I proposed a volunteer alliance between these children and our seniors who have time on their hands and want to feel purposeful."

"And? Was the vestry receptive?"

"Sadly, no."

"Why not?"

Vivian shrugged. "We live in dark times, Detective. The hope I once felt is gone. Self-interest and bigotry have regained legitimacy. You see it even here on the Upper West Side. Haven't you experienced an uptick in crimes of hatred and intolerance? Even our church is less interested in serving the needs of those less fortunate than ourselves. I remember when St. Paul's was a model of how people could bridge racial and economic divides. May I tell you a brief story from our past, Detective?"

Haggerty didn't see how church history was going to shed any light on two dead bodies, and yet he was curious. "Sure, go on."

"Are you familiar with Seneca Village?"

Haggerty shook his head.

"It was the oldest community of free blacks in our city's history. It was founded in 1825 only blocks from St. Paul's, and our church archives tell us that between 1826 and 1828, the affluent white congregation of St. Paul's helped the black residents of Seneca Village build a church."

Haggerty nodded.

"In 1856," she continued, "the city reclaimed Seneca Village by eminent domain so that Central Park could be built. The villagers had to move, and St. Paul's helped them build a new church, St. Augustine's Chapel."

Haggerty now regretted that he'd let Vivian go down this road. He frowned, and the junior churchwarden read his impatience. "It's all about community outreach, Detective. St. Paul's has always had the community in mind—with no concern for the color of people's skin, their economic status, or any other differences."

Haggerty ran his fingers through his hair. "And you're telling me this because . . . ?"

Vivian stretched her arm across the rector's desk and pressed her hand over his. "Because none of us can hope to understand the present without understanding our past." She pulled back her hand and crossed her arms. "I assume you're familiar with Mark 3:25, Detective? 'And if a house be divided against itself, that house cannot stand.'"

Haggerty nodded. Everyone knew that quote thanks to Abraham Lincoln, even if they didn't know it came from the Bible.

"The St. Paul's I once knew was committed to the community we served. But that is changing. While some of us remain dedicated to serve as the collective social conscience of our neighborhood, others now see that role as unsustainable—or no longer worth the sacrifice required to sustain it. It's the sad result of the times we now live in, Detective. I'm afraid I can't tell you what happened here tonight, but I do know that these deaths should be a warning to us all."

CHAPTER 17

Codella was reentering the Blue Lounge with a glass of water when Sergeant Zamora stopped her. "The ME's with the body, Detective."

She removed her hand from the doorknob. "Which body?"

"Philip Graves."

She pointed to the door. "Susan Bentley's in there. Make sure she stays put, and don't let her talk to anyone."

Codella handed him the water glass and headed out of the parish house. She followed the stone path through the garden and grabbed booties from the officer stationed in front of the crime scene. Rudolph Gambarin was holding a rectal thermometer as she approached. He glanced at her but offered no greeting before he returned his attention to the digital display. This was part of calculating the time of death, she knew, and she had to stop herself from asking him what the body temperature was. Gambarin worked his death scenes slowly and methodically, and he didn't share his insights until he was good and ready to. She stood next to Banks, and together they watched the small, meticulous man complete his visual inspection of the body.

Banks nudged her arm. "You scored a big one here," he said in a low voice as he looked at his watch. "Shit, it's almost one thirty. We won't even get to the minivan body for another hour. Get this, Codella. It's Parents' Day at my son's school tomorrow.

I get to tell them all about the exciting life of a crime scene investigator."

"Please tell me you're going to spare them these details."

He grinned. "You and me, Codella, we always end up at the same scenes, don't we? You think it means something?"

She rolled her eyes.

Ten minutes later, Gambarin signaled her over, removed his thick black glasses, and folded them slowly. His disposable jumpsuit rustled as he pocketed them. Under the superbright flood beam of a scene light, she noticed that a few gray hairs in his eyebrows badly needed trimming. "I have no doubt that the manner of death was homicide," he said.

"A head blow?"

He nodded. "Or two or three." He looked around. "Though I don't see any objects around here that a killer could have used."

"What sort of object are we looking for?"

"Something hard and flat, I think. But you can't expect me to say much more based on what's here, Detective. This is a significantly altered scene. Many hands have touched this body before me." His words were an obvious chastisement. "I'll have to get him on my table."

"But you did calculate a time of death," she said.

He nodded. "Assuming the victim was ninety-eight point six before he died, then we're looking at a time of death between ten thirty and eleven PM."

"That's around when he left the meeting. Can you be any more precise?"

"Come on, Detective. You know there are too many variables for that." Gambarin peeled off one set of nitrile gloves only to put on a second. "I'll go see the other body now."

Codella told Banks, "Find me whatever the killer used to bang this body over the head." Then she returned to the parish house and told Zamora to get Haggerty. When he appeared, she said, "Tell me everything you've learned before I talk to Susan Bentley."

CHAPTER 18

The doorman at the West End Avenue building was asleep at the front desk. Muñoz rapped on the ledge and the man's head shot up. Muñoz showed his shield. "Which apartment belongs to Emily Flounders?"

The doorman wiped drool at the edge of his mouth onto the back of his hand. "7C." He looked from Muñoz to Officer Dunn as he picked up the house phone. "You want I buzz her?"

"No. Just point us to the elevator."

As they waited for the car to descend from an upper floor, Muñoz stared at the petite uniformed officer in the bright lobby light. Her cap was a little too large for her head. They had talked amiably on the walk over, but now they were silent. She was flexing her slender fingers by her sides, and he guessed that she'd never done a death notification either.

The elevator doors opened, they got in, and Dunn pressed seven. She was biting her lower lip. "You watch cop shows on TV?" he asked.

"Never," she said.

"Me neither. Can't stand them." He smiled, and she smiled back.

The doors opened.

He let her step out first. They walked down a carpeted hall to 7C, and Muñoz rang the bell. On the other side of the door, light footsteps approached. The feet were bare or slippered, he guessed. The bolt clicked. The doorknob turned. And then a woman in her early thirties was staring at them across the threshold. Her eyes dropped to the shield in his hand. She took a step back and shook her head. She was ready for bad news, he realized, and this came as a relief to him. His task would be slightly easier if she already expected the worst.

She wiped away a tear. "My mother should have been home three hours ago. I don't know where she is."

Muñoz placed his hand on her forearm. "I'm Detective Muñoz, and this is Officer Dunn," he said gently. "May we come in?"

CHAPTER 19

Codella positioned a chair in front of the couch where Susan Bentley sat. The doctor's legs were crossed and her right hand rested on the hem of her pencil skirt. Her calves were lean and muscular, but her knees were scraped and speckled with dirt—from kneeling on the hard stone path hours ago, Codella imagined. "What kind of doctor are you?"

"A pediatric endocrinologist." Susan pushed hair behind her ear. She wore a perfume Codella couldn't identify.

"So you're not the sort of doctor who performs emergency CPR very often."

"As a matter of fact, I haven't had to perform it since my ER rotation twenty years ago. But I'm trained." She looked relaxed and composed.

"And you're a vestry member." Codella's eyes panned the room. On the wall to her left were three framed photographs of St. Paul's Church at different periods in the church's history. The oldest, a sepia-toned picture, showed parishioners stepping out of a horse-drawn carriage in front of the church's south gate long before that gate was made of wrought iron.

"That's correct." Susan's tone was affable, but she offered no extraneous information. She was like a well-coached witness on the stand.

"How long have you attended St. Paul's?"

"Seventeen years now," answered Susan. "Since my oldest son was three."

"So you live in this neighborhood?"

"No, I live on East Eighty-Seventh and Park Avenue, closer to my office and hospital." She placed her well-manicured left hand on the edge of the frayed blue couch.

"Then why St. Paul's?"

"I like it here." Susan shrugged. "It's relaxed and diverse. You won't find many churches in Manhattan with so many black, white, and Hispanic parishioners worshipping together." Codella heard obvious pride in her voice as she said this. "And we're not just racially diverse," Susan continued. "Many of our parishioners are refugees from less tolerant religions. Divorced Catholics who couldn't remarry. Gay people shunned by the faiths they grew up in. Former evangelicals. Mormons. We even have a family of recovering cult members." She sounded as if she were reciting promotional copy from a St. Paul's welcome brochure. "St. Paul's allows people to define their faith however they see fit," she concluded, "which is why our parish is filled with so many caring people."

And one of those caring people might be a murderer, Codella thought as she steered the conversation to the night's vestry meeting and listened to the doctor give a detailed account of everyone's arrivals and departures. Her chronology closely matched what Codella had heard from Roger Sturgis and what Haggerty had learned from Rose Bartruff and Vivian Wakefield.

"Did you speak to Mr. Graves after the meeting before he left the church?"

Susan Bentley smirked.

"What is it?" asked Codella.

"He'd correct you if he were alive to do it. He was a PhD, you see. He liked to claim the *doctor* title." Her tone was unmistakably derisive.

"I see. Then did you speak to *Dr.* Graves after the meeting?"

"Only to say good-bye."

"Where were you when you said good-bye to him?"

Susan paused before answering. "Between the coatrack and the Community Room. He was on his way to the door."

"How did he seem to you?"

Susan shrugged. "He seemed fine."

"Do you remember if Roger Sturgis was nearby?"

"Roger? No. I don't remember."

"What about Peter Linton?"

"Peter was in the lounge—I think."

"And the rector?"

"She'd gone to her office to get a book."

"What book?"

"On meditation." Susan reached to the floor for her cream-colored purse and brought out a slim paperback volume. "She lent it to me."

Codella stared at the title—*Finding Your Inner God*—and tried to envision the blonde endocrinologist cross-legged on a floor with her eyes closed. "How long was she gone?"

"A few minutes, I guess."

"And then what?"

"We sat at a table in the Community Room. She showed me some pages she'd flagged for me."

"I'm curious. What made her lend you that book tonight?"

Susan tucked the volume back in her purse and shrugged casually. "I happened to be in her office a few days ago. We got on the subject of daily meditation, and I told her I wanted to try it."

"I hear it increases the white matter in your brain," Codella said with feigned interest. "Do you meet with the rector often?"

Susan frowned. "No. Not often."

Codella thumbed a note into her iPhone. She could feel Susan watching her closely. She looked up with a smile. "How long would you say the two of you were in the Community Room discussing meditation?"

"Not long. Mother Anna was eager to get home. Todd—that's her husband—wasn't feeling well, and she was concerned about Christopher, her son. He's two. She was afraid he might be keeping Todd up."

"What did you do after the rector left?"

"I went back to the coatrack. Roger was there. We were chatting."

"How long would you say you were chatting?"

"Five minutes. Maybe a little longer."

"And that's where you were when Rose Bartruff ran inside to get you?"

"That's right." Susan crossed her arms and massaged her biceps as if she were cold. "She was in a panic. Roger and I followed her out to the side of the church, and she pointed out a body on the ground. I had no idea it was Philip until I rolled him over and Roger shined a light on his face. Philip had no pulse, but he was still warm. I knew the chances of saving him were slim, but I felt I had to try."

"You attempted to use an AED."

The doctor nodded. "Rose rushed inside to get it, but when Roger opened it up, we discovered that it wasn't properly charged."

"Had that ever happened before?"

"No." She shook her head. "We only installed the unit six months ago. It seemed like a smart thing to do since we have so many elderly parishioners. We trained five staff members to use it, but there hasn't been a need—until tonight."

"What went through your head when you realized the defibrillator wasn't going to help you?"

"Just that I was going to have to do CPR for as long as it took the EMTs to arrive."

Codella detected no defensiveness in the doctor's tone or manner—nothing to warrant her suspicion—but an unexplained fact remained: something had caused the defibrillator to fail, whether it was deliberate human intervention or an unfortunate mechanical flaw, and she would need to find out what it was.

She watched the doctor glance down at the buzzing cell phone in her purse. "I'm sorry," she said. "It's probably my husband leaving me a message. He's on West Coast time right now."

Codella nodded. "You said a moment earlier that St. Paul's was filled with caring people. In your opinion, Doctor, was Philip Graves one of those people?"

CHAPTER 20

Roger Sturgis stood at the corner of One Hundred Twentieth Street and dug the ring of keys out of his pocket. He counted seven keys in all, and one was obviously a car remote. Another one, small and silver, looked like it might open a file cabinet or desk drawer. It wouldn't take him long, he judged, to figure out which of the other five unlocked the apartment door. He knew what he was supposed to do with these keys, and if he didn't do it now, the window of opportunity would close. The question was, did he have the nerve?

He looked through the building's glass front door and saw no attendant within. The door was locked, but after two unsuccessful tries, he slid the correct key into the keyhole and let himself in.

The lobby was spacious and well lit, though hardly as inviting as the lobby of his and Kendra's building. Here, no elegant drapes framed the windows. No tasteful wallpaper adorned the walls. And no soft leather couches formed a comfortable waiting area. The small white hexagonal floor tiles had long ago lost their sheen and were outlined in time-blackened grout. A wooden table and chair just inside the door suggested that someone was usually stationed in this lobby, and he felt a ripple of adrenaline as he swiveled his head and listened for sounds. "Hello?" he called, but the only response was the echo of his own voice in the cavernous entrance hall. Maybe this was one of those cost-conscious buildings that only hired a daytime attendant to sign for deliveries and dry cleaning. Did closed circuit surveillance take over at night?

He peered up and around but did not see the telltale drop-ceiling mounts of wide-angle cameras. He spotted the elevator and was halfway there when he stopped abruptly. *Jesus fucking Christ. How could I be so stupid?* He stared at the keys in his hand—the promise of absolution—but without an apartment number, they might as well be garbage.

If there was no twenty-four-hour doorman, he thought, then there must be apartment buzzers. He returned to the outer door. A name was next to each buzzer, but not a number. He took a deep breath and straightened his shoulders. "Think, goddammit," he whispered, and then realization dawned. The small key on the ring he was holding did not open a file cabinet or desk drawer. It was the key to a mailbox.

Every Manhattan apartment building had a bank of mailboxes, and Sturgis found this building's discreetly hidden behind a wall on the right side of the lobby. The small square front door of each little box was labeled with an apartment number. All he had to do was match the key on the ring to one of these locks, and how difficult could that be? He moved to the far-left mailbox in the top row. The small key fit into the lock but did not turn it. He tried the key in every lock across the top row with no luck, and then he returned to the left and tried the second row of boxes.

Halfway through the third row, Roger heard the lobby door open and close on the other side of the wall. He froze as footsteps crossed the tile floor. Would the police have come so soon? He stared at his hand poised in front of a mailbox. *Breathe,* he reminded himself. *It can't be the police. They're too busy right now. And you're just a resident getting your mail. You've faced far more dangerous situations than this.*

The footsteps stopped. The elevator door opened, and when it closed again, Roger resumed his efforts with a sense of physical and emotional exhilaration. He continued along the rows, penetrating each lock with the key until he arrived at the second to last mailbox in the fourth row, and the key not only went into the lock but turned it. The door opened. He smiled. Apartment 6E.

CHAPTER 21

The door to the Blue Lounge burst open, and Peter Linton—red-faced and out of breath—stormed into the room followed by Officer O'Donnell. Codella noticed that the man's fists were clenched, and his mouth was so compressed that his lips were almost white. She stood as he charged toward her. Susan Bentley called out, "Peter! What are you doing?" He was only ten feet away from the couch when O'Donnell grabbed his arm and pulled him back. Peter turned and rammed his shoulder into the officer's chest. O'Donnell flung him to the carpet and pinned him like a wrestler.

"Get off me!" Peter managed to free one arm and flailed it in front of O'Donnell's face.

Codella stepped closer to the two men. "Stop resisting, Mr. Linton, or he's not going to let you go."

Peter finally stopped squirming. His breathing was heavy. His face was flushed. Codella waited several seconds before she gave O'Donnell the cue to release his grip. Then O'Donnell stood back, and the short, beefy man rose to his feet and rubbed his wrists. "That was unnecessary force," he accused.

Codella ignored the accusation. "Why did you barge in here, Mr. Linton? What's the problem?"

"The *problem*," Peter said as he turned his back to O'Donnell, "is that it's two in the morning and you've interviewed everyone *except* me. You're deliberately keeping me here because I pissed off that other detective. Don't think I don't know it."

Codella took a deep breath before she spoke. "What I know, Mr. Linton, is that you're throwing a temper tantrum."

"No. I'm expressing my constitutional rights."

"Oh, really?" She smiled in a way she knew would fuel his fury.

"You think that's funny? I'm an attorney. I know my rights."

"And I know mine. The medical examiner has confirmed that a homicide occurred here, Mr. Linton. Like it or not, you're part of a homicide investigation now. Everyone else has been patient, and you need to be patient too. You're *not* the only one waiting to speak with Detective Haggerty and me. In fact, your rector asked that *she* be the last person we see so that you could all go home first." She paused for him to take this in. "Any slight you may perceive is only in your head." And that head, she noted now, was as smooth and hairless as polished marble. Only a patchy fringe of dull brown strands still grew above his ears and at the nape of his neck. Why did balding men cling pathetically to their small weeds of hair?

"Bullshit!" He spit out the word. "I know how you civil servants think. It makes you feel so powerful to keep people waiting."

"You seem to have a deep disregard for the police, Mr. Linton. Or is it just that you have a deep disregard for anyone in a position of authority?" Codella watched the angry twitch of his upper lip.

"I don't have a problem with authority. But I have a problem with people who take *theirs* too far." He looked over his shoulder, letting Officer O'Donnell know he was one of those people too.

Susan Bentley rose from her chair. "The detective is just doing her job, Peter."

Peter glared at her and flicked his fingers as if he were shooing away a mosquito. "Don't talk to me, Susan."

Codella turned to Susan, "You can go now, Doctor. I'm sure we'll speak again."

As soon as Susan Bentley was gone, she turned to O'Donnell, thanked him for his help, and asked him to shut the door on his way out. When the door closed behind him, she turned back to Peter Linton, who was rubbing the bald crown of his head like a worry stone. "Why did you speak so dismissively to Dr. Bentley just now?"

"What?" he sneered.

"You sounded very angry at her."

"I'm not angry. I'm just upset. My back is killing me. I have a bad back, and it's not easy to sit for hours on end."

"I understand," said Codella. "Shall I have someone bring you some Advil?"

He smirked. "Advil's about as effective as a Tic Tac. This is Vicodin pain." He looked at his watch. "I need to get home. I start a trial in the morning. I still have a lot of prep work I was planning to do tonight. This is an important case for me. My client is depending on me to keep him out of prison."

"Well, two people are dead—your fellow parishioners, Mr. Linton—and they're depending on me. Detective Haggerty mentioned that you've been upset since he arrived."

"These vestry meetings always get me worked up."

"What got you worked up tonight?"

Sweat soaked the collar of his dress shirt. He glanced at the door.

"Sit down." Codella pointed him to the couch Susan Bentley had vacated. Then she pulled over a straight-backed chair and sat directly in front of him. "Roger Sturgis mentioned that you gave a cemetery report at the meeting. Is that correct? He mentioned that you want to make improvements to the cemetery but others don't agree. Is that why you're upset?"

"We have no more space for in-ground burials." Peter sighed as if explaining this to her were a huge waste of his time.

"But there's a strip of city land adjacent to the cemetery. It's been there for decades—the city will never develop it. I want St. Paul's to buy it, and I've spoken with the councilman from Sheepshead Bay. He's willing to advocate for us. If we got that land, we could bury five hundred more bodies and build a new aboveground mausoleum. That would mean a lot of revenue for the cemetery—and since the cemetery provides thirty percent of the church's operating budget, it's a lot of funding for church programs. But you know how vestries are. Everyone's got his or her own agenda."

"I see." Peter's profit-and-loss discussion of bodies struck Codella as far more ghoulish than the jokes CSU investigators often made while they processed grisly death scenes. Those investigators were defending themselves against their emotions, whereas Peter Linton seemed to have no emotion other than rage.

"And our crematory furnace is ancient," he continued. "We can barely process two bodies a day. If we had more capacity, we could burn bodies for the smaller funeral homes in the area. I've already investigated new cremation models. The technology has improved dramatically since St. Paul's purchased its equipment. I've done a return-on-investment analysis based on some very reasonable assumptions about the added business we could generate."

"And you thought the vestry would vote for your proposal?"

Peter nodded. "Any moron could see the advantage. We're facing tough fiscal times. We've had a shortfall in the budget for months now because of our boiler problems—we had no choice but to replace it in December. Do you have any idea what a boiler costs? Two months ago, we had to let our choir director go. We couldn't afford him full time anymore, and he wouldn't accept a part-time position. We had to replace him with a part-timer, Stephanie Lund. She's fine for now, but when the youth choirs start back up next September, we'll need someone full time again. We need a revenue stream. If we don't turn things around, we'll have to defund pro-grams, and no one on this vestry wants that."

"And how did the vote go tonight?"

"Well, let's just say that if I were running for president, they wouldn't call it a landslide." He smiled for the first time and shrugged. "Look, I'm sorry for being so difficult. I'm stressed out about this trial tomorrow. It's a manslaughter case. I need it to go well. Are we done here?"

"Not quite yet," Codella said. "Where were you when Dr. Graves left the vestry meeting to go home?"

"In the Blue Lounge," said Peter. "Oh, except when I stepped out to take a phone call."

"Stepped out where?"

"Into the hall. I just walked around out there while I spoke to my client. He's understandably nervous about tomorrow. He killed a young girl on her way to school. He's charged with vehicular homicide."

Codella touch-typed a note into her iPhone. "How long were you on the phone?"

"I don't know. A couple minutes, I guess."

Codella projected an expression of disinterest that she didn't really feel. "One other question. What were you text-ing tonight in the garden while the EMTs performed CPR? Sergeant Zamora observed you. You might as well tell me the truth. We'll be requesting your mobile phone records anyway."

"My records? Why?"

"You're a lawyer. You can figure that out, can't you?"

"No judge is going to give you a warrant for my phone records just because I was texting."

He was right, of course, Codella knew.

"But if you're so interested, I texted my wife. I knew I was going to be late. I told her Philip was dead and that she should go to bed without me."

"Sergeant Zamora told me you texted while the EMTs were still working. How did you know Philip Graves was dead if they weren't finished trying to resuscitate him?"

Peter gave her an "are you crazy?" expression. "Any idiot could see he wasn't going to reopen his eyes."

Codella stared at the perspiring man. "All right, Mr. Linton. You can go now," she said, "but I'm sure we'll speak again."

CHAPTER 22

This time, the woman who came to the door looked annoyed rather than anguished. She was an attractive middle-aged redhead wearing a blue satin robe. A man stood behind her in a T-shirt and sweats. "What's going on?" he demanded, his arm resting protectively—or possessively—on her shoulder.

Muñoz displayed his shield and apologized for the late intrusion. "Are you Jill Graves?" He addressed the woman.

"I used to be." She frowned. "My name is Jill Woodruff now. This is my husband, Robert."

Muñoz nodded at the man briefly and returned his gaze to the woman. "Philip Graves was your husband?"

"That's right. But we've been divorced five years now. What's this about?"

Muñoz sensed little need for delicacy. "Mr. Graves is dead."

"Dead?" She looked more confused than upset. "Philip?"

"May I come in?"

She stepped back and Muñoz entered. Beyond the door was a spacious and modern open-concept living area. The leather sectionals looked new and expensive. The light fixtures and glass coffee table were sleek and modern. Through the west-facing windows, he could just make out the lighted-up buildings across the Hudson River in New Jersey. During the day, the view through those windows would be stunning. "His death appears to have been a homicide, Mrs. Woodruff."

"You mean he was murdered," she stated rather than asked. "By whom?"

Muñoz was struck by how different this death notification was from the previous one. Martha Flounders's knees had buckled as he and Officer Dunn led her to her couch. The young woman was so distraught that he'd asked Officer Dunn to stay with her until her aunt—Emily Flounders's sister—could arrive from Union, New Jersey.

By contrast, this notification barely caused a snag in Jill Woodruff's emotional fabric. Curiosity appeared to be her primary feeling. Her question—who had killed him?—could just as easily pertain to a neighbor or a stranger on the street, he thought. Either Woodruff was a constitutionally detached individual or her relationship with her ex-husband had been so unpleasant that his fate engendered no pity in her at all.

"We're investigating that," he said. "Did you have any children with Mr. Graves?"

"We had a son," she said crisply, "but he died early in life."

Muñoz recognized the brittle tone of someone who didn't want to revisit a painful loss. "Is there anyone else I should inform about his death?" he asked. "A sibling? A parent?"

"Philip's parents are dead. He has a sister in Oklahoma, but they weren't close. Her name is Olivia. I wouldn't know how to put you in touch with her."

Muñoz jotted the name on his notepad. "Is there a friend?"

"He's on the faculty of Columbia College. In the history department. You could contact them."

Muñoz nodded. "When did you last see your ex-husband?"

Woodruff turned to the man behind her. "Was it four months ago we ran into him at the Fairway uptown?"

The man yawned. "Yes, three or four months ago."

"So you didn't see him often?" asked Muñoz.

"No. I've probably only seen him twice in the past five years." She shrugged. "It's funny, isn't it, how people can live within twenty blocks of each other in this town and never see each other."

"Yes, funny." Muñoz studied the rich blue silk of her robe. He noticed the carefully balanced high- and lowlights in her red hair and the subtle, appealing scent of her perfume. She was obviously a woman who liked to look good and be surrounded by beautiful things. Had she divorced Philip Graves because he couldn't provide those things, or had he divorced her because he found her too superficial? "Can you think of anyone who might have wanted to do your ex-husband harm?" Muñoz asked.

Jill Woodruff's eyebrows rose. "I imagine there were plenty of people who didn't *like* my ex-husband, Detective. He was"— she considered her words—"prickly. And pompous. He liked to be the smartest one in the room. And he didn't go out of his way to be tactful. He told you exactly what he thought about things. That got us scratched off quite a few guest lists, I can tell you, but I can't imagine it would cause anyone to kill him."

Muñoz nodded. "Thanks for your time." He turned to go. If Jill Woodruff remained awake after he left, it wouldn't be for need of solace.

CHAPTER 23

The light was on in the foyer—Susan always left it on—but judging from the darkness beyond, her husband hadn't returned. That meant he couldn't get a flight out of Seattle. Ordinarily she would sympathize—conducting a chamber orchestra, even a renowned one, wasn't as glamorous as many people assumed it was, and Daniel was often at the mercy of regional weather systems—but now she was relieved that she didn't have to face him.

She dropped her purse and kicked off her heels. Her toes ached from confinement. She stood still for several seconds, her whole body humming like an overworked electric grid. How much time did she have before the truth came out? So many incoming thoughts and emotions crowded her mind that she couldn't think straight. Short of a miracle, Philip's death ensured that her judgment day was near. She felt tears roll down her face as she thought of what she would lose. Daniel would certainly want a divorce. And her sons? Would they turn on her too? Or had she sufficiently opened their minds to the varieties of human experience?

She pressed her palms over her ears as if she could block out her own voice whispering terrible taunts in her mind: *Your whole life is a lie. You deserve what you're about to get.*

Meditate, Mother Anna would say. *Acknowledge the thoughts and push them away. Don't hold onto them.* As if letting go was the easiest thing in the world to do. Susan had tried a few times, closing her eyes and attempting to focus her mind exclusively on her breathing, but she had not found relief from her guilty conscience.

She walked into the kitchen she and Daniel had remodeled last summer. In less than six hours, she was supposed to be sitting across from the Grubers—Marilyn and Jack—in her consultation room. How could she possibly do that now?

She opened the Sub-Zero and stared at the too-familiar items on their biweekly grocery list. Organic Greek yogurt. Kalamata olives. Coconut milk. She'd eaten nothing since the PowerBar she'd consumed on her way to the vestry meeting. But nothing on the racks whetted her appetite now.

She sat on a stool at the island and stared out the window facing east. She looked at her phone, wishing for just a two- or three-word text message that would mean she was saved. But even if by some miracle her lies could be contained, there was her conscience to consider. How could she continue to live with herself?

She stood and poured a glass of water from the tap. Her future could unfold in three ways. She could face exposure within the next few hours. She could live days or weeks in constant fear of eventual exposure. Or she could end the burden of waiting right now. None of the options were pleasant, but one would get things over more quickly.

She set the glass on the granite counter and walked to the south end of the apartment, to the room that served as a study or guest suite. She stepped into the guest bathroom and turned on the faucet in the large whirlpool tub. Guests who stayed in this suite always marveled at the amenities, as if space and luxury were only available to suburbanites. She positioned her fingers in the flow of water and adjusted the temperature the way she liked her baths—warm, but not too hot.

She removed her skirt and blouse and folded them neatly on the seat of the toilet. She slipped off her panties and was removing her bra when she remembered that what she needed for this bath wasn't here. It was sitting on a shelf in the medicine cabinet of the master bathroom.

She didn't bother to wrap a towel around her body before she stepped out of the suite, walked past the closed doors of her sons, who were away at college, and entered the master bedroom. She stared at the empty bed where she and Daniel had slept together for the past twelve years. Daniel had been a warm and sensitive father to the boys she'd adopted between her first and second marriages, and she loved him deeply, but she hadn't been honest with him, and now she would pay for that.

She made her way to the bathroom, found what she needed there, and was back in the guest bathroom before the water had reached the halfway mark in the tub. When it reached the three-quarter level—she liked to immerse her shoulders when she bathed—she locked the door and stepped in.

In the soothing warm water, Susan felt weightless. She closed her eyes. Certainly no one who knew about her childhood would have predicted that she would become a renowned physician, sought out by families all over the country. No one would have imagined that she would live in an apartment so exquisitely designed that it had been featured on an *Architectural Digest* cover. And then there were her sons. She'd traveled to Russia twice to bring them home. One was now a nationally ranked tennis player who had been recruited by Stanford, and the other was a talented pianist who studied at the Boston Conservatory. To the outside observer, her life was perfect. But this whole perfect life was built on a landfill of lies.

Susan took a deep breath and pressed her husband's straight razor against the translucent skin of her right wrist. This method of suicide ranked high on the agony scale and low on effectiveness, but she knew the secret of success. You had to slice half an inch deep, cutting through skin and tendons to reach the radial artery. You had to carve a deep, long trench from your inside wrist to the elbow joint. And if you wanted to be absolutely certain that you succeeded, you had to cut the other arm as well. You would not experience the dreamy death of a narcotics over-dose. This death would hurt. But at least in death, you could show the courage you had lacked in life. This death would be a form of self-punishment and an apology to others.

CHAPTER 24

Roger Sturgis felt as acutely alert as he had driving across the Saudi desert at night. He rang the bell and pressed his ear to the apartment door. If someone was in there, he would hear them approach, and he would duck into the fire stairs before they saw him. But no footsteps sounded. No one was behind the door.

He slid a well-worn key into the top lock and turned it. Bingo. He slipped the same key into the lower lock, and that one turned too. He was gripping the brass doorknob before it occurred to him that he was leaving a full set of his fingerprints for one of those crime scene guys to lift, and like all current and former military personnel, his prints were in the national database. He let go, reached in his pocket for his handkerchief, and carefully wiped the knob clean before he continued inside and closed the door behind him.

He stood in the darkness and checked the time on his iPhone. He had to do this fast. He flicked on his iPhone flashlight. Only hours ago, this little beam had illuminated the face of Philip in the St. Paul's garden. Now it would light his way to whatever evidence the man had stored here.

Roger stepped lightly over creaking floorboards as he followed the light through a narrow entry passage. Inches before he collided with a wall, he turned left and the passage opened into a room. Two sets of windows on the opposite wall looked out on the northwest corner of Amsterdam Avenue. Light filtered into the room from the street below, and the full moon rising over the rooftop of Columbia Teacher's College made him feel as if this mission were sanctioned by some higher power. Not God, he thought quickly, but fate. Whatever that was. Fate was on his side. Things were going to work out.

The windows were shut, and a heavy odor of curry hung in the stagnant air. As his eyes adjusted to the dimness, the living room came into focus. What it lacked in square footage, it made up for in prewar ceiling height. A couch was pressed against the wall to his right. The far cushion, next to a side table and lamp, had been flattened by overuse. Apparently Philip sat his pomp-ous ass in that spot, and it never occurred to him to rotate or flip the cushions.

On a low coffee table in front of the couch was a Styrofoam takeout container. Roger moved closer. One uneaten shrimp lay in a puddle of curry sauce. A used fork rested beside a mound of basmati rice. Grains of that rice and shrimp were in Philip's stomach right now, Roger thought.

He looked from the container to the stack of books on the table next to the couch. These were the predictable titles of a twentieth-century Cold War scholar: *The Cambridge History of the Cold War, The Rise and Fall of Communism, The Crisis Years.* Even during vestry meetings, Philip had peppered his remarks with lessons learned from two superpowers overanalyzing each other. He liked to quote Reinhold Niebuhr's warning to gov-ernments to not try to play God to history, but Graves had never faced an incoming Scud missile. He was a boorish blowhard who liked to show how intelligent he was. And although he warned against playing God to history, hadn't he tried to play God to the church's future?

Roger scanned the rest of the room. What exactly was he looking for, and would he know when he saw it?

The window in Philip's bedroom faced an air shaft. How could this be the home of a tenured Columbia professor who'd written five or six books and spoke all over college campuses in the United States and abroad? Roger remembered Philip once bitterly describing the spacious apartment he and his wife had purchased together three years before their divorce. "I got screwed. That place has probably tripled in value since she bought me out," he'd said with obvious resentment.

Roger closed the curtain and twisted the dimmer switch on a halogen lamp in the corner to a low light he judged would go unnoticed beyond the curtains. As he stepped away from the lamp, he realized that he'd just left another set of fingerprints and quickly took out his handkerchief again to wipe the switch.

The modern black lacquer desk by the window did not suit the space at all. Stacks of loose papers and books covered the left and right sides. The inside of a Columbia University mug was stained by coffee. A pair of vintage Nikita Khrushchev and Fidel Castro bobbleheads grimaced up at him with bright-red puckered lips. The words "Kissin Kuzzins" appeared on the base of each bobblehead. Roger stared at the messy desktop. The proof had to be here.

He examined the papers in the left stack—student essays, photocopied and stapled readings, magazines, and journals. He pulled a folder from the bottom of the stack and began to read the opening chapter of a novel Philip was apparently writing. After two paragraphs, he flung it onto the seat of the desk chair. *You pretentious dilettante,* he thought. Using his handkerchief to avoid leaving prints, he opened each desk drawer and looked inside. He was contemplating where else to look when his iPhone screen lit up with the image of Kendra, and the vibrating phone slipped out of his hand and crashed onto Philip's laptop keyboard, causing it to come to life. Roger lifted the phone. Shit. He'd meant to call Kendra. Had she already spoken to someone else at the church?

He took a deep breath before he accepted the call. "Yeah, babe."

"I've been calling and calling you, Roger."

"I know. I'm sorry. My phone was on silent."

"Where are you? It's almost three."

"You didn't call Vivian?"

"Yes, but she didn't pick up either."

He took a deep breath of relief. And she hadn't gone to the church either, he told himself. She wouldn't have done that, not with Charlotte sleeping. Kendra was taking her new role as a mother very seriously. "I'm still at the church. Something bad has happened. Philip and Emily are dead."

"Oh, my God."

He gave her the basic facts. "I'll be able to tell you more in the morning—before I go to the airport. Now get some sleep. I'll be home very soon. Don't worry about me."

He hung up and stared at the illuminated password screen of Philip Graves's laptop.

CHAPTER 25

The restroom stall was cramped, the hot and cold faucet levers squeaked, and the clear plastic soap dispenser was filled with pink liquid that Codella recognized as generic-brand hand soap. She cupped cold water in her palms and splashed it onto her cheeks. Then she dried her face and hands on a paper towel and stared into the mirror. For someone who'd been up for twenty-one hours, she didn't look too terrible, she decided.

She pushed some hair out of her eyes and turned away from the mirror. As she made her way through the corridor, out the door, and down the steps to the garden, she thought about the three vestry members she'd spoken with. Roger Sturgis had tried to rattle her with overt sexual provocations. Susan Bentley's cautious, controlled answers had made her thoughts and emotions difficult to read. Peter Linton had been an open book of anger and resentment. Hardly anyone had mentioned Emily Flounders, and no one expressed the slightest sorrow for Philip Graves. Codella could only conclude that they hadn't liked the senior vestry warden, but had one of them killed him?

She ducked under the crime scene tape cordoning off Emily Flounders's minivan. In the years she'd known Rudolph Gambarin, she had seen him maneuver through thick brambles in Central Park, slide down slippery rocks to the edge of the Hudson River, and crawl into dumpsters of rotting garbage to lay claim to corpses. Now the small-boned medical examiner had turned contortionist, fitting his body inside the front seat of the minivan without disturbing the body. Codella was watching him run a bright flashlight over the dead woman's hair, face, and neck when Muñoz appeared at her side. As he filled her in on the two death notifications he'd delivered, Sergeant Zamora approached.

"Hey, Detective, can I speak to you?"

Codella turned, and Zamora stepped closer. "We just found a guy wandering around on the second floor of the church." Zamora pointed over his left shoulder.

Codella looked past him toward a tall man standing next to another officer on the sidewalk twenty feet away. A small child was in his arms. "Who the hell is he?"

"He says he's the rector's husband. What do you want me to do with him?"

Codella walked over to the man. In the glare from the crime scene lights, she could see that his hair was light brown and his skin was pale, but his eyes were dark. He looked part Asian. "Something bad has happened, hasn't it?" he asked.

Codella ignored the question. "What's your name?"

"Todd Brookes," he said. "I'm married to the rector."

"Who let you into the church, Mr. Brookes?"

"No one," he said.

"Are you saying you didn't come through the gate?"

"No. I came through a door from the rectory into the garden."

Codella frowned. "What door? Show me."

"Right now?"

"Yes, now," she said.

Codella and Muñoz followed Todd along the sidewalk past the south gate. They climbed the front steps of the rectory and watched him unlock the door. He gestured them inside as he flipped a light switch, illuminating the spacious parlor level of the brownstone. Without a word, he led them across herring-bone parquet floors into a large kitchen with a door that led to a side stair and a garden exit.

"Who has access to this staircase and door?"

"Just Anna and me—we have the first two floors of the rectory—and Mr. Curtis, the church janitor. He lives in one of the top-floor apartments. The other apartment is empty right now. The choir director moved out a few months ago."

Codella stepped through the door and into the dark night. Straight ahead of her were spiked wrought-iron bars of a fence separating the north side of the church from the sidewalk beyond. She rounded a corner and found herself in the garden, staring at the spot—not twenty-five feet away—where Philip Graves had fallen. Beyond that was the stone path that led to the parish house entrance on the south side of the church.

Codella turned back to the rectory door. "Where have you been this evening, Mr. Brookes?"

"Right here," he said. "At home."

"Alone?"

"With my son." He glanced down at the small child sleeping against his chest.

"Did you not hear the emergency vehicles arrive?"

Todd shook his head. "After I put Christopher down, I took a shower and went to bed. My allergies have been crazy this spring. I took an antihistamine."

"What brought you into the church just now?"

"Anna wasn't in bed when I got up to use the bathroom."

Codella studied his face. His dark eyes were close together in a way that made you want to keep staring into them. She smiled. "Wait here, please, Mr. Brookes." Then she gestured for Muñoz to step outside. She led him around the corner and toward the crime scene where they could not be observed or overheard. "Take him into the Blue Lounge. Play it nice and calm—a routine interview—but find out everything he's done since that vestry meeting started."

"Got it," said Muñoz.

"And don't let him utter a syllable to his wife or anyone else."

CHAPTER 26

Anna stared at Stephanie Lund's blue hair. Vivian, Roger, Susan, and Peter had gone now, and the part-time choir director was the only other person in the Community Room except for the yawning police officer propped against the wall of windows. How much longer would it be before the detectives got to her? She thought of Todd in their bed next door, unconscious and unsuspecting. She visualized Christopher sleeping soundly in his little bed. And then she pictured Philip's dead body for the hundredth time. Seeing it sprawled on the stones had forced her to acknowledge—to *name*—her feelings for him. She had *loved* him—or at the very least, she had loved the *idea* of loving him, and she had wanted him with a hunger no amount of prayer, Christian fellowship, or sexual fantasizing would have extinguished. If Philip hadn't died tonight, and if he'd extended even a subtle invitation for more, she would have given herself to him, she knew, ignoring all the warnings drummed into her in seminary and yearly Safe Church training sessions.

She rested her elbows on the round table and buried her face in her warm palms. She found it tempting to think that God had intervened to remove her temptation and save her from a career and marriage-ending mistake. But that would mean God had taken two lives to save hers from ruin. That preposterous—and narcissistic—thought contradicted everything she believed. God was not a puppet master sitting on a heavenly cloud staring down at earth and pulling the strings of individual lives. She thought of God more like the C. S. Lewis quote she had once highlighted: "God created things which had free will." Human beings had to choose the path toward God over and over. They made wrong choices all the time. In her four years at St. Paul's, how many parishioners had confessed their guilty consciences in her office? She knew all too well that when they left her, they would repeat those same offenses again and again. They came to her for temporary relief, for permission to be imperfect. Why couldn't she give herself that same permission?

She stared at Stephanie Lund's mascara-lined eyes. What could a man possibly find attractive about her heavily made-up face and the buzz cut on one side of her head? When Stephanie noticed her staring, Anna quickly dropped her gaze. The choir director probably wondered what any man would find attractive about her too, she realized. The silence between the two women grew, and Anna knew she had to say something. "How are you holding up?" she asked.

"I can't believe this is happening," Stephanie replied. "I mean, two people? Right here?"

Anna wanted to tell her that Philip and Emily were not just *two people*. What did Stephanie know about them? She was just a part-time employee with no stake in the church or its people. She would go home tonight having an interesting story to tell, but her life wouldn't be altered in any measurable way by what had happened.

Of course, Anna couldn't say any of that. "Yes. It's terrible," she agreed. "I can't believe it either."

She folded her hands on the table. She remembered Philip's voice last night when he'd phoned her at home and asked, "Did Peter call you yet, Anna?" Philip was the only vestry member who didn't preface *Anna* with *Mother* when he spoke to her.

"How did you know he called me?"

"He's calling everyone on the vestry tonight. He's lining up votes for his cemetery proposal, and I want to caution you." His voice had been a silky whisper, and she'd wished she could crawl through the phone to get to it. "He's not an evil guy," Philip acknowledged. "He's not like some of the backstabbing vestry members we had when you first got here, but we have a little problem with him. I'll stop by the church tomorrow and fill you in. It's complicated. I'm going to need your help at the meeting."

Philip had spoken with an intimacy that made her feel calm despite his news. She knew he would take care of things. He always had—ever since she'd come to St. Paul's. Without his "hand of God," she wouldn't even be the church's rector. Four and a half years ago, when the search committee had narrowed the field to two finalists, he'd confided, "I know you're the right leader for this church, and I'm going to help you."

They'd met for coffee at Edgar's Café, and he'd told her, "Some of the vestry members are still undecided. Vivian Wakefield, our junior churchwarden, wants to meet you again. She's very influential."

"She's the older African American woman," Anna had remembered out loud as she raised her cup to her lips. Her hand was shaking slightly, and she steadied the cup with her other hand.

"That's right. She's been a St. Paul's member since birth, and many people, particularly our black parishioners, look up to her. If she endorses you, so will her followers. But there's one small catch. The other finalist is black. He'll certainly use that to his advantage. What will your advantage be?"

In the silence after his question, Anna recalled now, she'd heard the hiss of steam from the espresso machine behind the café bar. She'd studied Philip's windblown hair. When he smiled, the lines in the outer corners of his eyes made him look boyish, although she guessed he was in his early fifties. He touched the edge of her hand for just an instant, and the touch traveled up her arm like an injection of some powerful, euphoria-inducing drug. "I don't know," she finally said.

He leaned in. The smell of his citrus cologne made her want him even closer. "Listen carefully," he said. "Your advantage will be your underdog status. You're going to make Vivian Wakefield determined to help you."

"How?"

"By making her see that you are just like her deceased son."

"But I don't even know her son."

"Get her to talk about him. It won't be difficult."

"That's it? That's all you're going to tell me?"

Then Philip sat back in the wrought-iron chair and smiled again. "That's all you need. The rest is up to you."

Anna's thoughts flashed to Vivian at the meeting tonight, her head held high as the conversation became more and more heated. She had held her head like that when Anna met with her four years ago. Like Anna, Vivian's son had been ordained five years before. He had served interim posts as an associate rector in three cities while searching for a permanent position, and he'd finally given up the search and accepted a pastoral counseling position in New Orleans. "He was killed by a drunk driver in the French Quarter six months ago," Vivian told Anna in a voice hardened to conceal her sorrow.

"I'm so, so sorry," Anna told her.

"I would have liked to see him interview for the St. Paul's rectorship." The junior churchwarden smiled wistfully. "But he went where the Lord wanted him to be, and now God has called him home."

For some reason, a quotation from Proverbs came into Anna's mind. "*Commit to the Lord whatever you do, and he will establish your plans*," she whispered just loud enough for Vivian to hear. She told the older woman she had taken comfort in this quotation during her long and so far unsuccessful search for a parish. "The seminary prepares us as spiritual servants, but it doesn't really prepare us for the politics of finding a place to serve. I sincerely hope you find the right rector for St. Paul's."

By listening to Philip's counsel, Anna had won Vivian's vote, and she had listened carefully to his advice ever since, including last night. But now he was gone, and she felt unmoored. How was she going to get through this? How was she going to make critical decisions for this church without him?

She jerked her head up when she heard footsteps approach. Detective Haggerty appeared in the doorway. "Stephanie Lund," he called out, "can you come with me please?"

CHAPTER 27

Muñoz closed the Blue Lounge door behind them. "Have a seat, Mr. Brookes."

Todd Brookes frowned. "Where's my wife? Is my wife okay?"

"She's fine," Muñoz assured him. "Please. Have a seat." He smiled.

Todd held his arms around his sleeping child. He didn't sit. "No one's told me what happened. Why are all these police officers here? I saw lights in the garden and a group of people around a van."

"Two people have died, Mr. Brookes. We're speaking to everyone who was here tonight. We need your—"

"Who?" Todd interrupted. "Who died?"

Muñoz controlled his irritation. *Play it nice and calm*, Codella had instructed. "The vestry warden, Philip Graves, and one of the vestry members, Emily Flounders."

"Jesus Christ." Todd closed his eyes and shook his head. Muñoz debated whether the gestures were spontaneous or calculated. He couldn't tell. People reacted in many ways when they heard shocking news. "How did it happen?"

"Sit down, Mr. Brookes. I need you to answer my questions. I need your help right now."

"Of course." Todd lowered himself to the couch in slow motion, as if the slightest jolt would wake his child. He shifted the small boy onto the middle cushion next to him and propped his head with a throw pillow. The boy's mouth hung open, Muñoz noticed. He was sleeping very soundly.

"You were on the second floor of the church when Sergeant Zamora found you, is that right? How did you get up there without one of our officers seeing you?"

Todd shrugged. "I came in through the north entrance. I would have come through the garden to the south entrance, but when I came out of the rectory, there were so many people standing around."

"The north entrance is where the homeless guests enter?"

"That's right."

"It wasn't locked?" asked Muñoz.

"It was, but I used the spare keys Anna keeps at home."

"You brought the keys with you when you left the rectory?"

"No. I went back for them when I saw all the police in the garden."

Muñoz jotted notes and gave no reaction. "How long were you in the parish house before Sergeant Zamora saw you?"

Todd shrugged. "I don't know. Not long. A couple of minutes, I guess. Why?"

Muñoz's instinct to seriously grill the man kicked in. *Why did you go to so much trouble to avoid those police officers? Why didn't you go up to them and ask what was happening? Were you looking for something? What are you hiding?* Instead, he leaned forward, looked at the worn Blue Lounge carpet, and shook his head like a man desperate for help. "You know this place, Mr. Brookes. You know these people. We've got two probable homicides. Did you see anything while the rest of these witnesses were holed up in their meeting? Tell me everything you did from the moment you entered the building."

CHAPTER 28

Codella wasn't at all pleased as she returned to the parish house. If Zamora's officers had failed to notice the door leading from the rectory to the garden, what else had they overlooked? This was an old church, and for all she knew, it contained secret rooms, hidden passageways, and any number of other unmarked egresses a murderer could have used. She walked into the Community Room where Anna Brookes now sat alone. "I'd like you to give me a tour of the church, Rector," she said in an amiable voice she hoped concealed her irritation.

The "tour" began on the first floor. The rector used her ring of keys to unlock each small first-floor staff office. She led Codella to the large commercial kitchen where Vivian Wakefield had reportedly rinsed out the tea service and where, according to Haggerty, Rose Bartruff had made a surreptitious phone call. From there, they entered the "dish room," where tall stacks of restaurant-style dinner plates, bowls, serving platters, and glassware sat on painted shelves. "We host a pasta dinner for the congregation once a month, and we serve two hundred or more homeless people supper every Saturday," the rector explained as if she needed to justify the massive inventory of tableware.

Down a side corridor from the kitchen was the church's nursery, equipped with three cribs, a round ABC rug, and shelves of toys. Codella stood by a counter just inside the door, reading a note posted in a clear acrylic sign holder: "Parents, please sign in and tell us your pew row in case we need to find you during the service!" On the counter below this note was a clipboard with a sign-in sheet.

They left the nursery and passed the restrooms, and the rector pulled open a heavy wooden door that led into the St. Paul's nave. Codella stepped inside, and the first thing she noticed was the cool still air. Then she heard the silence. The expression "pregnant silence" came to mind as she looked around. She had never considered herself a religious person. She did not pray—although she'd allowed a hospital chaplain to pray at her bedside while she was hospitalized for cancer—and she didn't believe in an idyllic afterlife, a "heaven." Still, there was no denying the energy she felt in this space.

She walked to the front of the nave, stopped just below the steps to the chancel, and stared down the central aisle between the symmetrical rows of pews. She gazed up at the high barrel-vaulted ceiling. This was no ostentatious Cathedral of St. John's the Divine, advertising its grandeur to the world. This was a hidden gateway to the divine, camouflaged from the street—*a holy rift in an unholy city*, she thought. And although she didn't miss the Catholic masses of her childhood, she could understand why stressed-out Upper West Siders would gravitate to this sacred space on a Sunday morning.

In the low light, she strained to make out the stained-glass depictions of Christ and his disciples in the lancet windows to her left and right. On Sunday mornings, she supposed, the sun would shine iridescently through these intricate panels and make worshippers feel exalted. She turned to the rector. "You have a beautiful church." And then her eyes moved to the staircase on the left side of the nave, and she walked toward it.

At the top of those stairs, Codella found herself in a corridor with several doors on either side. She turned to the left and entered what appeared to be a library. Dark bookshelves lined two of the walls. Identical blue spines across three of the shelves all read, "*Holy Bible.*" A portable chalkboard stood at one end of a scratched rectangular table that dominated the center of the room. "Our fifth- and sixth-grade Sunday school class meets here," explained the rector.

In a larger room directly across the hall were three low kidney-shaped tables and matching diminutive chairs. Another Sunday school room, Codella presumed, and she imagined small children piling in here to learn Bible stories. In the year following her father's murder conviction and incarceration—when she was eleven—her first foster family had taken her to mass every Sunday without fail, as if they feared her father's crime had tarnished her soul. They also enrolled her in a new school, St. Ann's Catholic Prep, where an older nun named Sister Mary Catherine placed herself in charge of Codella's salvation. Like the other students, Codella was assigned Biblical verses to memorize and recite, and all the verses assigned to her were harsh reminders that mortal sins—like the murder her father had committed—would consign her to eternal damnation. Codella recalled some of those verses now: "Whoever takes a human life shall surely be put to death . . . The soul who sins shall die . . . Do not murder, and anyone who murders will be subject to judgment." Sister Mary Catherine of course conveniently overlooked all the Biblical passages that sanctioned the killing of nonbelievers.

The rector led Codella into and out of two more Sunday school classrooms. As they headed toward the second-floor reception hall, Codella pointed to a closed door on her right. "What's in there?"

"Oh, that's just a storeroom for the Sunday school supplies."

"I'd like to see it," said Codella.

The door wasn't locked, and the rector opened it and switched on the light, revealing a walk-in closet about twenty feet deep. Floor-to-ceiling metal shelves on either side of the little room held every craft supply imaginable. Codella stepped in and ran her eyes over plastic bins containing markers, crayons, glue sticks, and safety scissors. She noted stacks of construction paper and clear plastic bags of Noah's ark stencils, minicrosses, and plastic lanyard string. And then something caught her attention.

Codella pulled her phone from her pocket as she backed out of the closet. "I'm afraid I have to cut our tour short." She gestured apologetically to the phone in her hand. "Would you mind waiting for me in the Community Room? I'll find you there as soon as I can."

She gave the rector time to return to the Community Room. Then she rushed outside and found the lead CSU investigator standing on the street near the hood of Emily Flounders's minivan. The hatchback and all four doors were open, and investigators wearing disposable jumpsuits were dusting for prints under harsh spotlights. She called out to him, "Can you come with me, Banks? I need to show you something."

"Fuck, Codella." Banks's face was a silent plea for sympathy. "Tell me there's not another body."

"There's not a third body," she assured him.

"Then what?"

"Just come with me."

Banks followed her back inside and up to the second floor. Codella stopped in front of the supply closet door and tugged on a pair of nitrile gloves before she grasped the doorknob. She pointed to some fine granules of sediment on the tiles a few feet inside.

Banks looked where she was pointing. "Yeah? So what? Anyone could have tracked dirt in here."

"Yeah, but not just anyone did." Codella took out her iPhone and photographed the debris. She pointed to the back left corner of the closet. "Go all the way in and look in the little pocket of space between the shelves and the wall," she told him.

Banks stepped in and peered behind the high wall of metal shelving into the tiny alcove of space. He looked back with a sober expression that told her he'd seen the garden shovel propped in the corner and understood its significance. Then he dropped to his hands and knees, and she knew he was examining the rusty-colored blood on the back of the steel shovel blade. When he finally stood up, he whispered, "Looks like you found the murder weapon."

"I just don't get why it's here."

"What do you mean?"

"If these deaths were the work of a random person outside the church, they wouldn't have come all the way up here and found this closet. The fact that this shovel is here points to an inside job. But if I were a church member who just killed someone, why would I bother to take the shovel upstairs and stash it here? I'd leave it at the scene so the police might think an outsider was responsible."

"Unless you knew your prints were on that shovel, and you didn't have time to wipe it clean, so you stashed it here hoping to find a more permanent resting place for it later."

Codella nodded. "Could be."

"Or the killer panicked and didn't think things through."

She smiled at him. "Why did you go into forensics, Banks? You'd have made a good detective."

"People are too complicated," he said as they stepped back into the hall. Codella closed the closet door, and Banks asked, "How much longer before you're done taking statements?"

"We should be done within the hour," she said.

"Okay. Then we lock down this whole church and go through it with a fine-tooth comb tomorrow."

CHAPTER 29

"What time did you arrive at St. Paul's tonight, Miss Lund?" Haggerty knew he sounded more like an interrogator than interviewer, but he was tired of asking the same questions and getting the same answers.

Stephanie Lund cleared her throat. "Around eight o'clock, I guess."

"What brought you here?"

"The Hook and Hastings," she said.

"The *what*?"

"I'm sorry. The church organ. It has a hundred stops and five manuals."

Haggerty looked at her blankly.

"Keyboards. Five keyboards. I'm still getting used to them. I've only been at St. Paul's a couple of months. I was practicing the processional hymn for Palm Sunday. I was in the choir loft for about an hour," she volunteered. "And then I went to the piano in the second-floor reception hall. That's where the choir usually rehearses."

"What hymn did you practice?"

"Hymn one fifty-four," she answered without hesitation. "'All Glory, Laud, and Honor.'"

The title meant nothing to Haggerty. "You were by yourself the whole time?"

Stephanie nodded.

"And no one saw you?"

"Playing the organ? I don't know. They might have. I wouldn't have heard or seen them way up there in the loft."

"Did you see anyone while you were playing the piano?"

"Some guy poked his head in for a second."

"Who was he?"

"I don't know."

"Describe him," Haggerty said.

"I didn't get a good look at him. He just peeked in, and then he was gone."

"What time was that?"

"I'm sorry." She gave an apologetic look. "I kind of lost track of the time."

"You said you got to the church at eight. Did you enter on the south side?"

"Yes."

"So you would have passed the Community Room and the Blue Lounge on your way to the choir loft?"

"That's right."

"And did you see any of the vestry members or the rector when you came in?"

"No, but I saw the janitor. I think his name is Mr. Curtis. He was sweeping the floor in the Community Room. The door to the Blue Lounge was shut."

Haggerty made a note. "Did you see anyone else inside or outside the church?"

She shook her head.

"How do you get to the choir loft?"

"There are several ways to get there. I took the staircase on the left side of the nave. It leads to the second floor, and from there, you take a smaller set of stairs to the loft."

"And once you went up those stairs, you never came down to the first floor again?"

"Not until those two police officers escorted me down."

Haggerty stared at the close-shaved side of her head, the blue tints in her hair, and the huge hoops in her ears. He studied the luminous midnight blue fingernail polish on her long thin pianist's fingers. *You don't look like the kind of person who plays the organ at a church,* he wanted to say. But what did church organists look like? The only one he remembered was an elementary school music teacher who'd played the modest pipe organ at Queen of Peace on Staten Island when he was a boy. "Did you hear anything unusual while you were in the church?"

Stephanie shook her head.

"Did you know Dr. Graves?"

"I knew who he was."

"And Emily Flounders?"

"No. Who is she?"

Haggerty squinted. He couldn't contain his question. "I'm sorry, but what are you even doing in a place like this?"

"The same thing you're doing," she responded testily. *"Working.* I was an organ major at Juilliard. Where else would I be?"

CHAPTER 30

At four AM, the lone waiter in City Diner didn't bother with pleasantries. He shuffled over, stopped at the end of their booth, and held his pen poised against his order slip. Haggerty asked for coffee and a cheddar omelet. Muñoz ordered pancakes and a side of scrambled eggs. Codella supposed her body was hungry, although she didn't feel like eating. "Green tea and a toasted bagel," she said.

When the waiter shuffled away, she leaned on the table. "Okay, let's go over what we know—or what we think we know."

Muñoz yawned and stretched his arms overhead. "Todd Brookes—the rector's husband—says he was home all evening before his wife came home from the vestry meeting, but no one can vouch for that—except a two-year-old. He used his wife's extra set of parish house keys to enter on the north side of the church."

Codella remembered her first sight of Todd Brookes standing on the sidewalk with his child against his shoulder. "Zamora found him upstairs—very near to where I found the shovel. That's not enough to call him a suspect, but it sure makes him someone we need to look at closely. What else?"

"Vivian Wakefield runs the outreach committee," said Haggerty. "She's the one who started the St. Paul's Saturday Supper program, a food bank, and the homeless shelter. I get the feeling she's not happy with the direction the church is taking these days. She went on and on about its glorious legacy of reaching across racial and socioeconomic divides."

He summarized his interview with Vivian and her needless story of Seneca Village. "She seems to think these killings are a sign of the times and that things are only going to get worse."

The waiter appeared with a Pyrex pot and poured coffee for Haggerty and Muñoz. When he left, Codella said, "Peter Linton was very resentful that his cemetery improvement proposal got voted down. I've never heard someone speak quite so passionately about cremation."

The waiter returned with a stainless-steel pot of hot water and a tea bag. Codella stuck the bag in the water and closed the lid to let it steep. Muñoz added sweetener to his coffee while Haggerty said, "Rose Bartruff, the one who found the body, seemed really shaken up by what happened. She started crying while I interviewed her. She was worried about her daughter, who's got asthma. She told me she hadn't planned to attend tonight's meeting at all, but they needed a quorum. Earlier, I found her in the kitchen sneaking a phone call to her babysitter while everyone else was sitting in the Community Room."

"You know for a fact she called the babysitter?" Codella asked. "Did you check?"

"No," Haggerty admitted, "but I'm sure she was telling the truth."

Codella didn't believe in ever taking people at their word during an investigation, and she let Haggerty know it with a what-were-you-thinking look across the table. "We need to piece together where everyone was right after Philip Graves left the parish house." She asked Muñoz for paper, and she began to consolidate their collective notes about everyone's reported comings and goings.

"Vivian told me Philip Graves got up at exactly ten forty-two," Haggerty said. "She claims she's a clock watcher. Emily Flounders left two or three minutes later, and then Vivian went into the kitchen. She took the tea service there to wash it out. Rose Bartruff confirmed that."

"Roger Sturgis did too," said Codella. "He says he went to the men's room."

Haggerty nodded. "Rose Bartruff put him in the men's room too, and so did Vivian Wakefield."

"Why did he feel the need to announce his intention to relieve himself?" Codella wondered aloud.

Haggerty sipped his coffee. "According to Rose, Susan Bentley walked Graves to the door. She doesn't think Susan went outside with him though. She said the doctor was looking for the rector, and then Rose didn't see her again until after she found the body."

"Susan Bentley told me that she and the rector were in the Community Room after the meeting ended," Codella reported. "Supposedly the rector got a book from her office, and they talked about meditation."

"Which means the rector was also alone for a time," pointed out Muñoz, "while she got that book."

"Right," agreed Codella. "And no one can confirm that she actually went to her office during that time—although Susan Bentley made a point of taking a meditation book out of her purse and showing it to me."

"What about Peter Linton?" asked Muñoz. "Did you notice how that guy kept sniffling? If I didn't know any better, I'd say he snorts cocaine."

"Maybe he does," said Codella. "Just because you go to church doesn't mean you're an angel. I bet every one of these people has something they don't want others to know. He claims he went into the hallway to take a call from a client. Let's try to confirm that. We need phone records. We need to know who he texted in the garden and who he spoke to in the hallway. And we need to know if Rose Bartruff really called her babysitter."

"I know she did," Haggerty insisted.

"But *how* do you know?"

"I just do."

"Gut instincts aren't facts," Codella argued. "I'll wait for the phone records."

"That could take a long time," Haggerty reminded her. "We might get a court order, but that won't get us calls and texts from the past hundred and eighty days."

"I know." Codella frowned. "We need warrants, and for that we need probable cause, and we don't have that yet." She turned to Muñoz. "Talk to Portino in the morning. He's got sources. Ask him to help."

"That blue-haired choir director was up on the second floor when Zamora's guys found her," Haggerty continued. "That puts her in the vicinity of the shovel along with Todd. And she says some guy stuck his head in the reception hall while she was playing the piano."

"What guy?" asked Codella.

"She didn't see his face. It happened too fast, she says."

"Or maybe it didn't happen at all," Codella conjectured. "What time does she claim she saw this face?"

"She didn't know. Says she lost track of time."

"How convenient," Muñoz commented as the waiter approached with their breakfasts. Codella stared at the messy graphic she'd constructed—part timeline, part list, and part map. Unraveling the facts from this intricate knot of stories wasn't going to be that easy.

Muñoz upended the ketchup bottle and slapped his palm against the side. "Virtually all of the vestry members were alone at some point after Philip Graves left."

"Except Rose Bartruff," pointed out Haggerty. "She was always with someone else until the body was discovered. If you ask me, Todd Brookes is the most obvious suspect. He had all the time in the world to move around without anyone else observing him."

"Did we check out the janitor yet?" asked Codella. "Mr. Curtis, the one who lives above the rector's family?"

Haggerty nodded. "Zamora's guys took his statement. Curtis confirms that Stephanie Lund entered the parish house around eight o'clock. He finished up his work at eight fifteen and left the church. Then he and his wife walked to Pearls—that Chinese restaurant on Ninety-Ninth and Amsterdam. They were there from about eight forty-five to nine thirty. He had a receipt from the restaurant. Then they walked home and were together the rest of the evening."

Codella removed the tea bag from her teapot and buttered her bagel lightly. "Okay, let's engage in speculation for a moment. We'll accept the premise that Todd had the best opportunity to be alone with Graves in the garden. Why would he want to kill Graves?"

Haggerty wiped his mouth with his napkin. "You might not be asking that if you'd seen the rector when she found out Graves was dead."

"What do you mean?"

Haggerty described how Anna Brookes had wept and prayed over the body.

"You let her do that?"

"She's a priest. How do you say no to a priest?"

Now Codella rolled her eyes. "You're still such an Irish Catholic boy."

Haggerty shrugged. "Hey, I hope someone cries for me like that after I take my last breath."

Codella glanced around the diner. The waiter was slumped in a booth, semiconscious, and no other customers were in the restaurant to overhear them. "You're suggesting she was in love with Graves—maybe having an affair with him—and her husband found out and took his revenge?"

"It's possible," he argued.

"Possible, but there are less drastic ways to get even with your wife's lover—*if* he's her lover. And it doesn't explain Emily Flounders lying in the front seat of her car."

"Maybe Todd had a different reason to kill Graves," suggested Muñoz.

"Okay," said Codella. "Let's suppose he did have a different motive. Are we going to assume he stood outside and waited for Graves to emerge, hoping he was alone? It seems a little farfetched."

"Unless Philip Graves is a creature of habit," said Haggerty, "and Todd knew his habit."

"Maybe Todd sent him a text message to come outside alone," speculated Muñoz just before he shoveled hash browns into his mouth.

Their speculation was getting a little too speculative, Codella thought. "Okay, I could see Todd targeting Graves for some reason, but why would he kill Emily Flounders? What's the connection between Philip and Emily?"

No one offered a theory.

Codella poured her tea and took a sip. "Maybe there is no connection," she finally supplied an answer herself. "Maybe Graves was the only target, and Flounders was unintended collateral damage."

They were all quiet for a moment. Haggerty yawned. Muñoz rubbed his eyes. "You know what bothers me about this?" she said. "Banks's guys found Philip Graves's wallet in his pocket. His money and credit cards were there. But no keys. Why not? How was he planning to get back into his apartment tonight—unless he keeps his door unlocked or a key under his mat, and who does that in Manhattan? I want to know where those keys went."

THURSDAY

CHAPTER 31

Codella opened the heavy door to Manhattan North, rushed past the glassed-in reception area, and flew up the stairs as if there had never been a time right after cancer when she couldn't manage this simple feat.

Lieutenant McGowan's door was open, and she expected him to look up and growl, "Give me an update, Codella," but all he said was, "What is it?"

"Did you get my messages?"

"Yeah, I got them."

She waited for him to say more.

"What?" he finally snapped. "It sounds like you've got things under control, Codella. Take whoever you need and keep me posted." He gave a dismissive flick of the wrist and returned to the papers on his desk.

He hadn't looked her in the eye even once, she realized, and although he was hardly her favorite person, she considered asking if he was all right. Before she could open her mouth, however, he was saying, "Close the door on your way out."

Codella shut the door and headed down the hall. What was going on with McGowan? If anyone knew, it would be Dan Fisk, the senior detective in the homicide unit. She glanced into his office as she passed it. He was sitting at his desk, but she didn't go in. Fisk warmed a barstool next to McGowan almost every night of the week, and on the weekends, they watched Liverpool matches together. Fisk wasn't going to tell her anything.

She continued past the large detectives' squad room crammed with desks and reached the little kitchen at the end of the corridor. No one was there, and she stared at the glass coffeepot sitting on a warm burner. Facing a day on two hours of sleep wasn't going to be easy with only green tea, but she hadn't had a sip of coffee since her cancer treatment. And even if she were tempted to return to old habits, she'd never touch the poison in *that* pot.

She opened the refrigerator and pulled out a bottle of water. She took several gulps as she stared back at McGowan's office. She needed someone to run background checks on the St. Paul's vestry members, but before she could concentrate on the case, she had to satisfy her curiosity. She went downstairs, entered the patrol officers' bullpen, and tapped the shoulder of Farah Assiraj. "Got a minute?"

Farah turned and smiled. She was a young uniformed officer who'd conducted research for Codella on a cold case last month. "What can I do for you, Detective?"

Codella led her into the first-floor women's room and checked the stalls for feet. Then she leaned on one of the two porcelain sinks. "What's going on with McGowan?"

Farah rolled her large almond-shaped eyes. She looked more like a model than a cop with her high cheekbones, sensuous mouth, and perfect olive complexion, although she kept her long dark hair discreetly hidden beneath a hijab. "Jane Young is suing him for sexual harassment."

"Jesus!" Codella pictured Jane Young, another uniformed officer, who dyed her hair blonde and wore more makeup on her shifts than Codella had worn in her lifetime. In the last three months, Jane Young had probably spent more time in McGowan's office than all the detectives combined—until her abrupt transfer from the precinct a week ago. "What does she claim he did?"

Farah shrugged. "Nobody knows—or if they do, they're not saying."

Dennis McGowan had made Codella's life miserable since the day she'd walked through the front doors of Manhattan North with so much enthusiasm, and Haggerty had talked her off the ledge too many times to count. *Wait him out*, he'd advised. *Sooner or later, he'll do something really stupid, and they'll ship him off to some other unlucky squad.* Was Haggerty's prediction coming true?

During the Lucy Merchant case, McGowan had assigned Jane Young to Codella's research team—even though the case was high profile and Young had no experience. She'd spent an entire briefing playing with her ponytail and making eyes at McGowan across the conference room. Codella didn't doubt for a minute that McGowan had made advances, but she also had no doubt that Jane had egged him on. More than a few female officers played the flirtation game. Occasionally, sexual chemistry dissolved the old-boy bonds and got you up a rank or two, but most of the time you gave a lot more than you ever got in return. Had Jane Young gotten a little more than she bargained for? Or had she gotten exactly what she'd set out to get and was now planning to trade it in for a nice payoff or a promotion?

Codella's first sergeant in Brooklyn had wanted her to play that game. "Let's have drinks and talk about your future," he'd whispered close to her ear her second day in his squad. She'd turned him down, but the invitations kept coming until he got pissed and said, "I get it. You're a dyke, aren't you, Codella?" and gave her the cold shoulder until she moved to Vice.

She almost felt sorry for McGowan. Almost. She thanked Farah for the information, walked to the door, and turned to look back at the uniformed woman. "I've got two dead bodies, and I need some research. You want in?"

"Hell, yes," Farah said. "That's my kind of proposition."

"Come up and see me as soon as you can."

CHAPTER 32

Susan Bentley stroked the smooth skin of her wrists. The impressive display of diplomas and certificates on the wall across from her desk attested to her world-class reputation, but it didn't change the fact that she was a coward. Five hours ago, she'd set down the straight razor; she hadn't been able to accept a few moments of agony to avoid years of shame and loss. She would have to live with the consequences.

She stood and willed herself to focus all her attention on the Grubers from Plainfield, New Jersey, as they entered her office. The husband fixed her with his dark eyes, nodded, and gruffly said, "Good morning." The wife, her belly still distended two weeks after childbirth, wrapped her pink cardigan tightly around her as she lowered herself to the navy couch. They would have to face their consequences too, she thought as she came from behind her desk to shake their hands and sit in a chair across from them.

"I've reviewed all the tests," she began matter-of-factly. In her particular subspecialty of endocrinology, forthrightness was essential during a consultation like this. She was not the support team that would help these parents process their complex emotional reactions to biological fate. Her responsibility was to present the facts and recommend a care plan for the child. Empathy only biased parents' reactions. Empathy told them, "You have my permission to feel bad about your situation." For the sake of their child, she would not hold open the door of negativity for them to walk through. She had made that mistake only once and had learned that parents like these needed to face reality quickly and calmly. Life didn't dole out rewards and punishments in equal shares—some parents faced a far stiffer test of love than others—but that didn't absolve the Grubers of their responsibility to love and care for the child they'd created.

"Your child has a condition called Partial Androgen Insensitivity Syndrome—PAIS."

Mrs. Gruber hugged herself.

"Partial *what*?" the father demanded.

"Partial Androgen Insensitivity Syndrome," she repeated. "It's a recessive condition in which the body doesn't respond to male hormones."

"You said 'partial.' So it's not that serious, right?"

"Partial refers to the level of androgen insensitivity, Mr. Gruber. It—"

"I don't get it," he snapped.

Susan felt his impatience. He didn't really *want* to get it. He only wanted to be told that everything was fine.

"What are you saying to us?" he demanded.

"Genetically, your child is male, Mr. Gruber, but—"

"But *what*? Do we have a boy or a girl? Just give me the bottom line."

Susan was offended by his tone and his words, and she struggled to keep disdain out of her voice. "As I just began to say, Mr. Gruber, genetically your child is male—XY—but your child was born with sexual characteristics of both sexes, and from a *gender* perspective, we will have to wait for your child to tell us what he or she is. Partial AIS is a congenital intersex condition." She used the language the Grubers would have to learn. "Some children with partial androgen insensitivity syndrome will end up identifying as male; others will identify as female. Time will tell. The good news is that your child is healthy."

"Time will tell? No." The husband shook his head. "No. Absolutely not."

Susan noted the cold resolution in his gray eyes. The wife placed a hand on his arm. He jerked it away from her. Some parents drew closer in moments like this, shoring each other up in the face of what fate and hormone receptors had dealt them. Those were the parents who joined support groups and scoured the Internet to educate themselves for the sake of their child. But these parents were already breaking apart, and their child could get swallowed up in the chasm they created.

"Please, Jack," the wife whispered.

"Please *what*? Please let me take home a hermaphrodite?" He turned back to Susan. "I want something done about this. I want to speak to a surgeon. We're going to make this right."

"Your child will tell you what's right if you just wait and listen," she said evenly.

"Bullshit."

"Listen to the doctor," the wife said too timidly to have an impact.

The husband trained his sights on Susan as if his wife were not even there. "You said this was a congenital condition. Which of us carried the gene?"

"Does it matter?"

"It matters to me." His tone said, *Give me my answer. I'm paying your fee.*

She held Gruber's stare. In his eyes, she saw the same uncompromising cruelty she'd seen in Philip's one week ago, and she felt nothing short of pure contempt for him. This new father would never bend to the needs of another. He didn't care if he wrecked a life. He had no conscience or compassion, and she found herself wishing he were as dead as Philip now was.

CHAPTER 33

Codella sat at her desk and called Haggerty. "Are you at the church? What's happening over there?"

"The CSU guys are already here, and so are three news trucks," he said.

"I'm not surprised. Two dead bodies at a local church might even sell more papers than a constitutional crisis. They'll work this one for all it's worth. Cordon them off. Don't let them through the gate."

"Don't worry. My guys are on it. I'll meet you at Graves's apartment in a couple of hours."

When Codella ended the call, Farah Assiraj was standing in her doorway with a notebook under one arm. Codella gestured her to a chair, filled her in on the events of last night, and passed her a list of names. "I need to know more about these people."

Farah scanned the names. "Okay. Does anyone take priority?"

Codella stared at the timeline she'd scrawled in City Diner four hours ago. She thought back to Susan Bentley's cautious answers. She recalled Roger Sturgis assessing her like a commodity. She saw Todd Brookes standing on the sidewalk with his child, and she replayed the moment in which Peter Linton burst into the Blue Lounge, rammed into Officer O'Donnell's chest, and ended up pinned on the carpet. Finally she looked across her desk at Farah. "It's a hard call, but start with Todd Brookes."

Farah opened her notebook to a blank page and began to write.

"He's the rector's husband," Codella said, "and he was home alone last night while the vestry meeting was going on. We found him wandering around on the second floor of the parish house near where the murder weapon was hidden."

Farah nodded.

"And look into Peter Linton too. He was pretty belligerent last night. Kept complaining that he had to get home, and his back was hurting, and he had a trial this morning. What kind of lawyer is he? Does he really have a case in court right now? Run him through the databases."

Farah said, "Will do."

"Oh, and Roger Sturgis," Codella added. "When I asked what he does for a living, he told me he rescues failing companies. Something tells me he isn't with the Small Business Administration. He's probably a vulture capitalist. How wealthy is he? What companies does he own? Who's he married to, and does he have a criminal record?"

Farah was writing furiously now, and Codella realized she was talking at top speed because Peter Linton and Roger Sturgis had both triggered her extreme antipathy. She paused to give the officer time. She had once been in the younger woman's position, taking notes in hopes of dredging up information that would make a difference to a case and gain her a superior's respect.

"I guess they're all a priority, Farah. I want to know more about Susan Bentley too. There's just something about her. I couldn't get a sense of who she really is." Then her mind went to Vivian Wakefield, who'd veered off on the long story about Seneca Village with Haggerty. "Something happened at that meeting, and no one's coming clean."

Farah lowered her pen and looked up. "This was a meeting of church leaders, right? Didn't someone take minutes?"

Codella stared into the officer's dark eyes. "Oh, my God, Farah, You're right." She remembered Roger Sturgis peering into the silver minivan last night to identify the body. *It's Emily Flounders. She's the vestry secretary.*

As soon as Farah left her office, Codella called Muñoz. "Before you get with Portino on the phone records, check the inventory of Emily Flounders's belongings. She took the vestry meeting minutes. We need those minutes."

CHAPTER 34

Roger Sturgis pressed his cheek against Kendra's smooth shoulder blade. She moved and resettled. He inhaled the scent of her soft skin. She turned onto her back, and he kissed the pulsing vein on the side of her neck. He moved his head down, and his lips found her nipple. It hardened against his tongue. "Roger," she whispered.

"Shhh." He touched her lower lip with his thumb.

She lifted her head. "I didn't hear you come in last night. I tried to stay up for you, but—"

"It's okay." He ran the top of his foot up her calf. Her leg was smooth, hairless.

"Do they know who killed Emily and Philip?"

"Not yet." He brought his head back to the pillow. "The police are working on it. Three detectives were there. They interviewed us one by one. They asked me to identify Emily's body."

"Oh, my God. That's terrible. How was Vivian? She must be so upset." Vivian Wakefield was Kendra's aunt—Kendra's mother was Vivian's youngest sister—and Roger supposed Kendra was thinking about how close Vivian and Emily had been. "You don't think it was someone from the church, do you?" she continued.

He could tell she wanted him to say no. "It was probably a crazy person who wandered into the garden." He kissed her soft earlobe.

"I hope it wasn't someone from our homeless shelter." She sounded worried.

"Shhh." He stroked her arm. "Don't think about it now."

She bent her leg, and he felt her knee press against his groin. "You must be tired," she whispered.

"Not that tired." He gently twisted her nipple with his thumb and index finger.

"Cancel your trip today," she suggested.

"You know I can't do that. I've got meetings scheduled."

She sighed and pushed him away.

"Don't be angry."

"You're never here for more than three days at a time. Can't you Skype those companies? Can't they come here and give *you* presentations?"

"I have to meet their management teams. I need to see their operations. Otherwise, I don't know what I'm buying. You know that." He pressed his palm against her taut stomach. Last year when he'd placed his palm there, he could feel the baby—his baby—flip and stretch. "Remember, it's the revenue I generate from these operations that's going to give Charlotte her private school education, her dance lessons, and anything else you want her to have. You knew the deal." His hand slid below Kendra's navel, and his fingers felt the small triangle of tight pubic curls her Brazilian waxes left behind for him. "I have to be on a plane in three hours," he reminded her. "So I'll go take a shower now—unless you stop me."

He sat up. She grabbed his arm—he knew she would—and pulled him back down. In a quick well-practiced maneuver, she raised his right wrist over his head—he didn't resist—and locked it to one of the open handcuffs dangling from the back of the bedposts out of sight. She reached for his other wrist, and he let her lock that one too.

He tested the cuffs. "I guess I'm your prisoner." *Your slave,* he wanted to say, but she might object to that word, and so he carefully avoided it.

Kendra had embraced this sexual scenario with more enthusiasm than he'd anticipated. He'd supplied the handcuffs—an
authentic prop acquired for the St. Paul's revels two years ago
when Vivian had asked him to play the cop in a skit. Kendra had
thought to add the blindfold one weekend after he returned from
a trip with a business-class overnight kit containing a black sleep
mask. Since their game had begun, her imagination continued to
exceed his expectations. Now she looked down at his erection.
"I didn't say you could get hard yet."

"I'm sorry." He smiled beneath his moustache.

"Don't smile. I'm not amused." She placed the blindfold over
his eyes. He had to admit, she played her role convincingly, but
when all was said and done, he was really the one in control.

CHAPTER 35

Todd Brookes was standing in front of the gas range when Anna walked into the kitchen holding Christopher. She put Chris into his high chair, handed him a sippy cup of milk, and cut a bagel into sections for him. Then she turned to Todd. "You weren't in bed when I woke up at five AM." She pulled out her chair at the table.

"I moved to the couch. I couldn't get to sleep." He lifted a pot from the left front burner and spooned his steel-cut oatmeal into a bowl on the counter. "I didn't want to wake you."

He set the pot in the sink and ran steaming water into it.

Anna watched him carry his bowl to the table, pour two cups of coffee, and slide one across to her in a silent motion that screamed contempt. She stared at the small brown mole next to his left nostril. She'd liked that little mark when they'd first met—the slight imperfection had seemed to give his face character—but now, as he sipped his coffee without making eye contact, she decided the mole was only an imperfection.

"Why do you think the police talked to you last night?"

Todd lowered his cup. "For the same reason they talked to everyone. It's their job." His tone was like a slap across the face, and she felt her eyes sting. He watched her spoon sugar into her coffee, and she could feel his judgment. He drizzled blue agave over his oatmeal and stirred it in. Was his precious blue agave any healthier than a little sugar? *You have food issues*, she wanted to blurt out. People with food issues always believed their choices were so much better than those of everyone else, and they conveniently rationalized whatever indulgences they did allow themselves. Like blue agave. *You're such a hypocrite*, she wanted to say.

The edge of his lips curled upward in a familiar snotty expression. He lifted his spoon to his mouth and took a bite, closing his eyes as if in rapture. When was the last time he had truly looked at her? When was the last time he'd smiled at her or touched her with affection? "Why did you come over to the church anyway?" she asked.

"Maybe because I woke up, and you weren't there, and when I looked outside, the place was crawling with cops." He didn't stint on the sarcasm.

"But you had to get Christopher up. Why didn't you call my cell? I would have filled you in."

"I don't know. Why didn't you think to call me?" he fired back.

She hadn't even considered calling Todd last night, she realized. Her mind had been on Philip, only on Philip. She sank lower in her chair feeling guilty and ashamed until she reminded herself that Todd *wanted* her to feel guilty—he was a master at turning things around—and she sat up again and looked him in the eyes. "Which detective did you speak to?"

"Muñoz. The tall one."

"What questions did he ask you?"

"Probably the same ones you got asked."

"Do you suppose they suspect you—because you were home alone and don't have an alibi?"

"I wasn't home alone. Christopher was here."

"Yes, but—"

"But what?" He let his spoon clank to the table. "What's with the third degree, Anna? Jesus! You're so naïve, you know." He shook his head. "They suspect *everyone* right now—including you, by the way. And if there's anyone in this family who's guilty of something, it isn't me." He lifted his eyebrows and smirked.

Christopher began to cry. She reached over and took her son's small hand. "Shhh. It's okay, Chris." He curled his soft little fist around her index finger as she willed herself to hold Todd's gaze. Nothing was okay, and what exactly was he suggesting that she was guilty of? Certainly he wasn't referring to what she'd done in the bathroom last night. Even if he'd been awake, he didn't have the power to see through solid doors. He couldn't read her private thoughts.

She pushed out her chair. "Sofia is coming for Christopher at ten. Can you get him ready?"

He gave her a look that said she was asking a lot of him. She was tempted to say, *Don't tell me you've got another meeting. When are all those meetings going to lead to a new job?* She stood and stared at the sweetened coffee she hadn't even touched. "I need to get to my office. If I don't send a note to parishioners soon, they'll hear about the deaths on the news." She turned and left the kitchen.

When Anna walked down the front steps of the rectory ten minutes later, police vehicles and news vans were double-parked on the street, and reporters with microphones stood as close to the south gate as the crime scene tape allowed. She approached the officer guarding the gate, and he held up his hand in a *stop* gesture. "Church is closed to visitors, ma'am."

"I'm not a visitor. I'm the rector."

"Doesn't matter," he said. "You still can't come in."

"Is Detective Codella here?"

"Detective Haggerty."

"Can you call him out here?"

"Why?"

"Because I need to talk to him."

"About what?" the officer demanded.

If she told him she needed to get inside, he'd just send her away. "I have to speak directly to him about it," she said.

The officer shook his head. "Lady, this is a homicide investigation. It better be important."

"It is," she assured him. She wasn't lying, she thought. Disseminating the sad news to her parishioners *was* important. "Please," she said.

CHAPTER 36

"Excuse me, Detective Haggerty," said the uniformed officer, "but there's a woman outside who says she's the rector, and she insists on talking to you. She won't leave. What do you want me to do?"

Haggerty turned away from the CSU investigator who was dusting for prints in the second-floor supply closet where Claire had found the murder weapon. "I'll handle it."

He walked downstairs, stepped through the parish house doors, and spotted the rector sitting on the bench between the church and the gate. Her shoulder-length hair whipped across her face in the April wind. The stiff tab collar of a clergy blouse peeked out from under her light spring jacket. She looked pensive. Maybe a little sad. Or was he only seeing what he wanted to see? Was he determined to be right about her feelings for Philip Graves?

He descended the steps. "Good morning, Rector."

Anna Brookes rose to her feet. "I need to get in my office, Detective."

"You can't. It's a crime scene, Rector. We're not done collecting evidence."

"But I have to send a note to my parishioners. My laptop's in my office. I can't get to the parish e-mail list without my laptop."

"We'll be done by tomorrow."

"Tomorrow's too late," Anna insisted. "They'll have read about the deaths in the papers by then. Reporters are swarming this place."

She was different this morning, Haggerty thought. She wasn't the vulnerable woman who'd folded into herself on the stones and prayed over the dead body last night. "I need to get in there now. Even if it's just for five minutes." She reached out and grasped his wrist. His first instinct was to pull his arm free, but he didn't.

"Please, Detective." She held his eyes without blinking. The eyes had a glass-hard determination, and he found himself wondering what kind of sermon Anna Brookes would deliver the next time she ascended to the pulpit. How would she filter these deaths through the lens of her Christian faith? He thought of the stale homilies he used to hear during mass as a boy. Something told him Anna Brookes didn't download her sermons off the Internet.

He stared at her clerical collar. He'd known priests who lied, gambled, bribed, and raped children, and yet this collar still did and probably always would activate his latent Catholicism and demand his consideration. He heard Claire's warning voice in his head. *Don't let her play you. You don't know what role she has in this.* But he wasn't Claire. He didn't have her superhuman powers of deductive reasoning—nobody else he knew did. Instead, he had his gut instincts, and right now his gut told him to trust Anna Brookes, just like he'd trusted Rose Bartruff in the kitchen last night. "Come on," he said.

He led her through the front door, past the Community Room and Blue Lounge, and they turned left toward her small windowless office. Anna sat at her desk, opened her laptop, and powered it on. He stood over her left shoulder as she opened an e-mail and began a note to her parishioners. "*With deep sadness, I write to inform you that our beloved senior vestry warden, Philip Graves, and vestry secretary, Emily Flounders, have died.*"

He watched her agonize over each word of the lengthy missive until she came to her conclusion. *"At times like these, we must seek our strength and solace in each other and in God. Please join me on Saturday at 11 AM for a prayer vigil of remembrance. May Emily's and Philip's souls, and the souls of all the faithful departed, rest in peace."*

She clicked the send button, closed her computer, and turned to face him. "Thank you, Detective. You have your work to do, and I have mine." She rose. "Please find the killer for us."

"We will, Rector. Don't worry. We will."

She walked to the door, stopped, and turned back. Her mouth opened, but she didn't speak. She looked at him for several seconds.

Haggerty sensed her indecision. "Is there something you want to tell me, Rector? Something you think I should know?"

Anna Brookes shook her head. "No."

She didn't sound convincing. "Are you sure?" he asked.

"Yes." But she didn't look him in the eyes as she answered.

Haggerty reached in his pocket, pulled out a card, and handed it to her. "If you change your mind," he said gently, "you can call me anytime."

CHAPTER 37

Muñoz phoned Codella as soon as he checked the evidence room. "Emily Flounders didn't have any vestry minutes in her possession last night when we found her," he said. "I have an itemized list of everything that was in her purse, pockets, and minivan. I'll bring it to you when we meet over lunch. And so far, CSU has found nothing like that in the church. But they're keeping their eyes open."

"Thanks, Eduardo," she said. "Let's hope you can get us some phone records."

"I'll do my best, Detective."

Vic Portino was on his way to his desk with a mug of black coffee when Muñoz found him. "Detective Codella said you might be able to help me get some phone records fast. She said you have sources."

"*Had.*" Portino slurped his coffee. "I'm down to one right now. It's not like the old days when I had a whole Rolodex to tap."

Muñoz watched the veteran detective lumber back to his desk. He needed knee surgery, but he didn't want to have it until he retired in three months. "Meniscus tear," he told anyone who asked why he was limping. "I wish I could say I was chasing a perp, but I was crossing Broadway to go to the bank, and I tripped. Son of a bitch."

Portino sat and sipped his coffee again. "Everything's digital now. You log into the system and leave a big fat trail. Most of my sources got spooked." He set the mug on his desk and sniffled. "Now I just got my cousin at Verizon. I've helped him with a few little law enforcement matters, so he owes me. But even he only does it if I really lean on him."

"This is a big case, Detective Portino. Two dead vestry members at St. Paul's Church. Looks like a double homicide. We're gonna need you to lean."

Portino flexed his stubby fingers and smiled. "For Codella? Sure. Can't think of anyone else I'd rather help on my way out the door." Muñoz heard detachment in Portino's voice. The older detective no longer shared Codella's hunger to lead the charge or Muñoz's urgency to prove himself. "You got the numbers?" Portino held out his hand.

Muñoz reached in his jacket pocket and pulled out a list. Portino ran his eyes down the eight names. "I can only help you with the Verizon ones. Find out which those are." He handed the sheet of paper back to Muñoz.

"How do I do that?" Muñoz asked.

Portino shook his head. "Don't let Codella know you asked me that. Go get on the Internet and figure it out. It's not rocket science."

Muñoz logged onto his computer, searched "how to get someone's cell provider," and found a site to look up carriers. One by one, he entered each of the eight numbers. Three were Verizon subscribers—Peter Linton, Stephanie Lund, and Vivian Wakefield.

Muñoz took the numbers to Portino. "How long do you think it'll take your cousin?"

"In a hurry to make an impression?" Portino smirked. "Sit down and take a deep breath," he said. "We'll get you something. Don't worry."

CHAPTER 38

The parquet creaked beneath Codella's shoes as she followed the narrow passage into the living room. In the center of the room, she turned in a slow three sixty, giving herself time to absorb the sights, sounds, and smells of Philip Graves's apartment. This was as close as she would ever get to the living man.

Haggerty came up behind her. "It stinks like rotten fish in here."

Codella pointed a gloved finger at the food container on the coffee table. "His Last Supper—sans disciples."

She watched Haggerty's repulsed expression as he stared at the decomposing shrimp. "What a fucking pig," he said. "You'd think he could carry his dinner to the garbage before he went to his meeting."

"He wouldn't get away with that in my apartment," she said.

"Uh-oh. Sounds like a warning." Haggerty grinned.

Codella smiled. Then she turned and stared at miniature tumbleweeds of dust next to the baseboard molding. She pointed to the pile of books on the end table, a stack of old newspapers next to the couch, and a teetering tower of dog-eared magazines on a chair. She lifted a copy of a book written by Philip Graves—*The Coldest Thirteen Days*—and scanned the jacket flap.

"He was a fucking hoarder." Haggerty pointed to the clutter. "I can't imagine what the rector saw in him."

She set down the book. "Maybe they liked to talk about religion and history."

"Yeah, right." Haggerty rolled his eyes. "I know what I saw last night, and I'm telling you, if you'd seen her kneeling in that garden, you'd have drawn the same conclusion. She was in love with him." He scratched the back of his neck. "I just can't figure out what she saw in him. The guy was a good twenty years older than her."

"Maybe she's got daddy issues."

"Or maybe they were fucking each other."

"One doesn't preclude the other."

"We need to find out. But how?"

"That's easy," said Codella. "We ask her."

"And she'll deny it."

"Maybe, but then we'll ask her if she's lying, and if she is, she's not going to be able to do it convincingly a second time."

"Her Christian conscience?"

"Right."

Codella's phone rang. Banks said, "That shovel you found, Codella? Somebody wiped the shaft of the spade clean. No prints."

"That's it? That's why you called?"

"No, I called because we did get something."

"What?"

Haggerty wandered into the kitchen.

"A tiny spot of blood on the handle grip. There was a metal edge jutting out. Whoever held that spade got a little cut. The blood is a different type from the blood on the back of the blade. Graves's blood is A positive. This blood is O positive."

Codella sighed. "That's about as common as you get, Banks. That's not going to help me all that much unless I can match DNA."

"Well, it's something," he said. "Don't shoot the messenger."

Codella hung up, and Haggerty called out, "Hey, come look at this."

Two empty wineglasses and a corked bottle of wine were on the kitchen counter next to the stainless-steel sink. Haggerty read the label on the bottle. "Who do you suppose sipped this lovely Central Coast Cabernet with him?"

Codella stared at the dried sediment in the bottom of the glasses and examined the lipstick print on the rim of one glass. "Looks like he entertained a woman."

"I bet it was Anna Brookes," Haggerty said.

"She wasn't wearing lipstick last night."

"She probably doesn't wear it when she's being the St. Paul's rector, but she might wear it to visit the man she's in love with."

Codella moved closer to the blotchy pink half circle and studied the small vertical creases the lower lip had left behind. It looked like any of a thousand other lipstick prints, but the creases, she knew, were as unique as a fingerprint, and the traces of DNA the print contained could be compared to other DNA samples, including the blood on the shovel handle.

"We need to know who was here." She stepped back and photographed the sink area with her iPhone. "Put that glass in an evidence bag, and get it to Banks right away," she told Haggerty. "Have him check for fingerprints and use whatever leverage he has with the medical examiner's office to get rapid DNA analysis prioritized."

"And then what?"

"And then we ask the rector if she'll give us a DNA sample."

While Haggerty bagged the glasses and wine bottle, Codella followed a passage from the living room to the other rooms in the apartment. The bathroom was long and narrow with floor-to-ceiling subway tiles. The toilet stood against the back wall next to a vintage tub from the 1950s. A clear vinyl shower curtain hung from a rusted rod bolted to the walls. Codella stepped in front of the porcelain pedestal sink, where Graves's toothbrush lay on its side next to the soap dish. His electric razor was plugged into the wall socket beside the medicine cabinet. She opened the cabinet with two gloved fingers. All he had in there was a bottle of cologne, a nail clipper, and a tube of bacitracin. It was like the man was living out of a travel kit.

She wandered into his bedroom. In her years of searching the apartments of the dead, she had seen messy unmade beds like this one and others meticulously staged with elegant throw pillows and fluffy duvets. For some people, she had come to understand, an apartment was merely a private repository for self and possessions. For others, it was a painstakingly constructed work of art. In both cases, it provided a window into its owner's customs and values.

Evidently, Philip Graves had cared little about this space. His clothes lay on the floor and on the radiator. His stand-up halogen lamp—which he'd left on—listed to one side. The black desk below his window looked like cheap office furniture. The chair was pulled out, and a binder lay on the seat.

Codella took out her iPhone and photographed the desk and chair. She snapped pictures of the unmade bed and the lit halogen lamp. Then she opened the binder, careful to touch only the upper right edge. *Moscow Nights*, she read. *A Novel by Philip J. Graves.*

She turned the page and started to read as Haggerty's footsteps approached.

"*Thomas Dexter peered silently out his fifth-floor window at the Four Seasons Hotel, steps from Red Square. The summer night sky glowed iridescently above the silhouetted Kremlin. A cold shiver of terror pierced his chest like a dagger as he pictured Vera smiling at him in her bed hours ago. How long after he'd left her had she waited to pick up the phone and call her handlers? How long would it be before someone knocked on his door? How painful would the interrogation be? He could try to run, but he knew they would find him.*"

Codella stopped reading. "Our dead man was a John le Carré wannabe." She closed the binder and stared at it.

"What's wrong?" Haggerty asked.

"Why is it lying on the chair? Why isn't it on the desk?" She turned and pointed to the halogen lamp. "And why is that light on?"

"For the same reason his dinner is still sitting in the living room."

"You mean because he's a slob?"

"Isn't it obvious?"

Codella studied the stacks of papers on either side of the desk. The surface between the stacks was empty except for the familiar connector end of a white Mac power cable. "Did we inventory a laptop for Graves last night?"

"Nope. Only what was in his pockets—wallet, coins, gum."

"And no keys," she remembered aloud as she pointed to the cable. "He powers a computer here. Look around. See if you can find a laptop."

Haggerty pulled a black laptop case from under the desk. "Empty," he said.

"Look in the closet. Look in the other rooms. Make sure there's no computer in this apartment."

Haggerty was gone several minutes before he returned empty handed. "It could be in his Columbia office," he suggested.

Codella stared at the dim glow of the halogen lamp. She studied the *Moscow Nights* binder resting on the chair. "Call Portino. Ask him to send someone up to Graves's office to check. I think somebody might have beaten us here."

CHAPTER 39

Roger Sturgis cradled the phone between his ear and his shoulder. "I don't know yet," he said in a low voice as he waited for a man blocking the aisle to lift his luggage into the overhead bin. "Keep your fingers crossed. Look, I have to hang up now. And don't call me again. I'll call you when I know something."

He found his main cabin row—he'd booked too late to get first class—and placed his carry-on bag on his seat. The man assigned to the middle seat next to him was extremely heavy and had raised the armrest to give himself more space. His beefy bicep completely concealed the armrest, and his torso and thigh usurped almost half of Roger's aisle seat. His head was turned toward the window—deliberately, Roger suspected.

Roger walked to the back of the plane where a flight attendant with long brunette hair was placing cans of seltzer and soda into storage drawers. When she noticed him, he smiled. "I wonder if you could help me."

"I'll certainly try," she said pleasantly.

He pointed over his shoulder. "I'm on the aisle in row fourteen, and there's a very large man taking up half of my seat. Do you think you might be able to find me a different aisle seat—or am I supposed to charge him rent?"

The flight attendant tapped her long pink nails against the lapel of her jacket. "It's not a full flight. Wait here," she whispered, "and I'll see what I can do."

Ten minutes later, Roger sat back and closed his eyes in a premium main cabin seat on the aisle of the spacious exit row. He felt intensely focused and alert. Sex with Kendra always helped him concentrate, and he was impatient for the plane to get off the ground so that he could get to work.

When they finally hurtled down the runway, the molded interior walls of the fuselage vibrated and the overhead compartments rattled. His mind flashed back to flying over the desert in rickety Apache helicopters while he was in Iraq and Kuwait. When the nose of the plane tilted skyward, the laptop case under the seat in front of him slid against his shoes. He closed his eyes and felt the surge of the jet engines.

As soon as they reached ten thousand feet, he removed the laptop from the bag, set it on his tray table, and powered it on. Seconds later he was staring at the same password screen from the night before in Philip's bedroom.

He pressed *enter* on the optimistic off chance that Graves hadn't set a password—but the computer rejected his effort. He took a deep breath and released it slowly. What were the usual sources of people's passwords? Children's names? Wives' names? Dogs' or cats' names? Philip had no children—at least none that he talked about—and his ex-wife, Jill, had divorced him and walked away with the co-op apartment he'd been so proud of. He still smarted over the loss of that river-view real estate. No way would he want to think of his ex-wife every time he accessed a document. In truth, Philip only ever wanted to think about one person.

Roger typed in variations on the name *Philip Graves*, but the computer did not lower its defenses. He entered Philip's initials, address, apartment number, and street name. Nothing happened. He thought back on all his conversations with the vestry warden over the past three years. Had Philip ever mentioned a favorite movie? A vacation spot? A book or author he liked? Then Roger remembered Philip once telling the whole vestry about the positive reviews he'd received on his most recent book, *The Coldest Thirteen Days*, his analysis of the Cuban Missile Crisis. "You can get it on Amazon," he'd said as if any of them wanted to read his academic tome. Roger typed in the title now—with and without spaces and capitalization—but to no avail.

As the drinks cart came down the aisle, he tried other words related to Philip's area of expertise. *Cold War. Russia. Soviets. Stalin. Khrushchev.* Each word was rejected. *Cuban Missile Crisis. Bay of Pigs. KGB. Arms race. Nuclear arsenal. Kennedy. NATO. Gorbachev. Glasnost. Perestroika.* None of them unlocked the computer, and he felt his jaw tighten with frustration. How would he ever pick out the right combination? For all he knew, Philip had used an obscure reference from his distant past, something no one would ever be able to guess.

The flight attendant who'd found him his new seat stopped the drinks cart next to his aisle. Roger ordered a seltzer, and as she poured it for him, she asked if he was comfortable now. He forced a smile and said, "Very. You saved me." But the only thing that could save him right now was the password, he thought as her cart rolled on.

He closed his eyes. *Think, goddammit. Concentrate.* He imagined himself back in Philip's bedroom. He stared down at the pencil holder, laptop, and stacks of papers on the man's cluttered desk. He visualized the unwashed Columbia College coffee mug. And then he saw the puckered lips on the Khrushchev and Castro bobbleheads standing by the mug. He read the words "Kissin Kuzzins" on the base of each bobblehead. He opened his eyes, set his seltzer on the floor between his feet, typed those two words into the password box, held his breath, and pressed *enter* again.

The password screen dissolved.

CHAPTER 40

The door opened, and Emily Flounders's daughter, Martha, hugged Anna so tightly that the rector could only take shallow breaths. When Martha finally released her, Anna noticed that the young woman's eyes were swollen and red. "Thank you for coming, Mother Anna," she said.

"Of course, Martha." Anna placed her arm around Martha's shoulder. "Of course I came."

They walked into Emily Flounders's living room where a thinner, slightly younger version of Emily sat on the edge of a gold couch. Anna approached the woman and held out her hand. "You must be Emily's sister."

"Edith." The woman nodded.

"Edith. I'm so very sorry to meet you under these circumstances. I'm the rector of Emily's church, Mother Anna."

Martha Flounders sat beside her aunt, and their hands found each other's. They were like a pair of symbiotic organisms drawing strength from each other. Anna sat beside them and joined their silence. Many inexperienced clergy found silence like this intolerable. They tried to fill it with words of comfort that weren't comforting at all. But Anna had always known not to make that mistake. When, as a deacon, she'd performed her first bereavement visit—to a couple who'd lost their child in a bus accident—she took her cue from the priest who'd sat with her twenty-eight years ago when her father died. She was eleven then, and she refused to speak to anyone. Rector Paul hadn't even tried to coax her to speak. He'd simply sat and shared her grief, letting her know without words that he honored her pain. Anna's job, she knew, was not to convince a grieving person to feel better or accept the will of God before they were ready.

She breathed evenly and waited for Martha and Edith to tell her what they needed.

"I didn't get to see my mother," Martha murmured after several moments. "I didn't get to say good-bye to her." The muscles in Martha's face tensed in a spasm of emotional pain.

"I understand, Martha." Anna stroked the daughter's arm. Even the very devout sometimes couldn't take comfort in the soul's eternal life until they'd said good-bye to the flesh and bones of their departed.

"Detective Codella told me they're doing an autopsy today. Can I see her after that?"

Anna could think of no delicate way to tell Martha that seeing her mother's body after an autopsy would not be comforting. Instead, she took Martha's free hand and squeezed it.

"Who would do this to Emily?" asked Edith. "My sister was such a good person. She never hurt anyone. She was so kind, so giving."

"She was all those things, Edith." Anna spoke with the sober respect she would expect for her loved one. She stole a glance at her wristwatch. She still had an hour before she was supposed to meet Vivian Wakefield at the rectory. She met Edith's tired eyes. "Emily will be mourned by so many people. She was a stalwart of St. Paul's."

CHAPTER 41

Muñoz was already seated when Codella and Haggerty got to Edgar's Café. They joined him at a round table in front of the pastry display. Codella peeled off her leather jacket, hung it on the back of the chair, sat down, and turned to Muñoz. "Well?"

Muñoz flipped to a page in his spiral notebook. "I've got last night's call records for Vivian Wakefield, Peter Linton, and Stephanie Lund."

The waitress came and they ordered. As she left, Haggerty unfolded his napkin and set it on his lap. Codella stared at the portrait of Edgar Allan Poe—the Edgar's Café namesake—hanging on the opposite wall. "I want to know who Peter Linton texted in the garden last night."

"His wife," answered Muñoz.

Codella let out a long sigh. She'd hoped for a more incriminating answer, one to justify her dislike of the man. "Well, he chose a pretty odd time to phone home, don't you think?"

"Except that everyone texts, tweets, or Instagrams everything these days," pointed out Haggerty.

"True." Codella picked up her water glass. "He said he got a call after the meeting too."

"He did." Muñoz stared at his notes. "From a two-one-two number listed to a Jules Partridge. I ran his name. He lives on East Seventy-Fourth Street. He was charged with vehicular manslaughter last September in the death of a schoolgirl on the Upper East Side. He phoned Linton at ten forty-six."

"How long did they talk?"

"Only about a minute."

"That doesn't account for very much of his time," pointed out Codella.

Haggerty leaned his elbows on the little round table, causing it to wobble. "What about Vivian Wakefield? She had time to let her fingers do some dialing while she was rinsing the tea service in the kitchen."

"Yeah, but she didn't. She made no calls," said Muñoz, "and she had only one incoming call at one forty AM. It went to voice mail."

"From whom?"

"From Roger Sturgis's home phone."

"So Roger called Vivian Wakefield?" said Haggerty. "That's interesting."

Codella nodded her agreement. "What about Stephanie Lund?"

"She got a call at seven forty-five last night. From the St. Paul's rectory."

Haggerty squinted. "You mean from the rector's home?"

Muñoz nodded. "That's right. From the landline."

Codella watched Muñoz smile as the waitress set down his vanilla milkshake. He ripped the paper off his straw.

Haggerty rubbed his bloodshot eyes. "The rector couldn't have made that call. Rose Bartruff told me she got to the church at seven forty-five, and she was the last to arrive. Everyone else was in the Blue Lounge waiting—including Anna Brookes."

"So who made the call?" asked Muñoz.

"There's only one person who could have," said Haggerty. "Todd Brookes." He turned to Codella. "Something must be going on between him and Stephanie Lund. Why else would he call her while his wife's at a meeting? So much for her story about coming to the church last night to practice on the Hook and Hastings."

"The *what*?" asked Muñoz.

"The Hook and Hastings—the church organ. She told me she came over to the church to practice for the Palm Sunday service. She gave me a whole song and dance about how complex the organ is. But she was obviously playing a very different kind of organ last night. Maybe Graves caught them going at it against the garden wall."

Codella sipped her water and stared through the pastry window at the key lime pie. Edgar's key lime pie was her favorite dessert. "So you're back to the theory we shot down last night—that the deaths boil down to a cheating husband who killed two people to keep his affair from his wife?"

"Don't most homicides boil down to something really stupid like that?" Haggerty asked.

Codella supposed he was right. Anyone—even the most devout churchgoer—was capable of the ultimate crime. The only ingredients required were opportunity mixed with a single episode of blistering rage, extreme panic, or gross misjudgment. What if Graves had observed the lovers? What if he'd said something derisive or threatening, and Todd reacted out of anger or fear? It was perfectly plausible that Emily Flounders had been in the wrong place at the wrong time and paid the price for it.

"But we can't know with absolute certainty that he made that call," she pointed out, "and even if he did, it doesn't necessarily mean that Stephanie and Todd are lovers, but I agree it looks suspicious—especially when you consider that he had a set of keys to the whole church and Zamora's guys spotted him on the second floor, right outside the closet where I found the murder weapon less than an hour later."

Haggerty nodded. "Remember at the diner I told you Stephanie Lund saw some guy stick his head in the second-floor reception hall?"

"Yeah, but you said she couldn't describe him."

"Right, and it's probably because he wasn't there. Maybe that was her feeble attempt at an alibi. Maybe she was at the rectory the whole time—which would explain why Anna Brookes looked so sad this morning. Anna probably knows her husband is fucking around on her."

Codella paid close attention as Haggerty described his encounter with the rector that morning.

"I had the distinct impression she wanted to tell me something but stopped herself," he said.

Codella stared across the restaurant at two women engaged in conversation below the painting of Edgar Allan Poe. She'd never sat across from another woman like that, she thought, with no other objective than to enjoy a meal and each other's companionship. Jean, her neighbor, was her closest female friend—only because she understood Codella's inability to acknowledge her vulnerabilities. A woman priest, she imagined, had to be even stronger than a woman detective, and she felt sympathy for the rector taking root in her heart and mind. She thought of the lipstick print on the wineglass in Philip Graves's kitchen. Was Haggerty right? Did the lipstick print belong to Anna? Had she gone to the vestry warden's apartment and secretly poured her heart out to him the night before the meeting?

Codella looked at Haggerty. "Pay Anna a visit sooner rather than later. Tell her we're trying to eliminate suspects. Ask her if she'll give us fingerprints and a buccal swab."

He nodded.

"And bring Stephanie to the station," she added. "Tell her that guy who peeked in at her in the second-floor reception hall could be the one we're looking for. Show her some arrays. And while she's sitting with you, find out whatever you can about her and Todd."

She turned to Muñoz. His eyes were on the waitress walking toward them with their lunches. She watched the waitress set down their plates. As Muñoz sprinkled cheese over his steaming lasagna, she told him, "You might want to go easy on that. You and I have a date with the medical examiner an hour from now." She smiled. "Time to watch your first autopsy, and we've got a double feature."

CHAPTER 42

Roger Sturgis exited the North Terminal baggage claim of Detroit Metropolitan Airport. Monique was waiting in front of the short-term parking structure on the other side of the drop-off lanes. As soon as she spotted him, she waved both arms like a stranded shipwreck survivor signaling to a rescue plane, and her obvious joy only increased the dread he already felt.

He crossed at the pedestrian walkway. When he reached Monique, she pulled him into a tight embrace. Her kiss was a wet, warm branding. "You look tired, baby."

"A little." He withdrew from the embrace. He wasn't going to do Monique the ultimate injustice of drawing things out. He remembered a guy in his platoon who'd been too close to a mine when someone stepped on it. The poor kid flew twenty feet in the air, and when he came down, his legs were shredded. They got him to a field hospital, where a surgeon hacked off the fragmentized flesh and bone. The amputations weren't pretty, but they were over quickly. Monique deserved a quick amputation too.

She pointed to her 2005 Ford Focus at the end of the row. Someone had slammed into her car at a stoplight five months ago, and the rear bumper was like a crushed aluminum can. Why had he not bought her a new car? Why hadn't she asked him for one?

He went to the passenger side, opened the door, and slid into the seat. Monique's dashboard had no navigation system, Sirius XM radio button, or Bluetooth. He thought of the Volvo XC90 that Kendra drove and felt ashamed of himself. He'd taken from Monique—affection, solace, sex—but he hadn't given her much in return. She'd refused his offer of an apartment on Jefferson Avenue overlooking the river. She didn't want the hundred-dollar bills and the credit card he'd tried to give her. And he'd had to shame her into letting him pay for her son to attend private school. She was prescient, he thought now. She knew that all things came to an end and that you couldn't miss what you never had.

Monique got behind the wheel, and he turned to face her—to say, *I've got to end this*—but she spoke first. "I took the afternoon off so we can be together." She squeezed his hard left quad and turned the key in the ignition.

Now. Say it now, he told himself as the car motor labored. "When was the last time you changed the oil, Monique?" he asked instead.

"I don't know. September?"

"Seven months ago? That's way too long."

She backed out of the space. They exited the parking garage, followed the road that looped around the McNamara Terminal, and took a left past the car rental agencies. *Tell her to pull over.* They passed the gas station on Middlebelt Road. *Say something.* They came to the I-94 East entrance ramp, Monique accelerated, and they merged into the right lane behind an eighteen-wheeler. Then his opportunity was gone, and he sighed with both relief and exasperation.

As Monique concentrated on the road, he surreptitiously studied her profile. Her lips were fuller than Kendra's. Her skin was darker, and her face broader. Each time he came back to her, he stole glances like this, readjusting his eyes to her features, recalibrating his brain to her particular beauty, her idiosyncrasies. He had never planned to deceive Monique. When he'd met her twelve years ago, he didn't even know that Kendra existed. He'd flown in to tour a potential acquisition, checked into his hotel, and realized he hadn't packed a tie. He went to a mall, and Monique was behind the register at Brooks Brothers. He wasn't accustomed to a saleswoman recommending ties for him. As she held each one up to his chest, he'd smelled her delicate perfume. He'd been aware of her large breasts only inches from his chest. She was almost as tall as he was, and when he tried to step back from her, she gripped his bicep and said, "Stand still!" with the force of an army drill sergeant or a mother.

Two hours later, he was sitting in her kitchen, drinking coffee across the table from her four-year-old son, Justin. After she tucked the child into bed, she tucked him into hers. Her naked body was thick and strong. Her skin was so dark that he couldn't see her at first when they turned out the lights. She rubbed the army tattoo on his bicep. "I suppose you got stories," she whispered with her lips against his.

"More than you want to hear," he said.

"Well, I'm listening." And in the blackness of the bedroom, years dialed back in his brain like mileage off an odometer, and what he'd witnessed on a stretch of highway between Kuwait City and Safwan was as raw and mangled as that soldier's exploded legs. She stroked his head as he described images he'd never shared with anyone before, and when he ran out of words, her fingers moved down and gave him an excruciatingly tender release.

Now Monique reached across the front seat and took his hand. "What's the matter, baby?"

"Nothing." He pulled his hand back and gripped the laptop bag at his feet. Monique certainly must know that he had another life, but she never asked him about it. She wasn't like Kendra—vigilant and proprietary. Was that because she'd been abandoned enough times that she'd abandoned her expectations? He wanted to tell her that he felt empty everywhere—even in his perfect life—except with her. In the important ways—the ways you couldn't monetize—he supposed he needed her far more than she needed him.

They drove under the blue steel arches of the Gateway Bridge. He stared straight ahead but focused on her profile in his peripheral vision. Monique wouldn't make trouble for him. She was too proud for that. When he said good-bye and left her today, she wouldn't follow him to New York, and that knowledge made shutting the door on her even harder.

He watched the green exit signs. Ecorse Road. Telegraph Avenue. The Southfield Freeway. Every exit they passed brought them closer to Monique's bed, and if he let her take him there, he wouldn't be able to keep the promise he'd made to end things. Why did a person always have to make either-or choices? Why did you always have to sacrifice one desire—no, one *need*—for another?

They were coming up on the Oakwood Boulevard exit, still miles from Monique's house. "Turn off here." Roger pointed.

CHAPTER 43

Vivian Wakefield was standing on the front steps of the rectory when Anna returned. "I hope I haven't kept you waiting long," she told the churchwarden. "I've been with Emily's daughter and sister."

Vivian didn't seem to be listening. She was staring at the NYPD vehicles and news vans double-parked in front of the church. When she finally turned to Anna, she said, "I see our sad news has spread."

Anna nodded. "They've been there since early this morning."

"Have you spoken to them?"

Anna shook her head.

"I think we should," said Vivian.

"You do?"

"I do." The churchwarden crossed her arms. "To let the public know that St. Paul's won't bow down in the face of violence." She descended the steps, turned, and stared up at Anna. "Come with me, Rector. Now's not the time for us to be timid."

Anna followed Vivian along the sidewalk. They passed the same police officer Anna had seen at the gate that morning. Vivian stopped in front of the news vans and Anna stood a step behind her. Within seconds reporters surrounded them. Vivian pulled Anna closer and placed her arm around Anna's shoulder. The gesture, Anna recognized, sent the unequivocal message that they were a united front. In truth, however, she and

Vivian had never been confidants. Anna had relied exclusively on Philip's counsel, valuing his opinion even above her own, she thought now, as if he were the strong father she had lost so many years ago.

Vivian cleared her throat. "Rector Brookes and I are deeply disturbed by the killings at our church." She spoke with the clarity and passion of someone preaching from the pulpit. "Never in our two hundred-and-twenty-five-year history has our little church experienced an unprovoked assault like this. We are shocked and saddened."

Hands gripping microphones inched closer to the church-warden's lips as cameramen behind the reporters pointed lenses straight at her face.

"In the past year, we have been the target of malicious acts of intimidation," Vivian continued. "Our church signs celebrating peace, love, and diversity have been defaced. We've received anonymous calls demanding that we evict our homeless guests or suffer consequences. Residents of Indigo Tower, the new luxury building on the corner, have falsely complained to our councilwoman that the hungry people who wait in line to dine at our Saturday Supper are an eyesore, a threat to their children. And we have been assailed by developers pressuring us to sell our air rights so they can raise yet another tower to overshadow our belfry."

"Are the police investigating these acts of intimidation?" asked a reporter.

"They should be," Vivian stated. "We've made our situation clear to them. But the detectives who came here last night treated us like suspects—not victims of a terrible crime. They weren't interested in the leads we had. They were only interested in pointing fingers at us. Some members of the church were held in a room until three AM."

Anna admired Vivian's eloquent defense of their congregation—she too wanted to believe that no one in the parish was responsible for last night's tragic events—but she wasn't naïve either, despite Todd's accusation this morning. She knew the people who filled the St. Paul's pews each Sunday weren't saints. Just last week, a parishioner had confided that her husband had a drinking problem and verbally abused her while he was drunk. Another parishioner had recently confessed that he'd used insider information to buy stock before an IPO that sent the stock price soaring. Even the vestry members had lapses in judgment, as last evening had so clearly proven.

"Do the police believe someone from the church is the killer?" a reporter asked.

Vivian ignored the question. "If outside forces of intolerance and intimidation succeed in destroying our parish," she continued, "then this block, like so many others in the city, will become one more canyon of extravagant high-rise luxury apartments squeezing the soul out of a neighborhood."

Vivian wished the reporters good day, took Anna's arm, and led her back to the rectory. When they reached the brownstone's front steps, she said, "Well done, Rector."

"I didn't do anything."

"Your presence does more than words. You represent the soul of this church."

Anna doubted that. She thought of the meeting last night and how she'd hardly spoken a word. She should have done something. "Don't you think we should at least mention to the police that—"

"No!" Vivian cut her off.

Anna was startled by her brusqueness. "But—"

Vivian wrapped her arm around Anna. "Airing the church's dirty laundry isn't going to help the police solve this crime," she said more gently. "It will only damage our credibility at a time when people already have too many reasons to walk away from the church."

CHAPTER 44

Monique couldn't find her insurance card or registration in the stack of papers she'd removed from her car's glove compartment. Roger took the stack from her and started to look while the sales agent made a phone call.

"Why are you doing this?" she whispered.

"Doing what?" he asked.

"This." Monique gestured around the showroom. "Buying me a car. I don't need it."

"Yes you do. That piece of shit you're driving isn't worthy of you." He set her insurance identification card on the sales agent's desk and continued to search for the registration.

"But why now?" she pressed. "Why today?"

He found the tattered registration. "That clunker's going to die before much longer, and I don't want you stuck on I-94 in Detroit when it happens." *When I'm not around to help you*, he thought.

He handed the registration to the sales agent, a small man in an off-the-rack suit that didn't fit him properly. As the agent dialed Monique's insurance company, Roger stroked the leather upholstery of the armchair he was in. Kendra always loved when he bought her things. Nothing made her happier than expensive couture, designer shoes, or Tiffany jewelry. But Monique was wary of his generosity.

An hour later, she drove them to her little rented house on Chandler Park Drive. The new Ford Edge—she hadn't let him buy her a foreign car—sat in the driveway like a diamond glistening in the dirt. The aluminum-sided bungalow reminded him of the dump in Allen Park where he'd grown up. The grass was patchy. The roof sagged. The houses on either side were in even worse shape. But he felt more at home inside this little bungalow than he did in his and Kendra's apartment overlooking the Museum of Natural History.

Justin wouldn't be home for hours—he had lacrosse practice—and Roger followed Monique into her back bedroom. The blinds were drawn, and as usual she struck a kitchen match and lighted votives sitting in little candleholders on the dresser and windowsills. Roger had always supposed the candles were meant to compensate for the room's lack of elegance. When she finished this ritual, she stood in front of him at the foot of the bed and began to unbutton his shirt. *Stop her*, he told himself as he watched her hands move from one button to the next. *You need to stop her.* But he didn't, and then Monique undressed herself. When she wrapped her fleshy arms and legs around him, he closed his eyes, and everything he was in New York, everything Kendra expected him to be, fell away like the shed skin of a snake. He felt the rawness of the past come back into focus, and he remembered who he had always been, and he didn't want to give this up.

"You came here to say good-bye to me, didn't you, baby?" Her words extinguished the mood.

"Shhh." He pushed her onto the bed and pressed against her as if all his flesh, muscles, and tendons could disappear inside her.

She turned her head to the left. "It's okay. You do what you got to do."

"It's just that—" What? What was it? Why didn't he just stay here for good? Instead of giving up Monique and Justin, he could give up Kendra and Charlotte. He could disappear back into the enervating bleakness he'd emerged from decades ago, this place of beguiling deprivation that still strangely called to him. But he didn't want to be trapped in his past. He merely wanted to inhale it in small doses, to resuscitate the part of his identify that felt numb when he wasn't here. He could have rescued Monique and Justin from their struggle, but he'd chosen instead to leave them behind over and over again, the way his father had left his mother and him all those years ago.

He touched the side of Monique's face. "It's just—"

"Shhh," she said this time. "You just go on back."

He heard what she was really thinking. Go on back *to her.* Monique knew him better than Kendra ever would.

He rolled off her and stood. "I'm sorry." He supposed he wanted her to stop him.

"Not sorry enough," she said, and her voice was so soft and resigned that all he heard was his own self-condemnation.

CHAPTER 45

Codella watched Rudolph Gambarin dig his gloved fingers into the incision and peel back the hair and skin from Philip Graves's skull. Muñoz averted his eyes and winced. He looked down and shook his head. She could see that he was dizzy, so she pointed to the restroom. She watched him duck inside. Behind the door, he would either bend over the bowl, she thought, or touch his toes until the blood rushed back to his brain. Autopsies were difficult until you figured out your strategy for getting through them.

Gambarin picked up a precision saw and turned bone into dust as he sawed off the crown of Graves's skull. He placed it onto a stainless-steel tray, where it wobbled like a primitive bowl made from a coconut. As he carefully detached the brain, Codella watched each snip of his surgical scissors like a transfixed neurosurgical resident. Her strategy for getting through autopsies was to focus so tightly on the medical examiner's hands that she ceased to think of the person on the table.

When Muñoz emerged from the restroom, the gelatinous brain was fully exposed. Gambarin examined the surface, pointed an instrument at a dark spot, and described the clotting and swelling he saw into a voice recorder. Moments later, he lifted the brain into his hands like a delicate and precious newborn.

When the autopsy was complete, the medical examiner peeled off his gloves and dropped the mask from his gaunt face. He apparently hadn't shaved that morning, Codella noticed, and his stubble was stippled with gray. He removed his glasses and rubbed his eyes. "This victim's organs were perfectly healthy." He spoke to Codella as if Muñoz were just an incidental fixture in the room, she noticed, making a mental note to tell Muñoz not to take it personally. Gambarin wasn't the most socially adept person. "But he had a very nasty head wound." Gambarin moved to the tray holding the sawed-off skull. "You can see the fracture. Right here." He pointed. "The striking instrument was blunt."

"When you examined him last night, you weren't sure if he was struck once or multiple times," said Codella.

"It was one blow," Gambarin stated decisively now. "He suffered a subdural hematoma in the frontal lobe—at the impact site."

"We found a shovel at the crime scene," Codella said, glancing over at Muñoz. "Traces of blood and hair were visible on the flat side."

Gambarin nodded.

"So I'm thinking either the killer stood in front of the victim and brought the flat side of the shovel straight down, or he stood to his side and swung the shovel like a baseball bat. Does that make sense to you?"

"If the killer swung the shovel in an arc parallel to the ground, he would have had to be almost as tall as your detective here to make contact where he did." Gambarin glanced over at Muñoz. "Otherwise he would have struck the forehead, not the top of the frontal bone. I think it's more likely he stood in front of the victim or just slightly to one side and brought the shovel in a downward arc."

"Is the blow what killed him, Rudolph?"

"No." Gambarin shook his head. "The victim was alive after the blow. You can tell from the bleeding and swelling in his brain—which isn't to say that the head injury wouldn't have killed him in the absence of medical attention. In fact, I'm confident it would have. But whoever administered the blow didn't wait for that to happen."

"What do you mean?"

"There's evidence of mechanical asphyxia too."

"What kind of evidence?"

"The victim's nostrils appear to have been compressed—by fingers, I think, based on the external bruising. And there are ruptures of the small vessels inside the nostrils. I think someone pinched his nose—and perhaps covered his mouth too—in an effort make sure he died."

Codella considered this information. "But according to a doctor on the vestry, he was still warm when she got to him. She performed manual CPR until the EMTs arrived."

"Even if his body was warm, he could have been deprived of oxygen too long before she got to him. It's also conceivable that his head injury impaired his ability to breathe so that CPR was useless."

"Is it also possible the doctor didn't really perform CPR?"

Gambarin frowned. "You're suggesting maybe she only simulated her resuscitation efforts?"

Codella nodded. "I don't want to overlook any possibilities."

Gambarin rubbed his jaw as he mulled over the question. "I've never seen a case in which someone faked CPR. It could be done, I suppose—particularly at night, under minimal light—but this body won't help you make that case."

CHAPTER 46

Haggerty was beginning to feel impatient. When he'd gone by the rectory after lunch, Anna Brookes hadn't been home, and now he was listening to Stephanie Lund's voice mail message for the fourth time. "I'm either out or at the piano. Leave a message, and I'll call you back."

He wasn't in any mood to wait and call her back again. He stood up from his desk in the squad room, swung his jacket over his shoulder, and told Portino, "See you later."

He signed out a car, drove across the park at Ninety-Sixth Street, and took the FDR to Houston Street. He rang the buzzer of Stephanie's Clinton Street apartment, but there was no answer. Luckily another tenant arrived, a woman folding a stroller with one hand while she held her child in the other. He showed her his shield and said, "I'm looking for Stephanie Lund."

"She's probably teaching a lesson. She doesn't answer her door if she's teaching, but the door is probably ajar."

Haggerty followed the woman into the building, carried her stroller to the third floor for her, and continued up one more flight.

Stephanie Lund's door was indeed ajar, but he heard no piano sounds from within. He pushed the door open with the toe of his boot and stepped into a narrow living room with a tiny adjoining kitchen. He stared at two doors to his right. "Miss Lund?" he called, and when there was no answer, he opened one of the doors.

Behind it was a carefully made bed with three stuffed bears—papa, mama, and baby, he thought—propped against decorative pillows as if a child slept here. He tried to square the Goldilocks scene with his mental image of the hipster choir director at the church last night. Had she fucked the priest's husband with these bears looking on? Were they props in some weird sex game? Before he backed out of the room, he scanned the bureau and nightstand just in case Stephanie Lund was the current keeper of Graves's laptop or the missing vestry minutes, but nothing caught his eyes.

When he opened the second door, he saw Stephanie Lund lying on a fake Persian rug at the foot of a black upright Baldwin. His first thought was, *What is she doing on the floor?* Then he rushed to her side. Her eyes were open and glazed, her jaw was slack, and her mouth hung open so wide that Haggerty could see the fillings in her back molars. He pressed two fingers to her neck. She had a faint pulse. He tapped her cheek, but her head only lolled to the side. He scanned her body but saw no evidence of blood or injury. He looked around and saw no drugs that she might have swallowed. He clapped his hands near her ear, but she didn't respond. He gripped her shoulders and shook her. "Stephanie, can you hear me?" When she still didn't respond, he took out his phone and called 9-1-1.

He photographed the scene before he grabbed pillows from a sleeper couch and positioned them under her legs. And then he phoned Codella.

"Yeah?" was all she said.

"Where are you?"

"With Muñoz at the ME's. He just started Emily Flounders's autopsy."

"Leave Muñoz to it. Stephanie Lund is unconscious in her apartment. Ambulance is on the way. Looks like somebody tried to kill her but didn't quite finish the job."

"I'll be there as soon as I can," she said.

CHAPTER 47

The rear doors of a red-and-white FDNY ambulance were open, and two EMTs were sliding a stretcher into the back when Codella's taxi swerved to the curb in front of Stephanie Lund's address. She climbed out. On the stretcher, she saw the contours of a woman's breasts below a gray blanket. The face was turned away from her and obscured by an oxygen mask, but the hand dangling off the side of the stretcher had fingernails painted midnight blue. It was Lund. "How is she?" she asked one of the EMTs as she pulled back her jacket to show the shield clipped to her belt.

"Alive—barely. Unresponsive."

"Where are you taking her?"

"Bellevue."

Codella rushed past the gawking apartment dwellers congregated at the front door and climbed the four flights to Stephanie's apartment. Haggerty filled her in.

"So what do you think?" she asked.

"It can't just be a coincidence, Claire. I think Todd's been here. I keep remembering the way Anna Brookes looked at me this morning at the church. She wanted to tell me something. I should have pushed her harder. Maybe she knows her husband was fucking around while she was at the meeting, but she can't quite bring herself to share her misgivings."

"You think he came down here and tried to murder her."

"What if she was with him when he killed Graves and Flounders? What if he got worried that she'd lose her nerve and confess?" He shrugged. "By killing her, he makes sure no one's alive who can tie him to the murders."

Codella walked around the apartment. "How long do you suppose she was lying in here?"

"The EMTs couldn't say. We'll have to talk to the doctors."

Codella stepped into the room where Haggerty had found Stephanie. "If Todd did this, when did he come down here?"

"I don't know."

"Is CSU on their way?"

Haggerty nodded.

"All right. Let's take a look around here while we wait. Maybe we'll find something to connect some dots."

Haggerty pointed to the cell phone lying on the top of the piano. "We could start with this. You got gloves?"

"You know I always have gloves." Codella reached into the inside pocket of her leather jacket and pulled out a pair of nitrile gloves. She handed them to Haggerty, and he put them on, lifted the phone, and pressed the home button to light up the screen. "It's not password protected."

Codella looked on as Haggerty tapped the messages icon, pulled up Lund's list of contacts, and found Todd's name. They read the most recent exchange from two days before the homicides.

Why are you so upset about it, Steph?

Because it was wrong. I told you.

I thought you'd like a good story.

Well, I didn't. I feel bad for her.

For HER? Oh, come on.

"I wonder who she felt bad for," Haggerty said.

"The rector?"

"What should we do?"

"Pick up the son of a bitch. Let's have a chat with him in an interview room."

CHAPTER 48

When Gambarin finished Emily Flounders's autopsy, Muñoz knew he had to ask the questions Codella would have asked if she were still here. "What can you tell us, Doctor?"

Gambarin pulled off his mask, removed his glasses, and massaged the bridge of his nose. "Frankly, I'm stunned this woman was even walking around. She had severe occlusive coronary atherosclerosis. She was a ticking time bomb."

"So you think she had a heart attack?"

"I don't just *think* it, Detective."

Muñoz pictured Emily Flounders's body sprawled across the front passenger seat of her minivan last night, her left cheek resting on the center console. "Then her death had nothing to do with Philip Graves's death?" Muñoz tried to fathom that. Had Flounders simply felt unwell on her way to her car, tried to call for help, and dropped her phone as pain radiated down her arm? Had she managed to crawl into the car just before she suffered a massive heart attack? "Are you saying she died of natural causes?"

Gambarin shook his head. "Your two questions are not necessarily mutually exclusive."

"What do you mean?"

Gambarin moved to the sink and picked up a water bottle. "A myocardial infarction—a heart attack—occurs when blood flow to the heart muscle is severely reduced or cut off. That happens because plaque builds up in the arterial walls." He sipped some water. "If the plaque breaks off, a blockage forms, and a myocardial infarction results. The question becomes, did the victim have the heart attack simply because a random piece of unstable plaque dislodged, or did an event contribute to that plaque breaking off?"

"What do you mean by an *event?*"

Gambarin set the water bottle down and massaged his neck as he spoke. "Remember, despite humans' so-called higher intelligence—which I seriously question these days, by the way, given our species' poor decision making—we're still just animals. When we feel threatened, our primitive sympathetic nervous system takes over and activates our fight-or-flight response. Without getting too technical, Detective, the sympathetic nervous system sends a cascade of hormones through our bodies, and any flood of chemicals through this woman's compromised coronary arteries could have triggered a plaque rupture that caused instantaneous death."

"You mean like someone attacking her on her way to her car?"

"Yes, like that, except that she wasn't on her way to her car."

Muñoz frowned. "But we found her in her minivan."

"I know, but she didn't have her heart attack there."

"Then where did she have it?"

"In the garden." Gambarin offered this information in the even, unemotional tone of someone describing the weather.

"How do you know that?" Muñoz pressed him.

"Because sediment and a small spiky leaf were in her hair, Detective. I'm not a horticulturist, but even I know rosemary when I see it. I believe she fell on the stones near the rosemary shrub. She has a bump and a slight abrasion over her left temple where she might have hit the ground. I collected the leaf and sediment samples from her hair for analysis, of course." He gestured toward a tray as he ripped off his gown, bunched it up, and threw it into a bin.

Muñoz followed his example. "So we don't know if the death was natural or not?"

"That's right." Gambarin smiled. "You and Detective Codella will have to figure that out."

Muñoz thanked him and left. He was on his way uptown when Haggerty called and told him about Stephanie Lund. "EMS took her to the Bellevue ER. Codella and I can't get there right now. Can you head over? Maybe we'll get lucky and she'll wake up and tell you something."

"I'm on my way," said Muñoz.

He was across from the hospital when Michael called. "I went shopping and bought us salmon for dinner. What time do you want to eat?"

Muñoz spotted a car pulling out of a parking space.

"How's eight?" asked Michael.

"I guess."

"Or nine. Is nine better?"

"I don't know," Muñoz snapped. How was he supposed to think about eating salmon—or anything, for that matter—with the odors of formaldehyde and rotting flesh on his clothing and skin? Michael didn't speak, and Muñoz said, "I'm sorry. I'm not feeling all that well right now. I just spent four hours in an autopsy room."

"Oh, God, and then I call you about salmon. I'm so sorry."

Muñoz backed the car into the small parking space and got out. "It's not your fault. I shouldn't have snapped. You're just trying to be nice." He remembered his words to Michael last night. *Why don't you move in with me?* Had he spoken too impulsively? Relationships were difficult in the best of circumstances. How could he ever hold up his end of this one? "Look, maybe you want to think twice about me. I don't have the kind of job that makes relationships easy. We can slow things down if you want to."

"You're already kicking me out?"

Muñoz sighed. "I'm just—"

"You're just a mess right now, aren't you?"

"You could say that."

"Well, you can't scare me off that easily. Forget the salmon. We'll have some ice cream whenever you get home."

Muñoz smiled.

"Okay?"

"Okay." Muñoz crossed the street and stood in front of the Bellevue ER entrance. He didn't want to hang up. "Thanks."

"Don't mention it."

"And forget what I said just now. I want you to move in."

"I wonder how you'll feel about that when you see all the boxes I brought to your apartment today."

Muñoz closed his eyes and took a deep breath. "*Our* apartment," he said.

CHAPTER 49

Codella's phone vibrated just outside Interview Room A. "Shit, it's McGowan," she told Haggerty. "I better take this before we go in."

She lifted the phone to her ear as Haggerty looked on. "Yes, Lieutenant."

"Where are you, Codella?"

"At the one-seven-one."

"Well, I want you here. Right now."

"Can it wait an hour?" she asked. "I'm about to interview a suspect in the St. Paul's homicides. I think we're making some—"

"No, Codella," he shouted. "I want you here now." He slammed down the phone.

She looked at Haggerty. "Fuck."

"What is it?"

"I don't know. But McGowan's still in his office, and something's got him wound up. I have to go."

"All right," Haggerty said. "Just keep your cool. We'll let Todd sweat in that little room until you get back."

Codella was sweating when she reached McGowan's doorway ten minutes later. He pointed to a chair and said, "Sit your ass down. I got a little video cued up for you."

He lifted a remote off his desk and aimed it at the flat screen on the wall behind her. She rotated her chair in time to see a New York One reporter saying, "The day after two apparent homicides at St. Paul's Episcopal Church on the Upper West Side, churchwarden Vivian Wakefield gave a scathing indictment of the NYPD's investigation."

Codella watched the camera cut to a close-up of the warden and rector at the St. Paul's church gates as Vivian Wakefield stated, "The detectives who came here last night treated us like suspects—not victims of a terrible crime. They weren't interested in the leads we had. They were only interested in pointing fingers at us."

McGowan pressed his remote and the screen went black. "That church lady is out there telling the world these killings are the work of someone who wants to shut down their homeless shelter and soup kitchen. Did you check that out?"

"There are no leads to check out, Lieutenant. There are no complaints on file. And she mentioned none of this last night. She's fabricating. The question is why."

"I don't give a shit why. People in the community think some nutcase is out there and we're not doing anything about it. The media are eating it up. Our phone lines are flooded, and I got a call from the brass."

Codella nodded. No wonder he was still at his desk. "I understand, sir," she said in a calm voice, "but these deaths aren't the work of a person who doesn't like homeless people hanging around. We think someone at the church is involved. This afternoon, we found the interim choir director of St. Paul's unconscious in her Soho apartment. There's evidence to suggest she was having an affair with the rector's husband. We were about to interrogate him when you called me up here."

"We? Who's *we*? Who are you working with on this?"

"I'm working with the detective who originally caught the case. Detective Haggerty from the one-seven-one and his second, Detective Muñoz."

"Them again? Shit, Codella. Are you starting your own little rogue homicide squad? We take cases *away* from cops like them. We don't *work* with them."

"They're good detectives."

"We've got better detectives in Homicide."

Codella's anger and frustration rose in her throat, and although she heard Haggerty's words in her head—*keep your cool*—she could tell she wasn't going to. "I wouldn't know about that, Lieutenant, since you never require any of them to bring me onto their cases."

"That's bullshit."

"Is it?" There was no backing down now. She didn't even want to back down. "Just last week, you handed me a year-old case file and told me to stir the pot and see what floats to the surface. And meanwhile, you send Dan Fisk and three other detectives to work with the FBI on the gangland shooting in that restaurant in Harlem."

"So?" McGowan gave an exaggerated shrug with his arms raised. "We have to clear those files. And you're good at doing that."

"You mean I'm good at doing what other detectives don't want to do—or fixing what they screwed up."

"That's enough whining, Codella."

"I'm not whining, Lieutenant. I'm telling you how it is. You have a problem working with competent women. If you can't fuck them, you fuck them over."

As soon as the words were out, she knew she'd gone too far—that referring, even obliquely, to Jane Young's sexual harassment charge against him was playing dirty. She held his enraged stare. He shook his index finger at her like a knife he wanted to plunge into her gut, and she waited for him to finally speak the words he'd wanted to say for the past year and a half. *Get the fuck off my squad.* But the words didn't come. His face just got redder and redder. She'd never seen him hold back like this. He was either too angry for words, or he was in too much trouble to risk speaking. He stared at her until his phone rang, and then he said, "Get the fuck out of here."

CHAPTER 50

Haggerty's desk phone rang, and he picked it up hoping it was Claire.

"Detective," said the desk sergeant, "there's a man down here who says he's the attorney for some guy you've got up there."

"An attorney?"

"Yeah. He wants to see his client."

"Tell him I'll be right there." Haggerty hung up and ran down the stairs to the lobby of the one-seven-one. Standing by the wooden bench just inside the front door was the short, bald man who had given him so much attitude on Wednesday night. "Mr. Linton," he said, "what brings you to my precinct?"

"I believe you're holding Todd Brookes," said Linton.

"We're not holding him. He's not under arrest."

"Then why is he here?"

"We just want to ask him some questions."

"What questions?"

"Related to the case." Haggerty shrugged.

"Have you asked your questions yet?"

"No, but—"

"Well, I'm his attorney, Detective, and I'd like to see him right now."

"You're his attorney? Since when?"

"Since he called me fifteen minutes ago to say you had him in a little room." Linton checked his wristwatch. "Don't look so surprised, Detective. I've represented quite a few church members over the years."

"Really? Are there that many felons in the church?"

Linton's smug expression made Haggerty want to slap him. "Blameless people need my services all the time when law enforcement can't tell the difference between the innocent and the guilty."

Peter Linton clearly enjoyed delivering this jab, and Haggerty wanted to get him on the ropes, but he wasn't sure how. "You didn't like Philip Graves very much, did you?"

"What makes you say that?"

"You were awfully quick to text your wife that he was dead."

"And you're drawing conclusions from that?" Linton wiped his nose with a handkerchief. "No wonder you're getting nowhere. Now can I see my client?"

Haggerty led him up the stairs to Interview Room A. Linton opened the door and said, "Come outside with me, Todd. There's no privacy here."

He led Todd down the steps and out the front door of the precinct. Haggerty watched from a second-floor window as the two men stood on the sidewalk and exchanged words for several moments. When they returned to the second floor, Linton faced Haggerty and said, "Detective, you have absolutely no evidence to assume that my client has any involvement in these homicides, and until you do, he won't be answering any of your questions. You're on a fishing expedition, and Todd is going home to his wife."

"If he's got nothing to hide, why won't he answer some questions that might help us move our investigation forward?" asked Haggerty.

Linton smirked. "You're not going to move this investigation forward by continuing to interrogate and harass St. Paul's parishioners." He gestured for Todd to descend the stairs. "And if you bring any more vestry members in here, I'll represent them too."

"You're not off the suspect list either, Mr. Linton. Who's going to be your lawyer?"

"Don't worry about me." Linton sniffled. "Worry about finding the killer. Go into the community, Detective. Start canvassing. Run the names of local offenders. You guys have all the resources at your disposal. Why aren't you using them?"

"We are," said Haggerty.

"Really?" Linton's eyebrows went up. Then he smiled with what Haggerty took as false sincerity. "Let me tell you something. I've been a member of that church for more than fifteen years, Detective. We're all pains in the ass, I grant you. We've each got our pet peeves. But we're people of God. We don't go around killing each other. How many more of our parishioners have to die before you realize that?"

When Linton disappeared down the stairs, Haggerty returned to the squad room. "Goddamn that fucking asshole!"

Portino looked over. "Lawyers. They're all the same."

Haggerty called Muñoz at Bellevue Hospital, and then he waited for Claire. Ten minutes later, she finally called to say she was on her way back. "Don't hurry," he told her. "Todd Brookes left."

"What do you mean, he left?"

"His *attorney* showed up and took him out of here—and guess who his attorney is?"

"Just tell me. I'm in no mood for a guessing game after the scene I just had with McGowan."

"Your favorite vestry member," said Haggerty. "Peter Linton."

"You're kidding me, right?"

"I wish I were. And I just spoke to Muñoz at the hospital. You won't like this either. Stephanie Lund isn't going to wake up and talk to us anytime soon. She's on a ventilator. Her heartbeat's erratic. They're trying to keep her blood pressure up. Muñoz will go back tomorrow, but right now he's on his way back here."

"Did you get to Anna Brookes?"

"Not yet, but I will," he said.

CHAPTER 51

Codella left Manhattan North and started walking down Broadway. She didn't know where she was going, but wherever it was, she was going there fast. Her boots pounded the concrete so hard that her knees hurt. She wanted to flatten McGowan into the ground like an ant, and she wanted to throttle Vivian Wakefield.

She couldn't throttle her, of course, but she certainly could confront her. And nothing would give her more pleasure than to see Vivian squirm the way she'd been forced to squirm in McGowan's office. She slowed down at One Hundred Twenty-Fifth Street, searching her e-mails for the list of vestry member addresses Muñoz had sent to her, and then she resumed her walk at a pace in proportion to her purpose.

She rang the churchwarden's buzzer and walked up three flights of stairs. Vivian was waiting at her door. "Detective," she said with an apparent lack of interest that must, Codella thought, belie her surprise at the evening visit.

"May I come in, Mrs. Wakefield?"

Vivian waved her in, and Codella wasted no time. "I see you had your own little press conference this morning."

"Some reporters asked me for a statement." Vivian shrugged. "So I gave them one."

"A statement or an indictment?" Codella snapped.

"I have a right to speak my mind, Detective."

"You told those reporters about some leads you think I should be pursuing, but you never mentioned those so-called leads to me or my team last night. I wonder why. Did you have a memory lapse?"

"My memory is perfectly fine," Vivian asserted. "You just didn't ask. You were too interested in rushing to judgment against me and the members of my church. We're *victims* of this crime, Detective."

"So I heard. The press loved that line, didn't they? Well, they'll love it even more when I tell them I came here in good faith to get those leads, and you wouldn't give them to me because they don't exist. If they did, you had ample opportunity to tell us about them last night. Instead, you gave Detective Haggerty a long-winded history lesson about Seneca Village."

The churchwarden's face hardened into icy defiance. "I don't have to stand here and tolerate your bullying."

"I'm not bullying you, Mrs. Wakefield. I'm simply speaking my mind too. Give me the so-called leads you spoke to the press about, and I'll be on my way." Codella took out her iPhone as if preparing to take down the information.

Vivian's eyes narrowed. Her closed lips quivered slightly.

"You can't give me any concrete leads, can you?" Codella stared into her eyes. "And meanwhile, another person associated with St. Paul's has been attacked. Did you know that Stephanie Lund is lying in Bellevue Hospital right now because someone tried to kill her?"

Vivian's eyes widened slightly. Her mouth opened, but she didn't speak.

"These killings aren't the work of some neighborhood crazy who doesn't like your church's social programs. How many more St. Paul's people are going to die before you help me?"

"I can't tell you things I don't know, Detective."

"No, but you know things you're *not* telling me."

"Are you suggesting I'm a liar?"

"Withholding information *is* a form of lying—whether or not the Bible covers that. Are you withholding information?"

"No."

Yes you are, Codella wanted to say as she stared into Vivian's eyes, and she felt an intense desire to expose the churchwarden's duplicity. "Did you go to Philip's apartment in the days leading up to his death?"

"Why would I do that?"

"Just answer the question."

"No."

"No, you won't answer, or no, you didn't go there?"

"I have no reason to visit Philip at home."

"Are you willing to let us take your fingerprints and a DNA swab so we can eliminate you as a suspect?"

The churchwarden raised her chin. "There you go again, Detective. You see? What I told those reporters was entirely true. You're determined to persecute the victims."

"You didn't answer my question."

"I'm not going to help you conduct a witch hunt. Now I'd like you to leave my home."

Codella moved toward the door and gripped the doorknob. "All I've asked for is your cooperation," she said as she pulled the door open. "All I want is to find the person or persons responsible for these deaths."

"No, Detective," Vivian countered. "What you want is personal glorification. You don't care about me. You don't care about St. Paul's. All you care about is your own reputation."

Codella pointed a finger at her. "We'll see about that, Mrs. Wakefield. Time is going to tell whose motives are truly self-serving." Then she stepped into the corridor, slammed the churchwarden's door behind her, and walked downstairs. She hadn't succeeded in making Vivian cough up information, but she'd put her on notice that she saw through her, that she wasn't going to back down on her investigation of the church members.

Dusk had turned to darkness by the time she walked back to Broadway. As she continued downtown, her thoughts returned to McGowan. She saw his index finger raised at her the way she had raised hers at Vivian moments ago. She heard his livid but uncharacteristically quiet voice saying, *Get the fuck out of here.* Why hadn't he fired her on the spot? Was he plotting a more humiliating form of revenge against her? She knew from experience that he wasn't the kind of man to let her have the last word, so she probably didn't have much more time before he shut her down. She had to solve this case before that happened—but how?

As she passed West One Hundred Twentieth Street, she gazed left toward Philip Graves's building on the corner of Amsterdam Avenue. She and Haggerty had searched the apartment just ten hours earlier, but that visit felt more like a decade ago. She thought about the laptop missing from his desk, the halogen lamp left on, and the lipstick print on the wineglass in his kitchen. Had Haggerty managed to get Anna Brookes's fingerprints and DNA swab? Was the rector having an affair with Philip Graves while her husband was lying in Stephanie Lund's bedroom with those teddy bears looking on?

She had to put the pieces together, but her mind felt sluggish. She was thirsty and hungry. She hadn't slept since yesterday morning. She should go home and climb into bed, but how could she, knowing that she had gone too far with McGowan and that Vivian's malicious sound bites would be airing again on the eleven o'clock news?

She phoned Farah Assiraj as she crossed One Hundred Tenth Street. "Sorry to call you so late, Farah. But tell me you found something—anything—on one of those vestry people."

"Not much," Farah said apologetically. "I ran background checks and credit reports on everyone, and I didn't see anything worth noting—except that Peter Linton's seriously leveraged, and Roger Sturgis went car shopping today."

"Car shopping?"

"Yeah, a dealership in Dearborn, Michigan, ran a credit report on him. Michigan Avenue Ford."

Codella stopped walking. "That's odd, don't you think? Why would he buy a car there? Did he go to Michigan today?"

"I don't know."

"Keep digging, Farah. Call me if you get something else."

Codella resumed her quick pace. She thought of all the vestry members she had spoken to directly—Roger Sturgis, Susan Bentley, Peter Linton, and now Vivian Wakefield. The only one she hadn't interviewed herself was Rose Bartruff. Would Rose be any more forthcoming than the others?

CHAPTER 52

Rose set a glass of water on the dining room table in front of Detective Codella. She watched the detective drink most of the water in a long series of gulps. Finally the detective set down the glass and looked across the table. "Stephanie Lund was attacked in her apartment this afternoon."

"Oh, no."

Codella leaned forward and stared at Rose. The detective's eyes were so blue that Rose couldn't help but stare back at them. She remembered how her husband's blue eyes were the feature that had drawn her to him in their senior year of college—before they'd ever exchanged a word.

"I need your help, Rose," the detective said, "before anyone else becomes a victim."

"Of course," Rose told her. "How can I help you?"

"We've found a little trace evidence that we can't identify."

"What evidence?"

"I'm not at liberty to tell you that. But would you be willing to go to the One Hundred Seventy-First Precinct tomorrow morning and give us your fingerprints and a DNA swab so we could eliminate you as a match?"

"You think I'm a suspect?"

"Absolutely not," Codella insisted, and Rose thought she heard sincerity in the detective's voice. "This is standard procedure."

"I see. Well, if it would help, of course. Is that all you needed?"

"No. That's not all," Codella said. "I want you to think back on last night, on all the things you saw after you tripped over Philip Graves in the garden."

"But I already told Detective Haggerty everything that happened."

Detective Codella shook her head. "Not everything."

The detective's phone was lying on the table, and it began to vibrate. Rose watched the detective lift it, glance at the screen, and put it into her pocket. "You gave Detective Haggerty a summary, yes, but you didn't tell him everything you saw. And sometimes it's only after the fact, when we have a little time to reflect, that we remember everything."

"All I keep thinking about is landing on Philip's body, how it felt underneath me." Rose hugged herself.

"Yes, but your brain recorded much more than that one incident, Rose. May I call you Rose?" The detective's tone was forceful yet soothing. "If you closed your eyes right now and let your mind go back to that moment, you'd see other details, I'm sure. Why don't you close your eyes right now?"

"You want me to close my eyes?"

"To help you concentrate," urged Codella.

"If you think it would help."

"I do."

Rose shut her eyes but felt immediately self-conscious. She reopened them. "I want to help, I really do, but—"

Codella reached across the table and touched her hand. She smiled in a way that seemed to acknowledge that she was asking a lot. "I realize it isn't pleasant for you to summon these memories, Rose, but can you give it a try? Close your eyes, take a deep breath, and let what you saw last night in the garden come back to you."

Rose shut her eyes again. She heard herself breathe. Pixels of color danced on the black backdrop behind her eyelids.

"You're in the garden. You've just fallen over the body." Codella's voice was a guided meditation.

Rose followed her voice back to the scene. She watched herself rise to her feet, horrified at her discovery. She saw herself rush from the body back to the parish house. "Susan was in front of the coatrack," she explained with her eyes still shut. "I tugged on her arm. I could hardly get my words out."

"Go on, Rose. What else do you remember?"

"Susan and Roger followed me back outside. It was very dark in the garden." Rose felt enveloped in that darkness now. "I've been complaining about the lighting in the garden for over a year."

"Stay there," urged Codella. "Let your eyes adjust to the darkness."

Rose felt her closed eyelids flutter. She saw Susan Bentley kneel on the stones. "She was so good, so composed," said Rose. "Susan, I mean. She didn't panic at all."

Rose could almost feel the cool night air against her skin and smell the scent of fresh rosemary. The detective was right. Her brain had recorded more details than she'd realized. "Roger turned on his iPhone flashlight so we could see the body," she continued. "Philip was lying on his side. We didn't know it was him. We couldn't see his face from where we stood. Roger called nine-one-one. Susan took Philip's pulse. Then she rolled him onto his back, and Roger shined a light on the face—Philip's face—and we all gasped."

Rose pressed her fingertips against her eyelids. The thin beam of Roger's iPhone flashlight bore through the blackness in her mind, and she replayed the instant when Susan recognized Philip and leaned away from his body. "Susan looked frightened or—" She couldn't think of an appropriate word.

"Or what?" Codella prompted.

"Or repulsed," Rose finally said. She opened her eyes and stared at the detective. "I know it sounds strange, but I had the impression she wanted to get away from his body."

Codella nodded encouragingly. "What else do you see?"

Rose stared into the detective's blue eyes. "I ran to get the defibrillator, and it didn't work, and Susan kept doing CPR until the police arrived."

Codella stood, moved around the table, and sat in a chair right next to Rose. "Close your eyes again. Don't rush. Let yourself see the details. Did Susan or Roger say anything when they saw that the body was Philip?"

Rose shut her eyes and took a calming breath. "No. They just stared at each other. No one said anything for a while. It felt like time stopped, you know? And then it restarted, and Susan told me to go get the defibrillator. She sounded so insistent. I'd never heard her speak like that before, and I felt terrified because my husband died of a cardiac arrest right here in this apartment, and I couldn't save him."

Rose covered her face in her palms. Codella placed her hand on Rose's back. "I understand, Rose. It must have been very hard for you last night."

Tears ran down Rose's face. She wiped them away with the back of her hand. "I'm sorry. I haven't had a meltdown like this in a while."

"It's okay," said Codella. "But I need you to be strong. Can you stay in that garden just a little longer for me?"

Rose nodded. She saw herself race back to the church. "I got the defibrillator from the Community Room," she told the detective. She had never touched a defibrillator before that night, and as she'd opened the glass case and lifted out the unit, she remembered now, she'd thought about all the defibrillators she'd seen but never paid the slightest attention to in public places. She flashed to all the times she'd sat in an airplane exit row and never bothered to read the instructions on how to open the emergency exit because she was so certain she'd never be called upon to actually perform the task. "I ran from the room holding the defibrillator, and Peter asked me what was going on. I shouted something—I don't remember what—and he followed me outside—he and Vivian." Rose felt her heart pounding in her chest as if she were running the defibrillator to the garden right now.

"So Vivian and Peter followed you back to Philip's body?" Codella asked.

Rose nodded. She relived those tense moments while Susan and Roger tried to get the defibrillator working. "Peter was behind me," she said, "and when Roger announced that the defibrillator wasn't working, Peter told us we had a lawsuit waiting to happen."

"And then what?"

"And then Roger told him to shut the f-word up."

"And Vivian? What was she doing?"

With her eyelids squeezed tight, Rose saw the St. Paul's junior churchwarden standing next to Peter Linton. She described how Vivian's lips had moved—in prayer, she assumed—while Susan Bentley performed CPR in the strained silence before the EMTs arrived to administer shock after unsuccessful shock.

"Did it seem unusual for Vivian to pray like that?"

Rose considered this. Praying openly was hardly unusual for Vivian. She was one of the old-school Episcopalians in the congregation. She didn't shy away from overt expressions of devotion. On Sunday mornings when the congregation prayed, she folded her hands and bowed her head. When her pew row was called to receive Holy Communion, she bowed on one knee before she walked up the central aisle toward the altar. And when she returned to her seat, she pulled out a cushion from beneath the pew in front of her, kneeled to pray, and made the sign of the cross before rising again.

"Vivian was just being Vivian," Rose assured Codella, "and Philip's death probably brought back her own tragedy."

"What do you mean?"

Rose opened her eyes. "Vivian's only son died about five years ago. I wasn't a member of the church when it happened, but I've heard the story from more than one member of the congregation. He was in New Orleans—crossing with the light—and a driver who'd been drinking on Bourbon Street all night ran the light and struck him. He was killed instantly. Vivian had his body flown back to New York and cremated at the St. Paul's Cemetery—Peter arranged everything for her—and now his ashes are housed in the columbarium behind the pulpit. Vivian once showed me the plaque that bears his name. I heard that his death sent her into a major depression and that Susan Bentley personally took her to a doctor and got her on antidepressants." And now Rose found herself wondering if she too was clinically depressed because of Mark's death. Would she also benefit from fifty milligrams of an SSRI?

Codella said, "Close your eyes, Rose. Stay in the garden."

Rose returned to the moment after the EMTs announced that they could do nothing more for Philip. She watched Vivian's hands rise to her lips. She saw Peter turn away from the body and rub the top of his bald scalp. She heard Susan tell Roger, "Well, that's that," and she saw Roger pat Susan's shoulder as he told her, "You did all you could."

It occurred to Rose that Roger had been Susan's constant helper throughout the entire terrible event—offering to take a turn at CPR if she was tired, draping his tweed jacket over her shoulders when she shivered, following her instructions for starting the defibrillator. "I've never seen Roger act quite so supportive or gentle," she said. "And I'm sure Susan appreciated his attentiveness, because after the EMS guys pronounced Philip dead, he patted her back and she reached out and took his hand for a moment."

"Susan took Roger's hand?"

"Yes. It was touching."

"Open your eyes, Rose." Codella's demand startled her. "Take my hand the way she took his. Show me *exactly* what she did."

CHAPTER 53

As soon as Rose grasped her hand, every drop of exhaustion drained from Codella's body, and her mind jolted into high gear. She felt as if the thick curtains concealing the truth were beginning to part, and she needed to part them further. Her phone vibrated for the third time since she'd arrived at Rose's apartment, but she knew it was probably Haggerty, and she didn't take it out of her pocket. "You were surprised when Susan took his hand?"

"A little. But you can't be thinking—"

"No. Of course not," Codella insisted with more fervor than she felt. She didn't need the landscape gardener censoring herself out of misguided loyalty. "Did anyone else at the vestry meeting do or say anything that struck you as odd or out of character?"

As Rose thought about the question, Codella studied her earnest-looking face. Codella had met many people who appeared artless when in reality they weren't, but she sensed no deceitfulness in Rose Bartruff.

"I don't think so." Rose bit her lip. "I mean, Peter was Peter. He's always unhappy. That's just who he is. And Roger—well, Roger doesn't take the vestry very seriously. He only joined because of Kendra."

"Kendra?"

"His wife," explained Rose. "Vivian's niece."

"Roger's wife is Vivian's niece?"

"She's actually more like a second mother to Kendra. Kendra's mother died when she was nine years old—she told me the story at coffee hour one time—and after that she went to live with Vivian."

The curtains dividing Codella from the truth seemed to part a little more. Was it significant, she wondered, that Roger and Vivian were related by marriage? "What about Vivian?" she pressed on as her phone vibrated again. "Did Vivian seem like herself last night during the vestry meeting?"

Codella watched the muscles in Rose's face tighten as she contemplated this question. "I guess so."

"You don't sound sure."

Rose hesitated. "It's just that—well, Vivian always makes tea before the vestry meetings, and at the end of the meetings, she and Emily always take the tea service back to the kitchen together. They're very close—they were, I mean. But last night when Emily started to clear the teacups, Vivian took them away from her and insisted that she go home."

"Can you think of a reason why she might have done that?"

"She said Emily should hurry home because her daughter was flying in, but Emily clearly wanted to stay and help her, and Vivian still wouldn't let her."

"Could Vivian have had a different motive for wanting her to leave?"

Rose tilted her head, and her eyes narrowed. "Maybe. Maybe she was upset with Emily."

"Upset with her why?"

Rose leaned forward. "Well, Emily and Vivian usually vote the same way on vestry proposals, but last night Emily voted against the cemetery proposal."

"And Vivian voted *for* it?"

Rose nodded. "Vivian might have been upset with her for that."

"Did Emily explain her reason for voting against it?"

"Not while I was there. But she might have said something while I was out of the room."

"What do you mean, out of the room?"

"Well, you see, I missed the whole cemetery discussion. My daughter's babysitter called."

Codella felt the words like ice-cold water waking every sleeping synapse in her brain. "You mean you left the vestry meeting while it was in progress?"

Rose nodded.

"How long were gone?"

"About fifteen minutes. My daughter accidentally flushed her asthma inhaler down the toilet, and she can't be without it. I had to get on the phone with the pharmacy. It was either that or leave the meeting, and we already had two missing members. There wouldn't have been a quorum without me. Philip held the vote until I got back."

"I see." Codella stared at two botanical prints on the wall behind Rose. Fifteen minutes was a substantial interval of time. What had occurred in the Blue Lounge, she wondered, while Rose had not been there?

When she got home half an hour later, she was still pondering this question. Haggerty was sitting on the couch watching basketball. "I called you," he said. "Five times, I think. Maybe six."

"I know. I'm sorry. I was busy." She kicked off her boots.

"Doing what?" he asked.

"I paid Vivian Wakefield a visit." She hung her jacket on the closet doorknob. "And then I went to see Rose Bartruff."

"Oh."

She could tell from his tone he was upset. "What is it?" she asked.

He didn't respond.

"Tell me." She stood in front of the couch.

"I thought we were a team on this case." He shrugged. "But I see you've gone rogue."

"No, I haven't. But Vivian Wakefield is spreading malicious information to the press, and I had to confront her."

"I could have gone with you."

"It wasn't a big deal, Brian."

He picked up the remote and turned off the television. "Whatever." He stood and walked out of the living room.

She followed him into the bedroom. "Why are you so upset about this? I think I made a little progress."

"Well, good for you."

She grabbed his arm. "Why are you acting this way?"

He rubbed his chin. "This was my case, Claire. You're on it because I called Manhattan North last night. If I'd waited to make the call this morning, I'd be working with a different detective. But I *wanted* to work with you. And now you're working without me. You don't even answer my calls. How do you think that makes me feel?"

She looked away from him. She remembered the vibrations of her phone and her single-minded focus on the facts, and she knew how she would have felt.

"You don't want to work with me," he said matter-of-factly. "You don't really want a partner of any kind these days, do you? I wonder why I'm even here."

"Why do you have to make this about *us*?"

"Because if we're not sharing this case, what are we sharing? When you're on a case, you don't have the bandwidth to think about anything else. When I'm out of sight, I'm out of your mind."

"That's not true." But even as she said it, she knew he was right—at least tonight.

He turned, walked into the bathroom, and closed the door on her.

FRIDAY

CHAPTER 54

When Codella entered the kitchen, Haggerty didn't look up from the *Times*. She made herself some tea and put half a bagel into the toaster. She was going to have to break the silence between them, but she wasn't sure what to say or if he'd even accept an apology.

She flipped open her laptop and went to the *Daily News* to see what the tabloids were saying. The headline was even worse than she'd anticipated: "Genius Detective or Bully With a Badge?" Her bagel popped up in the toaster, but she ignored it as she read.

> In an exclusive interview at her Harlem home, Vivian Wakefield, founder of three community outreach programs on the Upper West Side, questioned the integrity of the high-profile NYPD detective leading the investigation of two homicides at St. Paul's Episcopal Church. "In my opinion, Detective Codella needs retraining. She's a bully using her badge to attack innocent people."

"Goddamn that fucking—" Codella lifted the laptop and almost launched it across the kitchen, but Haggerty rushed over and took it out of her hands.

"What's wrong?"

"Vivian Wakefield is doing everything she can to ruin my reputation."

Haggerty stared at the laptop screen before setting the computer on the counter. "Don't read it." His voice was gentle. At least he was talking to her now.

"How can I not read it?" Her eyes burned with tears of rage. "McGowan will be eating this up. This is just the excuse he needs to rein me in. Wakefield is making all of this up—"

"Shhh." He put his arms around her. "You're doing exactly what she wants you to do right now, Claire. Don't you see? She's threatened by you. She wants you as far away from the case as she can get you. And that means she's scared of you. She's afraid you'll find out the truth."

Codella felt Haggerty's arms loosen their hold around her, and she pulled him closer. "I'm sorry," she said.

He didn't speak.

She looked him in the eyes. "I really am. I should've answered your calls last night. I should've looped you in. I was wrong. I—Never mind. No excuses."

He smiled. "All right. Apology accepted. I know you're under pressure. But don't do it again, okay?"

"I won't."

"If you'd taken one of my calls, I'd have told you that Anna Brookes came to the precinct and let us take her fingerprints and a cheek swab last evening. Banks thinks we can have results tomorrow."

"Did you ask her if she was at Philip's apartment?"

"I did, and she denied it, of course."

"But you don't believe her?"

"I don't know." Haggerty shrugged.

"I'm beginning to think the lipstick stain isn't hers," Codella told him. "And I don't think it's Rose Bartruff's either. Rose agreed to go to the one-seven-one this morning to be fingerprinted and swabbed."

"Then who did drink out of that glass?" Haggerty asked.

"I don't know, but I'm starting to wonder if it was Susan Bentley."

"The doctor? What makes you think it's her?"

While Haggerty spread mixed-berry jam on her bagel, Codella told him, "We got so focused on Todd Brookes and Stephanie Lund yesterday that we didn't have time to think about the bigger picture. But there's more going on here than Todd Brookes covering up his affair with the choir director." She told him about Susan and Roger joining hands in the garden, Roger shopping for cars in Dearborn, Michigan, and Roger's relationship-by-marriage to Vivian Wakefield.

"What do you suggest we do?" He handed her the bagel.

"I'm going to go have a heart-to-heart with Susan Bentley this morning. Can you find out why a car dealership in Dearborn, Michigan, ran a credit report on Roger Sturgis yesterday? And tell Muñoz to go down to Bellevue and check on Stephanie Lund's condition. Then we'll get together and figure out where to go from there."

She ate the bagel, showered and dressed quickly, and gave Haggerty a long kiss before she left the apartment. When she hit the street, a man she didn't recognize started to walk beside her. "Detective Codella?"

"Yeah? Who are you?"

All she heard were the words *Daily News.* "Do you have any comment in response to the accusation that you've been bullying St. Paul's vestry members?"

Codella stopped and faced him. "You should have asked me that before you printed your story this morning." She turned and continued walking. Then she reconsidered and stopped again. "I haven't bullied anyone." She shook her index finger close to his face. "Mrs. Wakefield's comment was calculated to make the press question the integrity of this investigation, and you should have done your homework before quoting her. Detectives ask questions. It's what we do. No one's been harassed or falsely accused of anything. We're searching for answers, and we're making progress. That's it."

She turned again and walked to West Eighty-Sixth Street to catch the crosstown bus.

CHAPTER 55

Susan Bentley's receptionist knocked lightly on her open office door. "Doctor, there's a detective in the waiting room—Detective Codella. She wants to see you. What should I tell her?"

Susan held her breath the way she imagined the Grubers had held theirs yesterday. *Tell her to go away,* she wanted to say, but she knew she couldn't avoid the detective forever. "Bring her in."

A moment later, Codella stood in the office doorway. Susan came around her desk, shook the detective's hand, and gestured her to the couch. So much adrenaline was pumping through her arteries that her body felt like a bomb about to detonate. "Please, make yourself comfortable," she managed to say.

She watched Codella sit on the same cushion Jack Gruber had occupied yesterday morning, and it occurred to her that maybe *she* should be the one on that cushion. She, after all, was the one who had to face difficult truths today. Instead, she took the chair across from Codella and waited for the detective to break the silence.

Codella didn't keep her waiting long. "Why did you reach into Philip Graves's pocket on Wednesday night, remove his keys, and give them to Roger Sturgis?"

Time seemed to stop. Susan's mind drained. Her body froze. "What?"

"You heard me, Doctor. Why did you take the keys? And why did you give them to Roger Sturgis?"

Say something, Susan commanded herself. *Tell her you didn't do it.* The only way out of this was an immediate and force-ful denial, she knew, but after living a fiction for decades, she now found herself curiously unable to summon one more falsehood.

"Well?"

Susan stared at her pale-blue office carpet and knew that Codella would recognize her silence as an admission of guilt.

"You can tell me here and now, Doctor, or we can go to Manhattan North and sit in a room with a tape recorder on. Would you prefer that?"

"No. Please."

Codella's gaze was more than penetrating, like a power-ful CT scanner illuminating a body's secrets. Susan's lungs screamed for air, but she couldn't breathe. A terrible irony occurred to her. Beyond these walls, politicians were fighting over immigration policy, health care reform, and Supreme Court appointments. They were invading countries, trying to strip away people's constitutional rights, and poisoning the environment. But all that mattered to her right now was self-preservation.

"Answer my question, Doctor."

How could she possibly answer? So much truth would have to be told, and she had worked so diligently to hide that truth. The lies had invaded her mind like a malignant ganglion chok-ing off the self she might have become if she'd been born in a different time and to different parents.

"Goddammit, Doctor. Why do I get the feeling you're not who you say you are?"

The question felt like the sharp pain of a needle plunging into muscle. Susan dropped her head. Her shoulders folded in. She began to sob.

Codella leaned forward. Her voice softened only slightly. "Tell me."

"I can't."

"Then I'm going to have to take you to my station. I need answers. I'll arrest you if I have to."

"But—"

"No buts, Doctor. I've got two dead bodies and a woman in a coma, and I know that you're hiding the truth from me."

"My truth has nothing to do with you or those dead bodies!"

"That's for me to decide."

Susan stared at Codella over an invisible wall that protected her natural self from the unnatural forces of harsh human judgment. The detective intended to breach that wall one way or another. "All right," Susan surrendered. "I'll tell you. Just—just give me a moment."

Codella sat back, waiting. Susan rested both elbows on the desk and hid her face in her palms for several seconds. Finally she looked up and began to speak. "As you know, Detective, I'm a pediatric endocrinologist. I'm recognized internationally as an authority on congenital intersex conditions. What no one knows is that fifty-seven years ago, I was an infant like so many of my patients—biologically male but with anatomy that would never look male."

Then Susan closed her eyes to the present and acknowledged her hidden past in spoken words for the first time. Weeks after she was born, she told Codella, her father had walked away from his wife and the crying anomaly he didn't want to acknowledge as his flesh and blood. Her mother had kept a diaper over the truth, too ashamed to take her infant for regular checkups and immunizations until the baby developed pneumonia at ten months old. Then she deposited the child at the door of a social services agency a hundred miles from her home with a note that read, "Has a bad cough. Needs medical attention." No pronouns in that message.

Susan's only knowledge of these earliest months of her life came from her adoptive parents, Ed and Katherine Harrison, devout Missouri Synod Lutherans in Wisconsin who "took her on in the name of God."

"We brought you to a specialist at Johns Hopkins," her adoptive mother had once recounted with obvious pride in her accomplishment. Years later, Susan read about that specialist and others like him, surgeons who, with no empirical evidence, believed that gender identity did not become fixed for life until a child reached the age of eighteen months and that, if they intervened before that age, they could—with hormones and a scalpel—make someone the gender of their choosing. They had, Susan came to understand, frightened the Harrisons into immediate action. As a result, Susan had endured a series of painful operations that didn't end until her adolescence. The truth, she knew from her study of medical history and her training at Columbia's medical college, was that she and other genetic XYs like herself had been unwitting lab rats in the hands of pompous doctors who believed they were scientific gods.

When Susan finished her story, she opened her eyes and squinted into the bright lights of the consultation room. For decades she'd felt an unearthly gravitational grip of guilt tugging at her body and soul, a constant reminder of the thousands and thousands of lies she'd told to her husband, her adopted sons, her colleagues, and her friends. Every Sunday at St. Paul's, she recited her confessions of sin along with all the other parishioners—*Most merciful God, we confess that we have sinned against you in thought, word, and deed*—but those words from the *Book of Common Prayer* never did anything to diminish the guilt she felt about her lies of omission and commission. Now that she had finally spoken the truth, however—as much of it as she dared—she felt the dark gravity loosen its hold a little.

She stared into Codella's expression of obvious shock. "They used to put people like me in circus freak shows," she said. "Thankfully I escaped that fate, but mine wasn't much better. They took away my ability to choose who I became. I, in turn, tried my best to accept the identity I was given.

I built a life around a lie. Maybe I would have acted differently if I'd come of age in a more forgiving time, Detective. Then again, are these times any more forgiving? I've consoled myself with the knowledge that I'm at least saving other infants from my own fate, but I'm not proud of my deceptions. They've haunted me."

Codella's forehead was a twisted map of confusion. Finally she continued, "I need to know what this has to do with your taking Philip Graves's keys."

Susan remembered slipping Philip's keys out of his pocket and into her own on Wednesday night while Rose and Roger weren't looking. "Philip knew my secret. He had evidence. I wanted that evidence back. That's all. I had nothing to do with his death. In fact, I hoped against hope that I could revive him—if only to demand his silence in exchange for saving his life. But I also knew that if he didn't survive, I couldn't let those documents fall into other hands."

Codella's eyes narrowed. "Those words sound well-rehearsed, Doctor."

"Maybe so, but I assure you, they're the truth." Susan glared into the detective's skeptical face. "I did not kill that man—although I'm hardly sorry to see him gone."

"When did you find out he knew about you?"

"A week ago. He sent me an e-mail asking me to meet him at a diner. His note read, 'Does your husband know?'" Susan recalled reading the note several times. "I'm sure he meant to frighten me."

"And you went to meet him?"

"What else could I do?"

"What happened at that meeting?"

"He pushed some papers across the table—my entire case study written by the Johns Hopkins doctors." Susan recalled skimming the dense typed pages that described her condition in the terms of a far less enlightened era and detailed every surgical procedure in her "successful" reconstruction. "He watched me read. I'll never forget his triumphant little smile as he sat there sipping his black coffee. When I couldn't bear to read any more, I pushed the pages back at him, and he said, 'No, keep them, Susan. They'll remind you of the agreement we're about to make.'"

"What agreement was that?"

"Philip promised never to print another copy of those documents, not to reveal my secrets and destroy my life in the process, if I cooperated with him."

"By doing what?"

"By voting against Peter Linton's cemetery proposal."

"But why? Why was that so important?"

"Because he wanted to use the church to take revenge on his wife. His ex-wife, I mean."

"Revenge for what?"

"For ruining his life," Susan explained. "His wife divorced him and walked away from their marriage with the apartment they'd bought together. She fell in love with someone else. He was a very bitter man."

"But how did his revenge rest on defeating that proposal?"

"Peter's cemetery plan would have solved the church's fiscal crisis," Susan explained, "and Philip didn't want the crisis resolved that way. He wanted the vestry to approve the sale of our air rights. You see, he'd made a side deal with a developer. He was going to get an insider price on a high-floor luxury co-op in one of the developer's other buildings."

"He admitted this to you?"

Susan nodded. "He was feeling pretty full of himself in the diner that night. He knew I couldn't blow the whistle on him. He told me how he'd run into his wife and her new husband a few months earlier in the bread line at the uptown Fairway. I could feel his rage as he described the encounter. I'm not a psychologist, but if you ask me, all his insecurity, bitterness, and jealousy coalesced in that chance meeting, and he became determined never to feel small again in her eyes.

I think he was desperate to win back the status she'd stripped from him, and he used his scholarly expertise to devise a plan. It's ironic, when you think about it. Philip used to lecture everyone about the dangers of tyranny. And it turns out *he* was the tyrant in our midst. He was making St. Paul's into his own little puppet state."

"And Roger Sturgis was being blackmailed too?"

"I can't think of another reason why he'd vote against the proposal. Peter's plan was solid. Vivian supported it, and Roger is married to Vivian's niece."

Codella didn't speak for several seconds. "That still doesn't explain why you gave the keys to Roger," she finally broke the silence. "You'd spent years hiding from everyone. Why suddenly trust someone else with the truth? Why didn't you go to Graves's apartment yourself?"

Susan had second-guessed this decision over and over since Wednesday night. She recalled how she'd clasped Roger's hand in both of hers and passed him the ring of keys after Philip was pronounced dead. "I knew there was very little time to search his apartment before the police went in there. I know myself well, Detective, and although I had the nerve to lift those keys from Philip's pocket, I knew I didn't have what it took to break into his apartment. But I believed Roger did."

"And did Roger go there? Did he find those documents?"

"I don't know." She remembered Roger's words yesterday. *Don't call me again. I'll call you.* But he hadn't called her. She watched Codella type notes into her iPhone. "I know what I did was wrong, Detective, and I'm sorry. I really am. But I felt so desperate. My husband—I—"

Codella cut her off. "Did you go to Philip's apartment a day or two before the vestry meeting to talk to him? Did you drink a glass of wine in his apartment?"

"Me? Why would I do that?"

Codella was watching her closely. "We have some evidence—some trace evidence—that may help us in our case.

Are you willing to give us your fingerprints and a buccal swab so we can confirm that you don't match this evidence?"

Susan massaged the base of her neck. "I don't see any reason not to, but I'll need to speak to my lawyer first."

"You mean Peter Linton?"

"Peter? Peter's not my lawyer."

She watched the detective's eyes narrow in concentration. "How do you suppose Philip Graves got the information he used to bribe you?"

"I wish I knew. The records he showed me were decades old. They wouldn't have been easy to come by. Because of my condition, of course, I take hormones, and I have certain screenings on a regular basis. If someone hacked into my current medical files, and if they were at all suspicious or medically astute, I suppose those clues might have sent them on a deeper dive. But they would've had to go into very old digitized hospital archives. I think whoever did that had far better technology skills than Philip had."

Codella leaned forward in a way that signaled her understanding. "You mean you think someone helped him."

CHAPTER 56

Michael walked Muñoz to the door. Before Muñoz turned to go, he pointed to the boxes in the living room. "Don't you think you should unpack your things before I get home?"

"I'll have to move some of your things to make room in the closet."

"I guess you will." Muñoz leaned in and kissed him good-bye.

A shift change had occurred in the Bellevue ER since yesterday evening. A nurse told Muñoz that Stephanie Lund had been transferred to the medical intensive care unit on the second floor. Muñoz found his way there, showed his shield to an ICU nurse, and asked to speak to Stephanie's doctor.

"Dr. Varghese is the attending. He hasn't started morning rounds yet. I'll see if I can track him down for you." The nurse picked up a phone. A minute later she said, "He'll be here in a few moments."

Varghese was a tall, slim Indian man with an affable smile. "I'll need permission from the family to speak to you, Detective," he said apologetically. "The parents have been here since late last night. They're in the ICU waiting room. Why don't we go and see if they'll give me permission."

Muñoz followed Varghese to a small room where a middle-aged man and woman sat on a couch holding hands. Muñoz introduced himself.

"You're the detective investigating what happened to Stephanie?" the mother asked.

"I'm one of them," answered Muñoz.

"Who did this?" demanded the father, a stocky man with puffy bags under his eyes.

"We're trying to figure that out, Mr. Lund. And it would help me greatly if I could ask Dr. Varghese some questions. Would you mind giving him your permission to speak with me?"

"We want to hear too," said the father.

"Of course," Muñoz said as he turned to the doctor. "We need to know how long Stephanie was lying in her apartment. If we can narrow the window of time when the attack could have occurred, it might help us figure out who could have done this."

"You have a suspect?" interrupted the father.

"Not yet," Muñoz answered patiently. He turned back to Varghese. "We know she was alive and well until just after three o'clock early yesterday morning when we finished questioning her at the church. We assume she went straight home, but we can't be certain, of course. The last cell phone call she received was on Wednesday evening—before she arrived at the church—and the last call she made from that phone was earlier in the day. The question is, how long after she left St. Paul's did someone go to her apartment?"

Varghese opened the medical file he'd carried to the waiting room. He glanced at the scribbled notes, closed it, and thought for a moment. "Her CPK level was high."

"CPK?"

"It's a protein that leaks into the blood when there's a muscular injury—from a fall, from dehydration, or from being on the floor too long. We see high CPK levels all the time in elderly patients who fall and aren't found for many hours. They lie in the same position so long that the skin breaks down. I'd have to guess that Stephanie was lying in one place without food or water for at least twelve hours."

The mother's sudden sob echoed the anguish of Emily Flounders's daughter, Martha, on Wednesday night. Muñoz turned and apologized to the couple. "I'm sorry to have intruded on you at such a terrible time." He thanked Varghese, left the room, and waited for the doctor to emerge. They walked to the other end of the corridor before Muñoz asked his last question. "What's her prognosis?"

The doctor's expression was grim. "She stopped breathing shortly after she was brought in. She went into cardiac arrest, and we resuscitated her in the absence of a DNR. She's had one flatline EEG, and she has no evidence of brain activity on physical examination. It's wait and see for the moment, Detective, but I think we know where this is headed."

Muñoz did. Stephanie Lund was about to be homicide number three.

CHAPTER 57

Todd was at the sink when Anna entered the kitchen. The faucet was running, and his professional juicer was spinning. She stared at his back while he plunged two fat carrots down the feed chute. Orange-brown liquid spilled from the spout. He turned and glanced at her clergy collar with a look that suggested he found it sexually repellent. He covered his disgust with a feigned smile. "You want some juice? Apple, celery, carrot, and cilantro."

"No." She pulled out a chair at the table and sat.

"Come on," he coaxed. "Let me fix you one. It's a great combination. You'll feel better." He pushed three stalks of celery down the chute and the juicer's motor roared. He poured a glass of the liquid and sipped it. "Mmmm. Here, try it." He held it out.

She pushed the glass away. Did he seriously think his juice concoction could compensate for betrayal? Was he going to pretend the police didn't think he was a suspect?

He came behind her chair and kneaded her shoulders. But his thumbs dug too forcefully into her muscles. He wasn't in tune with how her body reacted to touch. She pulled away. "What do you think you're doing?"

"Relaxing you," he answered in a specious tone. "Why didn't you come to bed last night?"

"You have to ask me that?"

He returned to the sink.

She went to the refrigerator, pulled out a block of cheddar, and set it on a small cutting board. She took a knife from the rack and returned to her chair. "I can't be married to you anymore." She unwrapped the cheese.

"What?"

"You heard me." She cut a thin slice that curled toward the cutting board.

"You're just distraught over what's happened at the church."

Anna squinted, holding the knife in front of her. "Do you ever notice how often you tell me how I'm feeling? You have absolutely no idea what I think or feel."

"Maybe not. But I know when you're acting like a child."

"I'm not the child in this relationship. *You* are. That's why you lost your job. You couldn't take any criticism. And what are you doing about it? Surfing the Internet. Running out to Starbucks for your so-called networking meetings. Fucking around with Stephanie Lund."

He stared at her.

"Your little episode at the police station yesterday only confirmed what I already suspected. I'm not blind, Todd. If you were actually going to job interviews as often as you claimed, you'd have a job by now," she said. "It's been nine months. Nine months. And you've got skills companies kill for."

"It's a shitty economy."

"Really? Because according to NPR, the unemployment rate is declining. You know what I think? You don't want a job. You want to breeze in and out of here and have your little affairs while I do all the work."

"I didn't marry a priest," said Todd. "I married a business major. I didn't sign up to be the 'first husband' of St. Paul's Episcopal Church."

Anna set the knife on the table and looked him squarely in the eyes. "My role at that church is important to me, Todd. It gives my life meaning. And if you loved me, you would want that for me." She felt both powerful and terrified saying this. Power, it occurred to her, came with facing your terror and discovering that it wouldn't destroy you. "You've never supported what I wanted."

"I married a woman who wanted to spend her time with me—to hike and go mountain biking and—"

"And whatever else *you* like to do." Anna finished the sentence for him. "But people change, Todd. They develop different needs, and if you love someone, if you *really* love them, then you make room for their change."

Todd's cold eyes glared at her, and she allowed herself to feel the full force of his resentment. When she was certain that no residual warmth accompanied his rancor, she spoke. "For the past four years, I've pretended our relationship was healthy and happy. I even gave birth to a child to convince myself we were meant to stay together. And it's all because I was too ashamed to admit—to myself and to this congregation—that my marriage is a failure." Hot tears spilled over the rims of her lower eyelids and rolled down her cheeks, but she didn't wipe them away. Let him see her shame. "But I won't hide the truth anymore, Todd. I'm no more perfect than any of my parishioners, and you know what? That's all right. In fact, it's liberating. I feel relieved knowing that I won't have to be the person you punish daily rather than accepting responsibility for your own failures."

His face tightened. "I wouldn't have had an affair in the first place if you hadn't been completely infatuated with Philip Graves."

Anna picked up the knife and waved it in front of his face. "Don't try to turn this around on me. You're the one who was shoving your dick where it doesn't belong. And an hour from now, I have to go and console your little girlfriend's parents and pray over her comatose body on life support. I just hope to God you're not the one who put her in that coma."

"How can you even suggest that?" he hissed.

"How can I not?" she answered.

"I'm your husband. I'm the father of your child, Anna. You need to stand by me."

"Stand by you?" She laughed until he took the knife from her hand in one swift movement, tossed it on the counter, grabbed her wrists, and pulled her close.

"You need to stand by me," he said again. "We need to get through this together, and then we can talk about the future."

Anna tried to wriggle free, but he held her wrists tighter.

"Are you with me, Anna?"

She was about to say no, but the look in his eyes made her stop.

"Are you with me?"

"Let go of me, Todd."

"You don't want them to know about your affair with Philip, do you?"

"I didn't have an affair with Philip."

"They'll think you did. And you'll never get another parish, you know. Are you with me, Anna?" His artificially gentle voice sounded so chilling that she froze, and an icy comet's tail of fear streaked down her spine.

She finally jerked her arm free. "I have to take Christopher to preschool." Did he notice the trembling of her voice? "And then I'm going to the hospital."

CHAPTER 58

Haggerty stared at his computer screen. Roger Sturgis's credit score was near perfect. He had an American Express Centurion Card—the infamous "black card"—as well as a Visa and MasterCard with large credit limits. He paid his monthly balances on time and in full. He had no mortgage or other personal loans, and he'd never filed for personal bankruptcy or been foreclosed on. Why, Claire wanted Haggerty to find out, had Michigan Avenue Ford in Dearborn, Michigan, run a credit report on him yesterday? Unless Haggerty went straight to Roger Sturgis, there was only one way to get the answer.

He tapped the dealership telephone number into his cell phone. A recorded message offered him the extensions for new car sales, used car sales, and the service department. He selected new car sales, and a man's too-chipper voice answered, "Michigan Avenue Ford. This is Bill Price."

"Good morning, Mr. Price." Haggerty tried to keep all traces of New York out of his voice. "Are you by any chance the salesman my buddy Roger Sturgis spoke to yesterday?"

"Who?"

"I guess not," said Haggerty. "My friend Roger was in there yesterday. Can you tell me who helped him buy a car?"

"Hang on." The salesman placed him on hold. When he came back a minute later, he said, "I'm transferring you."

Then another enthusiastic voice said, "Jim Johnston. What can I do for you?"

"You spoke with Roger Sturgis yesterday, Mr. Johnston. Is that correct?"

"Yes, Mr. Sturgis was here. Nice guy."

"He bought a car, I believe."

"Yeah. For his lady friend, Monique. She had an old Focus. She was way overdue for something new." He chuckled.

"That's Monique Vincent, you mean?"

"No. Her name was Wilson."

"Oh? So that's the name she's using now?"

"What do you mean?" The salesman's voice turned suspicious. "What's your interest in Mr. Sturgis?"

"Oh, I'm not interested in him," Haggerty lied. "It's her I'm interested in. I work for her ex-husband's attorney. Custody problem. She won't let him see his kids."

"You're joking, right?"

"Why would I joke?" Haggerty asked. "Men get screwed over too, you know. A lot more often than you think."

"But she seemed like such a nice lady."

"Maybe she is," said Haggerty, "but the father hasn't seen his kid for a year, and he wants his parental rights. Look, I can go through the channels and get a subpoena for the information you've got on file, or you can give me her address right now and save us all a lot of work."

"I don't know," said the salesman.

"Do it for all the men who get screwed over," said Haggerty.

He hung up three minutes later and smiled down at the Chandler Park Drive address he'd scribbled. "God, I can't believe anyone buys a phone scam like that anymore," he said to Portino. Half an hour later, he had Monique Wilson's life story as told through her DMV, Social Security, and credit records.

CHAPTER 59

Every time Codella opened the door to the one-seven-one, she remembered all the years when this had been her precinct. Captain Reilly, her former commanding officer, had been her champion—not her nemesis—and stepping into his precinct today was like stepping into a sanctuary at a church.

She waved to the uniforms behind the bulletproof partition and took the side stairs two at a time to the detective's squad room on the second floor. Haggerty, Muñoz, and Portino were already in a huddle.

Codella told them what she'd learned from Susan Bentley.

"Jesus Christ, that's a story I haven't heard in all my years," said Portino.

"What a bastard Graves was," said Muñoz.

"The important thing is that we now know Susan Bentley gave Roger Sturgis the keys to Graves's apartment. But we still can't prove that Roger actually used them." She looked at Haggerty. "Did CSU get any prints off Graves's doorknobs?"

Haggerty shook his head. "None that they could trace."

"If Sturgis's prints were there, they'd be traceable. He's ex-military." She turned to Portino. "Did you have someone go to Graves's Columbia office and make sure his laptop's not there?"

Portino nodded. "I drove up myself. Nothing."

"Susan Bentley is convinced Graves was blackmailing Roger too," Codella told them. "That's why she gave him the keys. She was hoping he'd go in and find whatever incriminating documents Graves was keeping there. But she couldn't tell me what compromising information Graves had on Roger."

Haggerty slapped the top of his desk. They all looked at him. "I know what Graves had on him—a woman named Monique Wilson."

"Who's that?" Codella asked.

"She's a woman in Detroit, Michigan. She works at Brooks Brothers. She's got one child, a boy. And yesterday Roger Sturgis flew to Detroit and bought her a car. I did a little digging, and guess what? Roger flies to Detroit about once a week."

"So he's got a woman on the side. Why doesn't that surprise me?" said Codella, remembering how Roger had looked her up and down on Wednesday night in the Blue Lounge.

"But what does it all add up to?" asked Muñoz. "Are we changing our minds about Todd? Are we thinking maybe he didn't kill Graves and that Roger Sturgis did?"

"I have no idea," Codella admitted.

"If Roger killed Philip and Emily," said Haggerty, "it might explain why Vivian is so determined to get you off the case. She might want to protect Roger for her niece Kendra's sake."

Muñoz raised his hand to get their attention. "The medical examiner isn't convinced that Emily Flounders was an intentional homicide."

Codella stared at him. "What?" And it occurred to her she'd been so focused on Stephanie Lund's death and Vivian Wakefield's scathing comments to the press yesterday that she hadn't spoken to Muñoz about the Flounders autopsy.

"She died of cardiac arrest," he explained. "She had four severely blocked arteries. Gambarin called her a ticking time bomb. He suggested that she might have seen something that frightened her and triggered the heart attack."

"But what could she have seen to frighten her in her car?" asked Haggerty.

"She didn't die in her car," said Muñoz. "She died in the garden. She had sediment and a little rosemary leaf in her hair. Gambarin thinks she fell on the stone path. She had a scratch on her head."

Codella combed her fingers through her hair as she processed the new information. "So perhaps Emily came out of the parish house and heard whatever scuffle was going on. Maybe she followed the voices to the side of the church and witnessed the murder."

"And the shock caused her heart attack." Haggerty finished her train of thought.

"Right," she said, "but if she died in the garden, who carried her into her van—and more importantly, why?"

"That's what I don't get," said Muñoz. "I mean, let's say I'm Todd Brookes. I'm in the garden with Stephanie Lund and Philip Graves shows up. I panic and kill him. Then I realize Emily Flounders has seen the murder and died. Am I really going to take the time to carry her body to her van? Doesn't it make more sense for me to send Stephanie back to the church—to her piano—and get myself inside the rectory as fast as possible?" He paused. "Unless—"

"Unless what?" she encouraged him.

"Unless I'm looking for something."

"Like what?" asked Haggerty.

"Like the vestry minutes," Muñoz answered. "We haven't found them yet. They weren't in the church, in her van, in her purse, or anywhere on her person. You didn't see them at Stephanie Lund's apartment either. Maybe the killer carried her body to the van so he could search for the minutes without being discovered."

Codella stood up and paced. "But if I'm Todd Brookes, why do I need those minutes? They're not going to give away any secrets about me and Stephanie Lund. They're only going to describe whatever occurred in the Blue Lounge that night."

"What if the deaths have nothing to do with Todd and Stephanie's affair?" Haggerty suggested. "What if Roger Sturgis is our killer? He might have wanted those minutes."

"Why?" Codella demanded. "They wouldn't have revealed his affair with Monique Wilson. He and Susan voted against the cemetery proposal. Graves had no need to expose their secrets. So what incriminating information could the minutes contain?"

Haggerty shook his head. "I have no idea."

"We need to figure it out."

She continued to pace as she searched her brain for an answer that made sense. She replayed the Wednesday-night interviews with vestry members. Susan Bentley had extolled the diverse and welcoming nature of the church but had shed little light on the meeting itself. Vivian Wakefield had talked Haggerty's arm off about Seneca Village. And Roger had dismissed the entire vestry agenda as much ado about nothing. Rose, he'd said, had wasted their time describing the Palm Sunday flower arrangements. Vivian had "pitched" an after-school reading program that he obviously didn't care about. And Peter had made his "usual complaints" about the vestry not investing enough in cemetery improvements.

She stopped pacing and stared at a scuff on her boot for several seconds.

"What?" asked Haggerty. "What is it?"

"Last night Rose Bartruff told me that Vivian Wakefield acted upset with Emily Flounders at the end of the vestry meeting. Rose seemed to think it was because Vivian wanted the cemetery proposal to pass and Emily voted against it."

"Did she say why?" asked Muñoz.

Codella shook her head. "Apparently, Rose left the vestry meeting for fifteen minutes. She missed the whole discussion before the vote was taken."

"Jesus Christ!" Haggerty banged his desk. "She didn't mention that when I interviewed her."

Codella ignored his apparent annoyance. "The point is, something obviously happened in those fifteen minutes, and no one wants us to know what. Emily Flounders's vestry minutes would probably shed some light on it."

Codella's cell phone vibrated, and McGowan's name came up on the screen. She declined the call. She hadn't checked in at

Manhattan North this morning, and she didn't intend to. Going there would only invite McGowan to strike back for what she'd said to him yesterday. He'd contained his fury, but he wouldn't contain it for long. He would be looking for a way to pull the plug on her. She turned to Haggerty. "Let's go find Roger Sturgis. We certainly have enough on him to justify asking some hard questions."

Then she looked at Muñoz. "Take a ride to Graves's office. We know the laptop's not there, but maybe something else is."

CHAPTER 60

When Codella called Roger's home number, Kendra Sturgis picked up. "He's at the gym," she volunteered. "Equinox Sports Club on Broadway."

Haggerty signed out a car and drove them to the club. They waited at the curb in front of the entrance until Roger emerged half an hour later carrying a gym bag. Dark sunglasses concealed his eyes. His curly black hair was slicked back, Codella noticed, and even his moustache still looked wet from the shower. Codella climbed out of the front passenger seat and called to him. "Mr. Sturgis, you're a hard man to find."

Roger turned, and his lips curled into a closed-mouth smile. "Detective Codella," he said.

"And Detective Haggerty." She gestured toward the car. "Shall we take a ride together?"

Roger looked at his watch. "I'm sorry, Detective, but I have some meetings very soon."

"Why don't you call and reschedule those meetings," Codella suggested amiably.

Roger frowned. "What's this about, Detective?"

"Oh, I think you know."

"I'd like you to tell me anyway," he insisted.

"All right, it's about those two dead bodies at St. Paul's, one comatose choir director at Bellevue Hospital, and a woman

230 I Carrie Smith

named Monique Wilson in Detroit." She crossed her arms. "Now, are you going to get in the car with us?"

Roger held up his free hand in a gesture of mock surrender. "I guess I have no choice, do I?"

Codella watched him climb into the back seat before she got in. "Where are we going?" he asked as Haggerty pulled away from the curb.

Codella turned to face him. "Well, we can take you to your place, and Kendra can make us all some tea while we chat about your other life in Detroit. Or we can go to Detective Haggerty's precinct. Which would you prefer?"

Roger didn't ask any more questions as they drove to the one-seven-one. They led him into the precinct, up the stairs, and straight to Interview Room A. Roger dropped his gym bag on the floor, propped his sunglasses on his head, and reluctantly pulled out a chair. In the small enclosed space, Codella could smell his freshly applied cologne, and it reminded her of the cologne her father used to wear, although Roger's was undoubt- edly more expensive.

She slipped off her jacket and hung it on the hook behind the door. Haggerty stepped out and returned sipping a bottle of water.

"I'd like some water too if you don't mind."

"Sure thing," said Haggerty, and Codella recognized his strat- egy. Make the suspect ask for something. Make him a supplicant.

Haggerty left the room and came back with two more water bottles. He set one on the table in front of Roger and handed the other to Codella, who twisted off the top and took a drink.

Roger, she could see, was already getting impatient. He obviously wasn't the kind of man who liked to operate on other people's clock.

As she and Haggerty took their seats, she felt them slip into the familiar rhythm they'd shared when they were partners at the one-seven-one. Now like then, they didn't need to rehearse their

game plan. She knew without looking at him that he was waiting for her to break the ice. "How was your little trip to Detroit
yesterday?"

"Great, thanks." Roger smiled, but his voice was noticeably
curt.

"And how was Monique? Did she like her new car?"

His fake affability dropped away instantly. "Did you speak
to her?"

"No," said Codella. "At this point, we haven't yet talked to
Monique about Kendra or Kendra about Monique, but of course,
if we don't get what we need from this little chat, we just might
have to talk to both of them."

Roger inhaled a long, slow breath through his nostrils. He
exhaled even more slowly. "What do you want to know?"

Haggerty stepped in. "Did you go to Philip Graves's apartment after you left St. Paul's Church in the early hours of Thursday morning, Mr. Sturgis?"

Codella watched Roger smooth down the edges of his mustache, twist the top off his water bottle, and take a slow slug.
"Yes."

"Good," said Haggerty. "We appreciate honest answers. Let's
see if you can continue along that line. Did you take anything
out of Philip Graves's apartment?"

This time Roger considered his answer for a longer interval
of time. He took another sip, set his sunglasses on the table, and
flattened the edges of his mustache again. "Yes," he answered.

"What did you take from his apartment?" Codella asked.

"You already know."

"I'd like to hear it from you, Mr. Sturgis."

Roger tilted the chair back and looked from one detective to
the other. "Are you planning to arrest me?"

"That depends," she said.

"On what?" he demanded.

"On what you've done," Codella answered. "We're not interested in a thief. We want to find a killer."

"I didn't kill anyone," he said.

"Just answer the question. What did you take from Philip Graves's apartment?"

"I took his laptop."

"Anything else?"

"No." Roger didn't conceal his irritation.

"Why did you take it?"

"Come on, Detective. You obviously know that already. Philip was blackmailing me. He had documents that belonged to me."

"Did you find the documents on his computer?" Codella asked.

"No, and believe me, I looked."

"We'll need that computer," Haggerty said. "As soon as this interview is over."

"Tell us when and how he blackmailed you," Codella continued.

And then Roger Sturgis told a story that was eerily like Susan Bentley's. "He met me at the Metro Diner last week. He was in one of his puffed-up moods. 'Who would have thought you were such a complicated man, Roger,' he told me. 'Two cities. Two lives.' Philip always thought he was so, so clever. He pushed some documents across the table. They were tuition payments I'd made on behalf of Monique's son. He threatened to show them to Kendra."

"What did he want in return for his silence?" asked Haggerty.

Roger took another swig from the bottle. "He wanted the St. Paul's cemetery improvement plan to go down the drain. He wanted his air rights deal—he'd been pushing for us to sell the air rights for two years, and he must have gotten impatient using the powers of honest persuasion. I'm sure Susan told you that too since you obviously spoke to her before you came to see me."

"Did Philip Graves blackmail anyone else?" Codella asked.

Roger shrugged. "Not that I know of."

"What time did you get home from your little B and E?"

"Around three, I think."

"Did you go anywhere else before you went home?"

"No."

"Can you prove it?" Codella asked.

"I took a taxi, but I don't have the receipt. Why?"

"Because someone went to Stephanie Lund's apartment and tried to kill her early that morning." She watched his reaction.

He stared straight at her, and his surprise looked genuine. "It wasn't me, Detective. Give me a lie detector test if you want. I hardly even knew that woman. Why would I want to kill her?"

CHAPTER 61

Anna felt an almost unprecedented relief when she stepped out of Bellevue Hospital and heard an angry chorus of car horns on First Avenue. The ear-splitting street noise was infinitely more welcome than the soft sobs of Stephanie Lund's mother as she weighed the difficult decision of whether or not to take her daughter off a ventilator. And then Anna remembered her own difficult decision—should she pick up Christopher from school and go home to Todd, or should she take her son somewhere else until she could get Todd to move out? She could still feel Todd's fingers clamped around her wrists. She could hear his voice: *Are you with me, Anna?*

She rode the Number Three train uptown. When she climbed the subway stairs at Ninety-Sixth Street, she still didn't know what to do. She stood on the corner and watched two Con Ed workers emerge from a manhole on Broadway. She walked two blocks north, toward St. Paul's, and stopped again. She didn't want to go home. She remembered Detective Haggerty gently holding her hand yesterday afternoon and telling her to relax as he rolled each of her fingers over the ink to take her fingerprints. She recalled staring at the small cleft in his chin as he swabbed the inside of her cheek to get a sample of her DNA. She heard his words from just before she left the station house, an echo of the offer he'd made after letting her write an e-mail to her congregants: *If you ever need to talk to me, Rector, call me any time at all.*

She dug in her purse and found his card. And before she could question her impulse, she entered his number into her phone.

He answered on the third ring. "Haggerty."

"It's Anna Brookes" was all she could say before she ran out of courage to continue.

"Rector." His voice sounded soothing—so unlike Todd's. "What can I do for you?"

She began to cry.

"Where are you?" he asked.

She blinked up at a street sign. "Ninety-Eighth and Broadway."

"There's a Starbucks one block north of you. Go there and wait for me. I'm on my way now."

Before she could change her mind, the detective ended the call. She slipped the phone into her pocket. The sun was hidden behind dense clouds. As she crossed to the west side of Broadway, she noticed that rain was falling across the river in New Jersey. She walked the one block north and stood against the outside wall of the Starbucks storefront like a homeless woman waiting for a handout. Passing pedestrians glanced at her with curiosity or concern until Detective Haggerty took her arm, led her inside, and found her a seat. He bought her a cup of coffee and sat across from her. "What's going on, Rector? Tell me."

His gentle voice teased out her fears, and she started to cry again. "I just came from the hospital. I saw Stephanie. I met her parents. I know Todd was seeing her. I—" She shook her head and stared into the steam rising from her coffee.

"What?" The detective reached across the table and covered her hand with his. "You can tell me."

She opened her mouth to say, *I'm afraid he killed her.* But she couldn't bring the words to her lips because Todd's voice was louder than her own. *Are you with me, Anna? Are you with me?* She felt Todd's fingers squeeze her wrists. She heard his threat. *Do you want people to know about your affair?* She hadn't slept with Philip, but she'd wanted to, and wasn't her deep desire for him virtually the same thing? If he hadn't died, wouldn't she have ended up in his arms? In his bed?

She stared at Haggerty and shook her head. "I'm sorry. I shouldn't have called you. I'm fine. Really. Everything's fine." She stood.

Haggerty stood too. "Anna," she heard him say, "was your husband home all night after the vestry meeting?"

Anna turned and walked to the door, pretending not to hear.

CHAPTER 62

A Columbia University security guard led Muñoz to the second floor of Fayerweather Hall and stopped in front of a closed door with a nameplate that read, "Philip Graves, PhD." "You're sure it's okay for me to let you in here?" the guard asked. "Don't you need a warrant or something?"

"No," Muñoz assured him. "Professor Graves was the victim of a crime. I'm investigating his death. We don't need a warrant to search his belongings. What's in here might help us solve the crime."

The security guard unlocked the door, and Muñoz stepped inside. A red light on Graves's phone was blinking, and Muñoz pointed it out. "It looks like Mr. Graves has some messages. I'd like to listen to them. Can you get someone up here to help me access his voice mail?"

The guard nodded. "Give me a few minutes."

When he left, Muñoz took out his phone and tapped the camera icon. How many times had he watched Codella photograph a crime scene? The first day they'd met, in the apartment of Hector Sanchez, she'd told him, *Your camera. Your eyes. Never rely on someone else.*

Bookshelves covered two walls of Graves's cluttered office. His desk sat below the window. Two chairs and a small low table formed a cramped sitting area between the desk and the door.

Muñoz took several photographs before he approached the desk. A stack of what appeared to be student essays lay on the left edge. Muñoz picked up the top paper and flipped to the last page. A note scrawled below the final paragraph of the essay read, "This is *not* graduate-level work, Mr. Henley." Next to this note was the circled grade: C−.

Muñoz returned the paper to the stack, happy that he wasn't one of Philip Graves's students. He sat at the dead man's desk and opened the top left drawer. Pens, thumbtacks, and the crumpled tinfoil wrappers of Hershey's kisses littered the bottom. In the second drawer were the desiccated remains of a bagel and cream cheese wrapped in a napkin.

Muñoz saw no documents attesting to Graves's blackmail of Susan Bentley and Roger Sturgis. He did not find the vestry minutes handwritten by Emily Flounders before her last walk into the St. Paul's garden. He shut the drawer, wondering when the mice would arrive. Then he turned to the portraits of world leaders taped to the wall beside the door. He was no scholar of history, but he recognized Khrushchev, Mao, Castro, and Stalin.

He was scanning the books on Graves's shelves when a woman's voice caused him to turn. "You're the police officer?" The young woman standing in the doorway had short, choppy hair and wore a sweat shirt over jeans.

"I am." He showed her his identification. "Detective Muñoz."

She slipped around him, picked up the desk phone, and showed him how to access the voice mail. "Is there anything else you need?"

"No. That's it." He smiled. "Thanks."

When she was gone, he sat in Philip Graves's desk chair and punched in the codes to access his new messages. The first voice was a student requesting an extension on a paper. The second was a dean of undergraduates calling on behalf of a student athlete who needed to reschedule a test due to a conflicting away game. Muñoz listened to three more new messages before he began to review the old messages Graves had not deleted. A moment later, he scrambled for his cell phone.

CHAPTER 63

Codella sat at Haggerty's squad room desk and recalled the *Daily News* headline. "Genius Detective or Bully With a Badge?" Had McGowan seen the headline? If so, he would be relishing her public humiliation. She could hear his voice in her head. *This is what you get when you work with precinct cops, Codella. What a mess you've made for us.*

She stared at her phone and wondered when his call would come. She needed to make an arrest before he got to her. But she didn't have enough evidence. The fact that Roger Sturgis had stolen Graves's laptop no more proved that he murdered Graves than Todd's affair or suspicious appearance in the parish house established his guilt. Roger wasn't going to confess, and thanks to McGowan summoning her back to Manhattan North yesterday, she and Haggerty had lost their opportunity to question Todd. The evidence she currently had would never convince a DA that either man should be charged. And where was she going to get more evidence if Peter Linton started serving as defense attorney to the vestry? Vivian Wakefield certainly wasn't going to help her. And Rose Bartruff couldn't.

She reached for the water bottle Haggerty had been drinking earlier. Had she missed a lead? Was there something more she could be doing right now? Playing the waiting game was not her style. Waiting reminded her of lying in a hospital bed tethered to a chemo pole. She called Farah Assiraj. "Have you uncovered anything new?"

Farah read off her findings. Peter Linton was a partner at Tabor and Higginbottom, a firm specializing in criminal defense. Roger Sturgis was on the board of the Randall's Island Alliance and the Harlem Academy. And until last July, Todd Brookes was a business intelligence developer for First National Bank. "He's also an elite amateur cyclist," said Farah. "Last year he won the—"

"Hold on," Codella said when a second call came in on her cell. She glanced at the screen expecting to see McGowan's name, but the name she saw was Dan Fisk. "I need to go, Farah. I'll get back to you when I can."

But she didn't take Fisk's call. She waited until a pop-up message on her screen told her he had left a message. When she played it, Fisk's grating voice boomed in her ear. "Call me, Codella. That's an order."

She set the phone on the desk. Since when was Fisk giving her orders? Had McGowan sicced him on her as revenge for what she'd said yesterday?

She flipped the phone face down. No way would she call him back. She still remembered McGowan trying to reassign the Sanchez case to Fisk only hours after he'd assigned it to her six months ago. *Let's give this to Fisk. You're just getting back on your feet.* That case had meant everything to her at the time—it was the opportunity she needed to prove herself all over again—and this case was starting to feel just as important. Her reputation was on the line, thanks to Vivian Wakefield, and if Fisk took over, the press would have a field day with her. She'd be the "bully with a badge" forever. She couldn't let that happen. She had to solve this before Fisk took it from her. Even if it meant McGowan slapped her with insubordination and mothballed her for a month—or worse.

When Haggerty returned to the squad room, she was still staring at her phone. "What's the matter?" he asked.

She played him Fisk's message.

"What are you going to do?"

"Nothing," she said.

"Good. Because we haven't run out of leads yet." He pulled up a chair and told her about his meeting with Anna Brookes. "She knows something, Claire. There's something about Todd that she's not telling us. We've just got to get her to open up."

When Muñoz rang ten minutes later, she put him on speaker so Haggerty could hear. "I'm in Graves's office," he said. "You need to hear this message on his voice mail."

Codella and Haggerty leaned closer to her phone and listened to the fuzzy voice of a woman saying, "I know what you did, and you should be ashamed of yourself."

"What do you think it means?" asked Muñoz.

"I don't recognize the voice," said Codella.

"I do," said Haggerty. "I spoke to her on Wednesday night. That's Stephanie Lund."

"You're sure?" asked Codella.

"I'm positive."

"What do you think she knows?" asked Muñoz on the other end of the line.

Codella could only think of one possibility based on the evidence they had. "She knew he was blackmailing people."

"But how would she have found out?" asked Haggerty.

In the silence, Codella recalled the text messages she and Haggerty had read on Stephanie's cell phone yesterday. *I thought you'd like a good story,* Todd had texted to her. *Well, I didn't,* she'd responded. *I feel bad for her.* The *her* was Susan Bentley. "Stephanie found out from Todd. He told her Susan's secret—which means he knew what Philip Graves was up to."

She swigged from Haggerty's water bottle. "When Susan met Graves at a diner last week, he set some documents in front of her to show her he knew her secrets. He told her to keep them as a reminder of why she was going to do what he asked her to do. And Roger basically told us the same story. Graves wouldn't have given Roger and Susan his only copies of the documents he had. He must have kept copies for himself, but we didn't find them in his apartment, and Roger didn't find them on his laptop either. Are they in that office, Muñoz?"

"No. I've looked through everything. There's nothing about Bentley or Sturgis, and there are no vestry minutes either."

Haggerty turned to Codella. "You're thinking maybe Todd was helping Philip Graves and he has the documents—at the rectory or on his computer."

Codella nodded. "He was a business intelligence developer at a bank until he got fired," she said, remembering Farah's words. "He might know how to access people's data. And if he did—if he went into Susan's medical records and Roger's financials—then he's at least guilty of a few class E felonies." She spoke close to her phone. "Muñoz, when you get back here, find us a judge and try to get us a warrant. Let's arrest Todd on suspicion of criminal possession of computer materials. And maybe if we're lucky, something on his computer will prove he murdered Stephanie Lund."

"I'll get on it right away," Muñoz assured her.

"Did you find anything else?" she asked him.

"Just a drawer of half-eaten food he was hoarding and a wall plastered with tyrants of the twentieth century."

CHAPTER 64

Haggerty reached for the toothpaste just as Codella turned on the faucet to spit into the sink. Her bathroom wasn't big enough for them both, but wherever she was tonight, Haggerty also wanted to be—on the couch, at the stove, even here. He was doing his best to keep her distracted, she supposed. He knew that if he left her alone, she'd rehash her run-in with McGowan or replay Dan Fisk's gravelly *That's an order* and worry about when her phone was going to ring again as they tried to track her down.

"We've still got an episode of *Grey's Anatomy* on DVR," he said now. "You want to watch it with me?"

"You're joking, right?"

He smiled. "Or we could climb in bed, and I could take you out of yourself."

She smiled back. "Why don't we catch the news."

"No." He shook his head. "Bad idea. You'll just get worked up." He stuck his toothbrush in his mouth.

Codella sat on the bed and watched him brush his teeth. When he shut off the bathroom light minutes later, he sat down beside her. "I keep thinking about Anna Brookes at the rectory with Todd right now. I think she suspects him of being the murderer. When she was sitting in Starbucks with me, I could feel how frightened she was. But she wouldn't tell me anything."

"Maybe she has a secret too," Codella suggested.

"What kind of secret?"

"Maybe you called it right that first night, and she was having an affair with Philip. Maybe she's hiding the biggest secret of all, and she wants to come clean, but she's afraid of the consequences."

"Then why let me take her fingerprints? Why give me her DNA?"

Codella's cell phone rang. Her whole body froze.

Haggerty picked up her phone and quickly declined the call for her.

"Who was it?"

"You know."

"I won't be able to hold him off indefinitely. He'll track me down, and then what? He's vindictive. I could lose my shield."

"That's not going to happen."

"How can you be sure of that? Look what he made me go through just to get back on active duty. He's been waiting for an opportunity like this."

She imagined the inevitable scene. McGowan standing in his office, grinning victoriously as he held out his hand and demanded, *Turn in your shield, Codella.* "I am *never* giving up my shield to that bastard." She couldn't give her shield up to anyone, she thought.

"You won't have to. You're going to solve the case, and when you do, he's not going to have a leg to stand on. Now get him out of your head, Claire."

But how could she get him out? She remembered something Susan Bentley had said that morning: *I tried my best to accept the identity I was given. I built a life around a lie.* The doctor had played the hand she was dealt, and so had Codella. She'd always known she would never escape the fact that she'd seen her father commit a cold-blooded murder. His crime lived inside of her; she couldn't erase the memory or undo whatever effects it had had on her body, mind, and soul. Like Susan, all she could do was try to make something positive out of her fate. Susan had become an endocrinologist, and Codella had become a homicide detective. They were both, ironically, trying to save others in order to hold onto something in themselves. Codella couldn't imagine who she would become if she couldn't be a detective anymore.

Haggerty took her face in his warm palms. "Listen to me, Claire. You're going to go to bed now, and in the morning, you're going to get up and keep working the case—we're going to keep working it together until we make a breakthrough. And we will. Remember, we're only forty-eight hours into it."

"McGowan doesn't care about that."

"And you shouldn't care about him. Trust me. We're going to solve this case."

SATURDAY

CHAPTER 65

Claire tapped his shoulder. "Wake up," she said. "We need to get moving."

Haggerty groaned.

"Come on. It's seven."

He rolled on his side, reached his arm around her waist, and moved closer to her warmth until she sat up and swung her legs off the bed. "I had an idea in the middle of the night," she told him.

He sat up too. "Of course you did. Did you sleep at all?"

She stood. "We need to walk that parish house again and think about where everybody was at the end of the vestry meeting. We're missing something. I feel it. Let's get over there before anybody shows up for the eleven o'clock service." He watched her move toward the bathroom. "Call Muñoz," she said. "I'll take a quick shower."

Muñoz was standing at the south gate of St. Paul's when he and Claire arrived forty-five minutes later. Claire led them up the parish house steps, past the Community Room, and down the corridor to the Blue Lounge. She stared into the room from the doorway. "This is where it started. Everyone was sitting in here. They all agree on that much at least."

Haggerty and Muñoz stepped aside and let her enter first. "Philip Graves sat over there." She pointed to the long three-cushioned couch against the window. "Susan Bentley and Rose

Bartruff sat next to him, and Vivian Wakefield was over there."
She pointed to the right cushion of the blue love seat perpendicular to the couch. It was like she was reading a map that wasn't
there, he thought as he watched her pull details out of her brain.
"The rector was next to Vivian. And Roger, Emily, and Peter
were on chairs." She tapped the backs of two chairs upholstered
in blue fabric.

Haggerty was tempted to say, *Okay, but so what? How does
this help? What are we looking for?* But he'd worked with Claire
long enough to know you didn't interrupt her when she was
piecing things together. She'd probably been up most of
the night, frustrated by her inability to navigate through the
thicket of disparate facts and details the three of them had
accumulated. And she was determined to find her way before
McGowan found her.

He watched her step over to the long blue couch. "Graves
sat right here," she said again as she lowered herself onto
the far-right cushion. "And at around ten forty-five, he got
up to leave." She stood as she said this. "He walked to the
door." She walked to the door. "And then he took his coat
off the rack." She walked to the coatrack across from the Blue
Lounge door. "Everyone must have seen him go. And then
they all made their moves." She turned to him and Muñoz.
"And each of those vestry members had specific motives to
their movements."

"Beyond their *reported* motives, you mean," said Haggerty.

"That's right," said Claire. "Susan Bentley walked Philip
to the door." Claire moved in that direction now. "And
then—supposedly—she turned into the Community Room."
Claire pointed through that door. "We're supposed to believe
that she waited in there for Anna Brookes, who went to her
office to take a book on meditation from her bookshelf."

"Are you thinking that maybe the rector didn't do that?"
asked Muñoz.

"It's a possibility we can't overlook. I mean, everyone at that meeting has made claims, and they can't all be true. Susan did show me a meditation book—*Finding Your Inner God*—when I interviewed her on Wednesday night, and my instincts tell me she and the rector are being truthful, but we can't be certain. It's possible that book had been in Susan's bag for weeks and they made up a convenient story. Susan was awfully quick to show it to me."

Haggerty watched Claire retrace her steps back to the coatrack outside the Blue Lounge. "At about the same time that Susan was walking Philip to the door," she said, "Vivian was so adamant about taking the tea service to the kitchen without Emily Flounders's help that she pretty much ordered Emily to go home—even though she and Emily had cleared the tea service together at every meeting since Rose Bartruff joined the vestry."

Claire's intently focused eyes stared into the Blue Lounge. She was seeing into that night, Haggerty thought. "Rose Bartruff stayed in this room," she said, "until she got her coat, went outside, and decided to check on the Moroccan mint in the garden."

"Which led her to find the body," supplied Haggerty.

"And Peter Linton claims he was also in the Blue Lounge—until he got a phone call from his client and went into the corridor."

Claire walked to the end of the corridor and turned left in the direction of the kitchen. She stopped in front of the men's room door. "Roger claims he left the Blue Lounge to go in here. Rose and Vivian both recall him saying he was going to the men's room."

She ran her fingers through her hair. She always did that when she was thinking. "Somebody's lying to us." She turned left, entered the commercially outfitted kitchen, and leaned on the long granite island. "Let's assume for a moment that Vivian really did come into this kitchen. After all, she certainly fought hard to keep Emily out of it. Why would she have wanted to be in here alone?"

She looked from Muñoz to Haggerty. Haggerty knew there was no point in answering her question, because she already had the answer in her head. Seconds later she looked at him. "As you learned from Rose Bartruff, this kitchen is a very convenient place in which to make a phone call without being observed." She turned to Muñoz. "But we know from the call records you got that Vivian *didn't* make any phone calls that night, and she didn't receive any either—until she got a call hours later from Roger and Kendra's home phone, a call that Kendra must have made because Roger hadn't come home. Why did Vivian need to be alone in here?"

"To meet with someone," Haggerty responded on cue.

"Right," said Claire. "And the question is, with whom did she meet? There are only four contenders if we accept Rose's claim that she remained in the Blue Lounge. Roger could've sneaked in here while he was supposedly in the men's room. Anna could've come in while she was getting a book from her office down the hall. And it's possible Susan joined her in here after she sent the rector to get the book. It would have been easy enough for her to slip through the same passage Rose used Wednesday night when she came here from the Community Room to make coffee and a phone call."

"What about Peter Linton?" asked Muñoz.

"Yes. He's the fourth contender. He could easily have ducked in here after he spoke to his client." She crossed her arms and let out a deep breath. "So the next question is, which one of them did Vivian want to speak with alone?"

Claire stared at him. In all his years of working with her, he wasn't sure he'd ever seen her quite this focused and determined.

"Vivian and Peter were on the same side of the cemetery vote," she continued. "Vivian wouldn't have needed to speak with him unless it was to commiserate on their loss, but I don't get the sense that Vivian commiserates with too many people. According to Rose, Vivian was angry at the end of the meeting. So I'm thinking she would've wanted to let out her anger at someone. Rose and the rector abstained from the vote. Vivian probably wasn't happy about that, but I don't think she would have targeted them. I don't think she spoke to either of them in the kitchen. I think she would have wanted a word with Roger or Susan. They're the ones she'd counted on to vote with her. They're the ones who really let her down that night." Claire's eyes focused on the granite island in the center of the kitchen. When she finally looked up at him again, she said, "I think Vivian wanted a private conversation with Roger that night."

"What makes you think it was him?" asked Muñoz.

"First, no one actually saw him enter the men's room."

"And second?" prompted Haggerty.

"He's married to Vivian's niece," she said in a tone that suggested this was obvious. "Vivian would've expected him to support her position. And she probably felt justified in giving him holy hell when he didn't."

"So where does that leave us?" Haggerty asked.

"Presumably it leaves us with Susan and the rector in the Community Room, Vivian and Roger here in the kitchen, Rose in the Blue Lounge, and Peter wandering in the corridors."

Haggerty and Muñoz accompanied Claire out of the kitchen, down the hall, and up the stairs to the second floor. They stopped in front of the supply closet. "And then there's the issue of Stephanie Lund and Todd Brookes," Claire continued. "Both of them were up here. Sergeant Zamora found Stephanie at the piano in the reception hall." She looked in there now. "Todd was found here in the corridor—after the murder, of course, but we don't know how long he was actually in the building."

She turned and pointed to the supply closet. "And the shovel used on Philip Graves was in here—with two people's blood on it." She paused. "Who put it there? Was it Todd Brookes? Did he kill Philip Graves, take the shovel to the rectory, and then bring it over to the parish house and slip it into the closet? Did Stephanie put the shovel in the closet for him? Or are we totally wrong about Todd being the killer?"

Claire rubbed her temples. "We still have way more questions than answers."

CHAPTER 66

At ten thirty, Muñoz leaned against a double-parked patrol car to watch parishioners arrive for the eleven o'clock prayer service. His one good suit felt tight across the shoulders. He hadn't worn it in almost a year—since before the afternoon he'd taken a bullet to the shoulder chasing a suspect through the Frederick Douglass projects, back when he was still working narcotics. Rehab after his gunshot wound had made his arms and shoulders even more muscular than they'd been before the injury.

Two uniformed officers stood outside the gates, ensuring that reporters didn't enter or impede parishioners from entering the church.

Keep your eyes and ears open, Codella had instructed him, and he now watched an elderly black woman with a cane emerge from a car and make her way to the gate. The old woman's shoulders were stooped, and her black velvet hat made him think of his long-deceased grandmother dressed for church on a Sunday morning.

He watched a white family walk up the block—mother in a navy blazer and pencil skirt, father in gray pinstripes, daughter in a black dress with matching black ribbons in her ponytail. The mother's face was a knot of severity. The father was talking on his cell phone. The little girl smiled at Muñoz as she passed, and he smiled back at her.

Mourners streamed through the garden gate for the next ten minutes until Muñoz recognized the familiar face of Peter Linton stepping out of an Uber. He stood on the curb, and his eyes darted up and down the block as his wife, a tall brunette of about fifty, emerged from the other side of the car. The two did not look at each other as they walked through the gate.

Rose Bartruff introduced Muñoz to her daughter, Lily, before she passed through the gate. Roger Sturgis wore a handsome black suit, and his wife, Kendra, was on his arm. Below Kendra's open coat, Muñoz could see her body wrapped in a tight black sheath dress that might have been more appropriate on a red carpet. She was, he thought, a remarkably beautiful woman.

Just before eleven o'clock, Vivian Wakefield strode up the street wearing an elaborate church hat and a dark trench coat. As she approached the south gate, she avoided his gaze and didn't acknowledge the uniformed police, but she made a point of nodding to the reporters assembled behind a barricade. "Mrs. Wakefield!" one of the reporters called. "Do you have any comment?"

Vivian stepped closer to them. "This is a sad day for everyone who loves St. Paul's. We continue to wait for justice." She nodded, stepped through the gate, and walked deliberately up the stone path and into the parish house.

Susan Bentley, in a tailored black pantsuit, arrived less than a minute later, and Muñoz followed her into the church.

CHAPTER 67

A greeter just inside the nave was handing out programs. Codella took one and glanced at the grainy black-and-white headshots of Emily Flounders and Philip Graves on the front cover as Haggerty nudged her farther into the dim church. The pews on either side of the central aisle were packed, so they settled for a discreet standing position along the right wall and listened as an organist in the choir loft—a stand-in for Stephanie Lund—played a solemn prelude.

Moments later, a bold sustained chord introduced the processional hymn, signaling the congregants to rise. Their hands reached for hymnals, and mouths opened wide to sing as the procession made its way slowly up the central aisle—the crucifer and torchbearers in front followed by robed choir members and an Episcopal flag bearer. Rector Anna Brookes brought up the rear, her hymnal open in one palm, her other hand following the bars of music as she sang the lyrics and cast her eyes from left to right.

Acolytes lit candles on the altar, and a gospel reader ascended to the lectern on the right side of the chancel. The reader was not a well-practiced orator, and through the speaker system, her words—timid and monotone—sounded more like whispers from a white-noise machine.

As a second reader took his turn at the lectern, Codella studied the churchgoers. Susan Bentley sat in the third row on the far side of the central aisle. Roger and Kendra Sturgis were four rows behind her, and Peter Linton and his wife occupied a pew on the right aisle only twenty feet from Codella and Haggerty. Codella couldn't find Rose Bartruff, and it took her several moments to locate Vivian Wakefield seated near the back of the church, where, curiously, most the black parishioners had chosen to sit. Codella wondered what to make of this visible racial divide in a church where diversity was so proudly celebrated, and as she watched the churchwarden, she thought again of their unpleasant encounter yesterday.

When the last reader finished, the choir and congregation sang "A Mighty Fortress Is Our God," and by the time the hymn was over, Rector Anna Brookes had ascended into the pulpit. As she lifted her arms to bless the congregation, her chasuble became a pale-purple half-moon. The audience sat, and Anna Brookes stared down at them with a bittersweet smile. "Tomorrow we will celebrate Palm Sunday," she pronounced in a strong, steady voice. "The day when Jesus rode into Jerusalem and people covered the ground with branches and palms, singing, 'Blessed is He who comes in the name of the Lord.'"

She paused, allowing the congregation to absorb the significance of those words. "When Jesus entered that city," she continued, "he knew that he was coming there to face a violent and angry end. He knew that his purpose on this earth was to secure everlasting life for us—so that on mournful days like this one, we might still have hope."

The parishioners were silent now, their eyes focused on Anna as if she alone could make sense of what had happened on Wednesday night.

"Today we've gathered to mourn two beloved family members, friends, and colleagues—Emily Flounders and Philip Graves. We are horrified and deeply saddened that these two cherished people suffered such a violent end, and we can't quite believe that they have left us for good. In our hearts, we believe they should still be here, and we keep asking ourselves, 'Why would anyone want to take them away from us like this?'"

Codella watched the rector gaze directly into the eyes of parishioners as she spoke. "We'll be asking ourselves this question for a long time—I know I will—but as we mourn Emily and Philip today, we can at least take comfort in the knowledge that Jesus, having also faced his violent death, secured a place for Emily and Philip—and all of us—at the right hand of God."

As Anna continued her sermon, Codella surveyed the parishioners again. Rose Bartruff, she finally noticed, was sitting next to an older black man with white hair. Codella was still staring at her when the cell phone in her pocket began to vibrate. McGowan, she thought. McGowan was looking for her, and when he found her, he wouldn't show her any Christian compassion.

"Tomorrow we celebrate Jesus's triumph," Anna Brookes finally concluded, "but today we celebrate the lives of Emily and Philip. While they no longer walk among us, we can feel their spirits filling this sacred space."

Vivian Wakefield rose from her pew as if those words were her cue. She wore an elegant black jacket and matching pleated skirt, and the gold scarf at her neck was a ring of warm light. She moved toward the central aisle with calm dignity, and when she reached the chancel, the waiting congregation was so still that Codella could hear the churchwarden quietly clear her throat several feet from the microphone.

She stepped to the lectern and gazed into the faces staring back at her. "In all my years at St. Paul's, I've never stood here except to read the Gospel to you," she began with a resonant musicality that could not, Codella thought, be learned in any public speaking class. "I'm not an eloquent preacher like Mother Anna, but I feel called to speak my own mind today."

Codella looked at Haggerty and discreetly rolled her eyes. She wasn't fooled by Vivian's false humility. This was hardly the first time the churchwarden had been *called* to speak her mind since Wednesday, and there was no debating her effectiveness.

"In Matthew 18:20, the Lord said, 'Where two or three are gathered together in my name, there am I in the midst of them.' And I do feel the Lord here with me today. Don't you?" Vivian smiled into the crowded pews.

Several *amens* came in response. Many of them, Codella noted, came from the African American parishioners in the back rows.

"I feel Emily and Philip's presence as well. I hope you do too."

Vivian cast a knowing look from one side of the nave to the other. She raised her chin and acknowledged the choir in the loft. She turned to the acolytes and the deacon sitting behind her on the altar. "Never again will I feel the warm embrace of my dear, dear friend Emily, who was such a comfort to me in my darkest moments. Never again will I hear the impassioned voice of my cowarden, Philip. In times like these, I know from too many past experiences, we must call on our faith to give us strength to go on. 'Trust in the Lord with all your heart and lean not on your own understanding.'"

She paused. Heads nodded. "Emily and Philip did not die in vain," she declared. "God had a plan for them. God always has a plan. We may find his plan hard to understand or accept, but our faith compels us to accept it." Vivian's voice crescendoed to match her rising passion. "And we take comfort in the fact that their spirits remain with us." She shook her index finger in front of her face. "Remember, we share a collective memory. We are the body and soul of this church. We hold in our grasp the stories of our fathers and mothers, our sisters and brothers, our children and our friends. Today we add to our collective memory the stories of Emily and Philip, and we take comfort in the knowledge that so long as St. Paul's survives, they will still be with us."

Codella heard many more *amens*. Heads all over the church nodded as Vivian Wakefield stepped down from the lectern. On the other side of the central aisle, Susan Bentley's expression had not changed. Kendra Sturgis, however, was dabbing the corners of her eyes with a tissue. As Codella studied her, Roger Sturgis turned, and their eyes met, but he quickly looked away.

Anna Brookes spoke from the pulpit. "Thank you for those comforting words, Vivian." She turned to the congregation. "I invite family and friends of Emily and Philip to come forward now and share a memory or a prayer."

The first man who stepped to the lectern had a helmet of thick silver hair. "I'm Tom Farrell, and I've been a member of this congregation for twenty years," he began. "Emily Flounders was my friend. We taught together in the Bronx. When my wife died of cancer, I was, well, inconsolable. Emily lifted me up. 'Tom,' she said, 'you're coming to church with me this Sunday.' The music and sermon soothed me, and I still remember how Emily took me by the arm during the coffee hour and introduced me to everyone. The people I met that day have become my new family. I've come here every Sunday since. St. Paul's is a special place, and Emily was a special person. I'm going to miss her so much. God bless you and keep you, Emily."

He descended from the altar, and a brunette woman with a cast on one wrist climbed the three steps up. "Can you hear me?" She spoke so close to the microphone that her words were distorted. "All three of my children attended St. Paul's Sunday school," she began without introducing herself. The deacon moved swiftly from his bench on the altar and adjusted the microphone's position. "Emily was a saint. There's no other word to describe someone so good.

My youngest—Meghan—has autism, as many of you know. One day when she was little, she threw a terrible tantrum in Sunday school. I was so mortified I stopped bringing her to church. A month later, Emily called me. 'We miss Meghan,' she said. 'Why hasn't she come to Sunday school recently?' Emily already knew the reason, of course, but she begged me to bring Meghan back. 'We all have our bad days,' she assured me. That was Emily Flounders."

Codella let her thoughts wander as a steady succession of parishioners spoke, but she tuned back in when a heavyset man with a shaved head reached the lectern. "Philip Graves is one of the most brilliant men I've known in my life," he proclaimed in a slight British accent. "A Fulbright scholar. A tenured professor at Columbia. A man of impeccable character."

Codella watched a few heads nod. She saw Susan Bentley glance over her shoulder. Was she looking at Roger Sturgis? If so, Roger didn't look back at her. Vivian Wakefield sat expressionless.

"Philip was also a godsend to this church. He oversaw the altar renovation six years ago, and he devoted hours to helping Vivian set up the Weekday Beds program. Last summer, he faced down the objections to our Christianity-Islam study group with a cautionary lesson on despots throughout history who flourished in the fertile soil of xenophobia. I'll never forget his fascinating lecture. And more recently, he has been facing down our fiscal challenges, doing everything he could to keep our programs alive. Philip was Mother Anna's right-hand man. He loved the church, and I can't understand why anyone would do something so terrible to someone who did so much good."

Haggerty whispered in Codella's ear, "Oh, God, can this be over soon, please."

On the opposite wall of the nave, Muñoz was checking his phone.

Then Peter Linton stood, squeezed past his wife, and made his way up the side aisle. Roger Sturgis, Susan Bentley, Rose

Bartruff, and two other people Codella didn't recognize—the vestry members who hadn't attended the Wednesday-night meeting, she assumed—also stood and moved toward the lectern. Peter Linton leaned into the microphone. "We, your vestry members, cannot express the depth of our shock and sadness at the events that have touched our church." He blinked several times. "We've lost two important leaders, but we don't intend to let all their good works die with them." He made a fist in the air as if he were delivering an impassioned closing argument in front of a jury. "In their memories, we are more committed than ever to ensuring the survival and growth of St. Paul's. We grieve for our dear friends Emily and Philip, and we offer this prayer on their behalf."

Peter took a folded piece of paper from the breast pocket of his suit, opened it with jittery fingers, and cleared his throat. "Dear God, whose mercies cannot be numbered: Accept our prayers on behalf of your servants Philip Graves and Emily Flounders, and grant them an entrance into the land of light and joy in the fellowship of your saints; through Jesus Christ your Son our Lord, who lives and reigns with you and the Holy Spirit, one God, now and forever. Amen."

The church was silent as Peter and the others returned to their seats. Anna, still in the pulpit, stared into the congregation to see if anyone else wished to come forward. As Codella watched her, the rector's expression turned from calmness to confusion and then to apprehension. Codella followed her eyes to a figure moving up the central aisle. When the figure paused midway, Codella recognized him as Todd Brookes. As he resumed his walk up the aisle, Codella looked alternatingly from him to his wife. The rector's apprehension, she saw, was turning into fear.

When Todd stepped behind the lectern, Codella squeezed Haggerty's arm in a *get ready* signal. Her own hand moved instinctively to the Glock in her shoulder holster. Todd stared across the chancel at his wife. "Anna has spoken to you about Emily and Philip as a rector, but I know that her feelings for each of them were so much deeper." He turned to his wife. "Weren't they, Anna?"

Anna looked too stunned to speak.

"Let me tell you how she really felt about them."

Codella wondered if she was the only one who heard the menace below the false affection in his voice.

"Emily was warm and nurturing. She was like the mother Anna wished she'd had when she was growing up. Wasn't she, Anna?"

Codella's fingers tightened around the gun grip as she felt the sharp blade of Todd's words.

"And Philip," he continued. "He was like the father Anna lost when she was eleven." He paused, turning to his wife. "You were eleven, weren't you, sweetheart, when your father died suddenly?"

Anna's open mouth expressed her surprise—or was it horror?—but Todd seemed not to notice. He looked back at the congregation. "Philip was a strong and forceful father figure for Anna, and I know she mourns him deeply." His frown of concern struck Codella as calculated and insincere.

"But she still has me," he continued. "And she has all of you. And we can be Anna's collective right arm as we move forward and get through this terrible time together."

With that, Todd descended from the lectern and returned to the back of the church. Codella let out the breath she'd been holding and eased her hand off her gun.

CHAPTER 68

Codella, Haggerty, and Muñoz huddled outside the second-floor reception hall. "Go downstairs and keep an eye on anyone coming or going," Codella told Muñoz. As he turned to go, she looked at Haggerty. "I'll stand over here. You take the other side of the hall." She pointed. "I'm not sure what we're looking for, but let's hope we see it."

Codella stood just inside the doorway as parishioners streamed out of the church, then climbed the stairs and entered the hall.

A serving line had been set up on long rectangular tables covered with cream-colored tablecloths, and Codella watched as men, women, and children waited to fill their plates. They dug into homemade lasagnas, scooped meatballs, forked slices of ham and turkey, and piled tossed greens, bean salads, and cut-up fruit onto their plates.

The round tables from the Community Room downstairs had been arranged throughout the hall. On the raised stage at the back of the room sat the grand piano that Stephanie Lund claimed to have played on Wednesday night. A man now sat on the piano bench playing soft baroque music.

Codella leaned against the wall and lifted her phone out of her jacket pocket to see who'd phoned her during the service. She expected McGowan's name to stare back at her, but the number on the screen was unfamiliar. She played back the voice mail message.

"Got your lab results, Detective." She recognized Banks's voice. "The lipstick stain on that wineglass belongs to a woman. No surprise there. But the fingerprints and DNA don't match the samples from Rose Bartruff or Anna Brookes. They're not in the database either. So I guess that's a dead end. Sorry."

Codella returned the phone to her pocket and gazed around the reception hall. Her eyes landed on Rose Bartruff making her way through the food line. Rose had told the truth. She hadn't visited Philip Graves. She hadn't sipped wine with him.

Codella spotted the rector on the other side of the room. Anna might have been in love with Philip, but when Haggerty asked her if she'd gone to Philip's apartment, she'd told the truth. She hadn't sipped from that cup.

Then Codella saw Susan Bentley in a cluster of parishioners. The DNA on the wineglass from Philip's kitchen belonged to a genetic female. But Susan's DNA would have XY chromosomes. She hadn't touched that glass. She hadn't paid Philip a visit. So who had?

Vivian Wakefield stood against the far wall, engaged in deep conversation with a woman Codella had never seen before. Codella moved a few steps closer and saw that Vivian was holding a clear plastic cup. As Vivian listened to her companion speak, she raised the cup to her lips and took a sip of something. And when she lowered the cup, Codella saw the bold imprint of Vivian's lipstick on the rim. If any vestry woman had gone to Philip's apartment, Vivian had to be the one.

Codella approached the churchwarden and spoke close to her ear. "I need a word with you in private, Mrs. Wakefield."

"Now, Detective?"

"Now." Codella held her eyes.

Vivian excused herself from her conversation, set her glass on a table, and walked with Codella out of the reception hall. They stepped into a Sunday school classroom, and Codella closed the door behind them.

"What do you need so urgently that you have to interrupt me now, Detective?"

"The same thing I needed yesterday," Codella told her. "The truth, and I don't intend to leave this room without it. Since Wednesday, you've done virtually nothing to help my investigation, and you've done as much as you could to publically question my skills and integrity. Last night you—"

"Detective, this is hardly the time for you to defend yourself!"

"I'm not defending myself, Mrs. Wakefield. Last night you looked me in the eye and denied that you've lied to me, but I know that you have. Why did you go to Philip Graves's apartment before the vestry meeting on Wednesday?"

Vivian's face revealed nothing. "We're at a prayer service for the dead, Detective. I don't intend to be interrogated here."

"Would you prefer to speak to me at Manhattan North, Mrs. Wakefield? Because I can easily arrange a little ride for us uptown."

The muscles in Vivian's face stretched and pulled.

"Why did you go to see him, Mrs. Wakefield?"

Vivian still said nothing.

"You drank a glass of wine in his apartment," Codella said. "And that wineglass contains your fingerprints and DNA."

Vivian sighed. "All right, I went there. So what? It's not relevant to your case."

"That's for me to decide."

"It was just a vestry matter."

"What matter?" Codella demanded.

Vivian glanced at her watch. "Emily had mentioned to me that Philip asked her to send him all of last year's cemetery financial statements. She thought that was odd, and so did I. I figured Philip was trying to build a case against the proposal."

"And?"

"And nothing. I went there to see what he was up to. He served me a glass of wine. We sat on his couch for a few minutes. He wasn't forthcoming."

"But now you know what he was up to," Codella insisted. "And you need to tell me. What happened at that meeting during those fifteen minutes when Rose Bartruff wasn't in the Blue Lounge?"

Vivian didn't speak.

"Does this have something to do with Roger? Are you protecting him?"

"Why would I protect Roger?" asked Vivian.

"Because protecting him protects your niece. Come on, Mrs. Wakefield. I'm not a fool. You sent your best friend home that night so she wouldn't follow you into the kitchen. You wanted to talk to someone. I think it was Roger. I think you wanted a private conversation with him so badly that you sent your dear friend out into the garden. To her death."

"Stop!" Vivian's eyes were watery now, and her chin was trembling. "Just stop!"

Codella knew she had to continue. "But it's true, isn't it? Whether or not you realized what you were doing, you sent Emily to certain death."

Vivian's stony façade was crumbling.

"And you feel guilty about it. I see that," said Codella. "It torments you. So why don't you unburden yourself, Mrs. Wakefield? It's hard to live with a death on your conscience. What was so important that you had to speak to Roger alone? Tell me—for Emily's sake."

The churchwarden crossed her hands in front of her face. "I was just trying to save the church."

"From what?"

"From greedy people who put their own interests first. I didn't love Peter's cemetery proposal. I don't enjoy the idea of firing up our crematorium and burning bodies for every little funeral home in Brooklyn. It strikes me as ghoulish, in fact. But that and the additional burial plots to sell can save us financially without ruining the church. After Philip killed the proposal, he was going to sell our air rights to a developer who gave him the sweetest side deal."

Vivian removed a tissue tucked inside her sleeve and wiped her nose. "I don't expect you to understand my feelings, Detective. You don't seem to value beliefs and a higher power, so you can't even open your mind to the importance my church and my faith have for me. You probably look at me and think how simple I am. How silly to put my faith in the idea of God. People usually disparage what they don't understand. But I guess that's to be expected."

"Oh, you're really something, Mrs. Wakefield." Codella didn't hold back her anger anymore. "First you accuse me of being a bad cop, and now you try to make me out to be some religious intolerant. I don't judge other people's beliefs, but you're certainly judging me."

Vivian seemed not to hear these words. Her eyes were hard black diamonds. "You don't know what it's like to be moved around and ripped from the ones you love, generation after generation. You have no idea how difficult it is to hold onto an identity when you're never allowed to sink lasting roots."

Codella thought about her own past—shuttled from one foster family to another from the age of ten to eighteen. But Vivian, she knew, was talking about a legacy of enslavement—a far worse fate than she had suffered—and she remained silently respectful in the face of the churchwarden's righteous indignation.

"You intimated that I wasted your detective's time with a meaningless history lesson. Well, the history of this church is *my* history, and that's what I care about, Detective. My great-great-grandparents found their way north to freedom in New York City. I can't be sure of this—I have no records to prove it—but I believe they were residents of Seneca Village. Their daughter, my grandmother, was a founding member of St. Augustine's Chapel, the little church St. Paul's helped to build after the city repossessed the Seneca Village land in 1857. My grandmother worshipped at St. Augustine's Chapel all her life, and when she died, her ashes were placed in the St. Augustine's columbarium. After the stock market crash, St. Augustine's folded, and the mostly black parishioners were once again displaced. St. Paul's opened its doors to them, and my grandmother's ashes were moved to the St. Paul's columbarium."

Vivian paused and took a deep breath. Her expression reflected pain and exhaustion. "People have moved my ancestors too many times, Detective. And now it's up to me to keep them together. I'm the last one in my direct line. Someday—not that far in the future, I suppose—my ashes will be in the St. Paul's columbarium with my grandmother, my mother, and my son. And I don't intend to have my family uprooted again. This is my church, and I will make sure it stays where it is and what it is so long as I walk this earth. St. Paul's could never survive in the shadow of a forty-story luxury high-rise that displaces the neighborhood residents we've served for two centuries."

"What did you do about that, Mrs. Wakefield?" Codella asked quietly.

"I supported Peter's proposal," Vivian answered. "That's all. What more could I do?"

Codella watched every shift of Vivian's eyes, every movement of her fingers. "What did you discuss with Roger in the kitchen?"

"I told him I was disappointed in him." Vivian glanced toward the door. "Now I've answered your questions, Detective. I need to get back to the reception hall. I have an obligation to the parishioners right now."

Codella shook her head. "No. There's more."

Vivian's fingers found the gold cross around her neck. She lifted it to her lips.

"Come on, Mrs. Wakefield. You told me you're not a liar. Liars don't withhold information. Tell me what you know."

Vivian's fingers released the cross. Her lips parted. "I was angry with Roger. That's all."

"Did he tell you why he voted the way he did?"

Vivian said nothing.

"Did he tell you Philip blackmailed him into voting against the proposal?"

Vivian still didn't speak.

"Come on, Mrs. Wakefield."

The churchwarden finally nodded.

"And then what?"

"And then nothing," she asserted with vehemence. "Nothing happened. There was nothing to do. The vote was taken. It was over, and Philip had gone."

"Where did Roger go when he left you in the kitchen?"

"I know what you're thinking, Detective, but you're wrong. Roger didn't do this. Philip's death was just a convenient act of God."

"Bullshit, Mrs. Wakefield. It was no act of God, and you know that as well as I do."

CHAPTER 69

Anna had no appetite for food or conversation, and she didn't want to smile at or console one more parishioner. She slipped out of the noisy reception hall, ducked into the Sunday school classroom across the corridor, and pulled out a chair at the end of the long table farthest from the door. No one would bother her here.

She leaned forward and rested her head in her arms on top of the table, closed her eyes, and tried to clear her mind with every exhalation, but the image of her husband at the lectern and the sound of his mocking voice breached the barrier of her meditation: *Philip was a strong and forceful father figure for Anna, and I know that she mourns him deeply.* She did mourn him deeply, she thought now. She mourned the man she had wanted him to be.

Anna jumped when she opened her eyes and saw Detective Codella standing in the doorway.

"I didn't mean to startle you, Rector. May I join you?" The detective walked around the table and sat in the chair next to Anna's. She rested her arms in her lap and crossed one leg over the other. "I take it you needed to escape the crowd for a moment."

For more than a moment, Anna wanted to say. Codella stared at her, and Anna felt a growing urgency to speak. "I just can't do this anymore," she heard herself say.

"Do what?" the detective asked gently.

"Stay here. Be the St. Paul's priest—be anyone's priest. I'm not good at it. I don't know how to run this place. Everything's falling apart, and it's my fault."

Codella said nothing.

"Todd was right about one thing. I should never have gone to seminary. I'm not a decision maker. I let Philip make all the decisions. I—" She shook her head. "Never mind."

Codella continued to stare at her with impartial eyes. She and the detective were around the same age, Anna guessed, but they were nothing alike. The detective was forceful and determined—she would never have let herself end up in Anna's position. "I trusted him. I was wrong. I see that now."

"Tell me what happened, Rector. Tell me what happened in the fifteen minutes before the vote was taken."

Anna considered her words for a long time, and Codella did nothing to hurry her along. It occurred to Anna that police detectives were like priests in certain ways. Codella seemed to understand what Anna had learned in all her con-fessional conversations with parishioners—that sometimes you didn't have to bulldoze through people's walls to get to the truth; you could just sit back and wait for their ramparts to crumble on their own.

Anna felt her own resistance to the truth begin to crumble. "It was such a terrible scene."

"Terrible how?" Codella's voice was a whisper.

"Everyone was at each other's throats."

"Who?"

"All of them—except Rose. She'd gone out. She missed the whole confrontation over the cemetery proposal." Anna recalled Peter reviewing the plan and promising that it would increase church revenue and make a big impact on operating expenses. She could still hear Philip's contemptuous rebuke: "The church's operating expenses, Peter, or your own?"

"What are you talking about?" Peter had demanded.

"You know as well as I do why you want the cemetery expansion," Philip responded. "You've been cooking the cemetery books, and you've run out of ingredients. Bodies, that is."

Anna could still see Peter's blood-red face. "That's absurd!"

"Oh?" Philip pulled some documents out of a file folder in his lap. "Then look at this. The proof's right here. You didn't do a very good job of covering your trail." He turned to Vivian. "Peter's got a steady little stream of about five thousand dollars trickling into his pocket each month. Ask him."

Vivian turned to Peter with an "Is that true?" expression while Emily cupped her palm over her mouth. Susan winced as if the confrontation was physically painful to witness, and Roger just shook his head as Philip explained the mechanics of Peter's scheme.

Peter squirmed in his seat. He knew he was caught. "My wife lost most of her portfolio in the 2008 recession," he said. "And my firm didn't do well last year. And—" He started to cry.

"And you've been snorting away your paychecks, haven't you?"

"I'm—I'm sorry. I'm really sorry."

Philip made deliberate eye contact with each vestry member. "Peter has an addiction, and he's pilfered from the church. He's endangered our fiscal health."

"Oh, my God!" Emily Flounders exclaimed. "What are we going to do?"

"I believe we should forgive him and help him," Philip said. "That's what Christian people do." Philip stared at Anna with an expression that said, *Trust me.* He looked at the others. "Peter has been a member of this congregation for years. I think we should forgive his crime and let him pay back what he's taken—with interest, of course—over time. I've taken the liberty of drawing up a simple IOU that he can sign right now. Do we all agree?"

Then Philip turned to Anna. Everyone waited for her response. As soon as she nodded, the others agreed, and Philip passed the IOU to Peter. "We'll need your signature." He held out his Montblanc pen. "Emily, you brought your notary stamp?"

"Peter signed the IOU?" Codella asked.

Anna nodded. "He hardly had a choice."

"Why didn't you tell us about this sooner, Rector?"

"I was going to, but Vivian convinced me not to say anything. She felt that it would only damage the church's reputation."

Codella frowned. "Where is the IOU now?"

"In my office. In the file drawer on the left side of my desk, tucked in a hanging folder."

"And what happened after Peter signed it?"

At that point, Anna remembered, Philip held up a thick document and explained that he had a plan that would benefit the church rather than Peter's personal portfolio. "I've negotiated a very favorable sale of our air rights—with many givebacks for the church."

"Givebacks?" Emily asked. "What kind of givebacks?"

"He'll build a daycare center on the north side of the new high-rise," Philip explained, "and our parishioners will receive discounted tuition for their children."

Emily nodded with enthusiasm. She scribbled notes into her minutes.

"And there'll be a state-of-the-art playground adjoining the daycare center, and—you'll love this, Emily—it will be accessible from the second-floor Sunday school classrooms. That means children will be able to play there on Sunday mornings—with supervision, of course—while their parents enjoy the coffee hour after the service."

Emily's eyes had widened in delight, Anna recalled, until Vivian Wakefield interrupted Philip's laundry list of promises. "Three companies have been vying for our air rights, Philip," she said. "I want to know what this developer promised you personally to seal his deal."

"Nothing," Philip assured her as he looked toward Anna with another *trust me* expression.

"Well, I for one am not voting to sign that contract," Vivian declared. "Peter's proposal may have been self-serving, but it was also revenue generating, and we've got the votes to pass it. I suggest we get to it."

"Fine. Let's vote on the cemetery proposal right now," Philip agreed with a smile. "And next month—if the proposal doesn't pass—we'll vote on the air rights deal."

"So you took a vote?" asked Codella.

Anna nodded. "As soon as Rose returned. She abstained. She didn't feel it was right for her to vote after missing the whole discussion. I abstained too, of course. Emily voted against the proposal. I could tell Vivian was upset with her for that. But she was even more upset with Roger and Susan. She hadn't counted on them siding with Philip, and she stared at each of them as if they'd personally betrayed her."

Anna stood now, walked to the window, and stared down at the street. "I was as wrong about Philip as I was about Todd," she heard herself say. "The day of the meeting, he stopped by the church and warned me things were going to get ugly. He told me what Peter had done and that I'd have to have an iron stomach if we were going to save the church. He squeezed my hand and asked me to trust him even if it seemed as if he was being hard. He assured me he would make everything right. He told me Vivian was too stuck in the past to have a vision of how to take the church into the future. He assured me Susan and Roger would get on board with his ideas."

"And you put your faith in him."

Anna collapsed back into the chair.

"You loved him."

Anna looked down.

"You loved him," Codella repeated.

"Or I wanted to *be* loved by him." Anna hid her face in her hands. "Oh, God."

"There's nothing shameful about that."

"He was so kind and gentle, and I felt so alone with Todd." She realized her words sounded like a lame apology. "Todd is so angry all the time, so critical," she explained. "And I had a feeling he was probably seeing someone—"

Anna hugged herself as if the temperature in the room had plummeted. She stared at the long nicked table where fifth-grade students yawned into worn Bibles each Sunday morning. She bit her lower lip and remembered biting it three nights ago in the bathroom while Todd was sleeping—but he hadn't been sleeping, she was certain now. Anna covered her face in her palms.

"Anna." Codella's soft voice startled her. "Anna, I think you're asking yourself, did Todd kill Philip, and did he try to kill Stephanie?"

Anna looked up and nodded. Codella's hand moved to her shoulder. "Tell me why you think this. Tell me what you've been keeping inside."

And then Anna confessed. "Todd wasn't in our bed at five AM the morning after the vestry meeting. I don't know if he was home or not."

CHAPTER 70

Haggerty felt the vibration of his phone in his pocket. Claire's number came up on the screen. "Yeah?"

"You're still in the reception hall, right?"

"Right," he said. "Where have you been?"

"Talking to Vivian and the rector," she said. "I'll fill you in as soon as I can."

"Muñoz just called," he told her. "A judge granted us a warrant to search Todd's computer. Muñoz is waiting outside for someone to drive it over here."

"Good. That's progress," she said. "Can you find Roger Sturgis and bring him to the Blue Lounge?" Then she hung up.

Haggerty panned the reception hall and spotted Roger in a circle of parishioners with Vivian at his side. Vivian's hand was gripping Roger's arm as if she were trying to pull him away from the group. Haggerty rushed forward and grabbed Roger's other arm. "You're needed for a moment." He smiled.

Roger looked from Haggerty to Vivian. Vivian's eyes gave Roger a silent warning as Haggerty led him out of the hall.

Claire was waiting for them in the Blue Lounge, and Haggerty could tell that Roger wasn't happy to see her.

"Have a seat, Mr. Sturgis," she said, and Haggerty pushed him toward the long blue couch under the window.

Roger turned to her. "Are you going to let him handle me like that?"

"Detective Haggerty is a lot like you," said Claire. "He has a short fuse. I wouldn't test it if I were you."

"I don't have a short fuse," Roger insisted.

Claire pulled a chair right in front of him. "Drop the facade, Mr. Sturgis. I know what happened at that vestry meeting."

Roger said nothing.

"And I know what happened after too."

"Well I'm glad someone does," he said.

"You spoke to your aunt in the kitchen."

"She's not my aunt."

"All right, your wife's aunt. You went in the kitchen after the meeting. Tell me about your conversation."

"I thought you already knew. Didn't Vivian tell you?"

"I want to hear your version."

He shrugged. "She wanted to know why I voted to kill the cemetery proposal."

"Go on."

"So I told her."

"About the woman in Detroit?"

"And she slapped my face. Vivian can slap very hard."

"And then what?"

"Nothing." Roger smoothed his moustache. "That was it."

"Bullshit." Haggerty watched Claire rise from her chair and turn to him. "Detective Haggerty," she said, "see that Mr. Sturgis doesn't move from that couch until I get back."

CHAPTER 71

Codella climbed the stairs and returned to the second floor. The crowd in the reception hall was thinning, she noticed as she ducked back into the Sunday school classroom where Anna Brookes still sat. She took her seat next to Anna and said, "You have a chance to do the right thing, Rector. You can still be the strong leader of this church."

Anna shook her head. She was holding a wadded-up tissue, and Codella could see that her spirit was broken. Codella thought of all the times when she'd felt this helpless, sitting in a hospital bed and thinking that she wouldn't be able to make it through the next chemo treatment. "Listen to me," she said and pointed across the hall. "You have to find a way to reclaim your identity. You've got to find your inner strength. Everybody has to do that over and over again in their lives. Those people in that reception hall? They trust you. They love this place. It means something important to each of them. They come here because they're lonely, they need comfort, or they're afraid. And they find something here that keeps them coming back. Those are the people you need to think about right now. Tell me what happened *after* the meeting. Tell me what you know."

"I don't know who did this."

"I think you do. I think some part of you suspects but doesn't want to admit it. You have to find the part of you that knows the truth, and you have to tell me."

"How am I supposed to do that?"

"Be the person who went to seminary, Anna—the person who had a passion to lead. Stop being the victim of Todd or the weak little girl who needed to be loved by Philip Graves. Stand back and regain your perspective. What happened that night?"

Anna blew her nose, took a deep breath, and composed herself. "Right after Philip left, Susan stopped me in the hall and said she needed to talk."

"About what?"

"It wasn't clear to me. She said she was having terrible trouble sleeping, and she wondered if I could lend her a book on Christian meditation that I had on my office shelf. I got her the book, and she pulled me into the Community Room and asked me to recommend some passages that she could meditate on."

"And then what?"

"I flagged a few passages and got up to go—I was upset that I hadn't gotten to see Philip before he left, and I wanted to see him—but then she said she needed to confide something in me."

"What? What did she confide?"

"Nothing. She just told me she had a secret from her husband, and she wasn't sure whether to tell him. She wanted my advice. But that's all she told me."

"How long were you there with her?"

"About ten minutes, I'd say. Susan definitely wasn't her usual self. She seemed almost desperate to keep me there."

"When you did finally come out of the Community Room, where were the other vestry members?"

"Rose and Vivian were by the coatrack. Roger and Peter were standing in the Blue Lounge."

"How did they look?" asked Codella.

She watched Anna think for a moment. "As if they'd been fighting."

Codella stood. "I'll be back," she told the rector.

She returned to the Blue Lounge and motioned Haggerty into the corridor. As soon as he closed the door behind him, she whispered, "I don't think Todd Brookes killed Philip Graves."

"Who did? Roger Sturgis?"

"I don't know yet." She stared at the closed door and visualized Roger sitting on the couch. "But I'm going to try to get the truth out of him."

"Good luck with that," said Haggerty. "He's a hard son of a bitch."

"Yeah, but we all have a weakness, and I think I know what his is." She hoped she was right.

Haggerty touched her arm. "Go to it then," he said. "I'll be out here if you need me."

"No. I'll be fine here. You go help Muñoz execute the warrant." She touched his bristly jaw and watched him smile. Then she turned and entered Blue Lounge.

CHAPTER 72

Codella crossed the room and stopped five feet in front of him. "I know what happened, Mr. Sturgis."

"Oh, you do? Then tell me, please." Roger took a deep breath and let it out slowly. He'd been in tighter situations than this, he reminded himself. He had breached deadly minefields in Kuwait. He could certainly handle this minefield.

"You went outside to the garden."

"We all went outside, Detective."

"I mean *before* Graves died," said Codella. "You left Vivian in the kitchen—after you promised her you'd end things with the woman in Detroit."

He could feel her watching for his reaction. He didn't intend to give her one.

"You left Anna Brookes in the care of Susan Bentley, and you slipped outside to deal with your problem."

She continued to stare at him. Was she telling him what she *knew* or what she believed and needed him to affirm? "Should I be calling my lawyer right now, Detective?"

"That's up to you," Codella said, "but I hope it's not Peter Linton."

"I see you have a sense of humor." He smiled, but he felt no warmth inside.

Her eyes narrowed. Her stare made him feel exposed. "You loved that Monique woman, didn't you?" she asked, but the words, he could tell, weren't really a question.

That Monique woman. He bristled at the phrase.

"She meant something to you, something deep."

He rose to his feet. "Don't psychoanalyze me, Detective."

"Is that what it feels like I'm doing?"

"My personal relationships have nothing to do with Philip Graves's death."

"But I think they might."

Roger said nothing. He hadn't anticipated this.

"Your relationship with Monique wasn't just a simple affair. You paid her son's tuition. You sent him to a very nice and very expensive school in Grosse Pointe, Michigan. And you've been flying to Detroit almost once a week for years."

He shrugged.

"You went to see her on Thursday to break things off, didn't you? Vivian demanded that you do that immediately, or she was going to tell Kendra. Am I right?"

He crossed his arms.

"But when you got there, it wasn't so easy to say good-bye, was it? And you felt so guilty that you ended up at a car dealership. You bought Monique a car. A parting gift. Something she needed."

Roger held up his hands in a stop gesture. "That's enough!"

"Why is she so important to you, Mr. Sturgis?"

"That's none of your fucking business."

"Homicide is my business, and you were directly involved in a homicide—possibly two or three. You took your revenge on Graves for revealing your relationship with Monique Wilson. Monique. It's a pretty name, isn't it?"

Roger flashed an irate look. *Fuck you, Detective,* he wanted to say.

He could still hear Philip using Monique's name in the garden that night. *Kendra and Monique,* he'd said. *You've got yourself*

*a little harem of black beauties, don't you, Roger? You must really like
those tight black pussies.*

Then Roger had thrown the right hook that sent Philip to
his knees. Roger was about to walk away, but Philip was tougher
than he'd imagined. He got right back up and charged at Roger
like a linebacker determined to make a tackle. The two of them
were locked together when Peter Linton appeared behind Philip
with the shovel raised. The shovel came down at them so fast that
Roger barely had time to duck before it struck Philip squarely
against the skull, and Philip dropped in a heap. And then Roger
heard the gasp of Emily Flounders twenty feet away as she collapsed to the ground.

"What happened?" Codella insisted.

"I intended to rough Philip up," said Roger. "I intended to
give him a piece of my mind. But I never intended for him to die
that night. It wasn't me."

Codella pointed her index finger at him. "Don't even think
about moving from that couch, Sturgis. I'll be back for you."

CHAPTER 73

Peter Linton's wife was sitting at a table in the reception hall with two other parishioners, but Peter was nowhere to be seen. Codella searched every Sunday school classroom—including the one Anna Brookes was still in—and she even peered into the storage closet where she'd found the shovel on Wednesday night.

She returned to the first floor. He wasn't in the Community Room, the "dish room," or the kitchen. She entered the men's room and called out, "Mr. Linton?" but no one answered, and she saw no feet below the partitions of the stalls. She stepped into the nursery, but he wasn't there either.

Returning to the corridor, she listened for sounds, but all she heard was the murmur of the parishioners in the reception room above. She turned into the narrow hall that led to the rector's office. The door was unlocked, and she opened it, but Peter wasn't inside. She passed two other small offices—both empty—and came to a narrow staircase she'd never seen before. She studied the steps leading up and down and chastised herself for not completing her tour of the church with the rector on Wednesday night.

She climbed up the narrow stairs. They led to a passage behind the reception hall where the second-floor restrooms were located. She checked all the stalls in the men's and women's rooms. She glanced into the reception hall once more in case she'd missed him the first time, but his bald head wasn't there.

She took the stairs back to the first floor and gazed at the steps leading down. Her hand reached instinctively for her service weapon, but pulling a gun out of her holster in this place of worship felt strange, so she just kept her hand on the grip as she took one step at a time and listened.

When she got to the bottom, she saw a fast-moving blur out the corner of her eye. She turned, and the blur became a solid mass that crashed into her chest and stomach so hard that she crumpled to the floor, her eyes burning with tears of pain. Peter Linton stood above her with a wooden chair in his hands that she never would have guessed he had the strength to hold, let alone heave. He brought it down again, and she narrowly ducked its full force, but one chair leg landed squarely on her ankle. She heard a loud crack of bone and then her own voice howling in pain.

She took deep breaths as she drew her gun. "Get the fuck back, and drop the chair."

But Peter moved closer. His eyes were tiny pinpoints. The muscles in his face twitched. *You've been snorting away your paychecks,* Philip Graves had told him at the Wednesday-night meeting, according to Anna Brookes. Was he on something now?

"I'm not taking the rap for this," he said.

"For what?"

"For killing Philip."

"But you did kill him," Codella asserted. "You swung the shovel against his head just like you're swinging that chair at me. Why attack me if you didn't do anything?"

"It wasn't just me." His eyes darted from side to side as he continued to grip the chair so tightly that his knuckles were white. "They were all part of it—Roger, Susan, Vivian—"

"Maybe so," she interrupted, "but they didn't kill Philip. *You* did." She breathed in and out through her nose and tried to ignore the intensifying pain in her ankle. "You're the one who swung the back of the shovel blade into his head. And then you took the shovel upstairs and hid it in the supply closet. That was your mistake, Mr. Linton."

Peter was breathing heavily now. "You can't prove any of that."

"Why? Because you killed the one person who saw you with the shovel?"

"I don't know what you're talking about."

"Oh, yes you do." Codella kept her hands relaxed around the gun grip. "You didn't expect Stephanie Lund to be at the piano when you sneaked the shovel upstairs. She heard you pass by the door, and your eyes met, didn't they? Just for an instant. She didn't know you by name, so you were confident she wouldn't identify you to us that night, but you figured she'd tell us she'd seen someone up there, and you couldn't be sure she wouldn't identify you later if we showed her some photos. So you didn't take any chances. When you left the church that night, you went straight to her apartment and waited for her to get home, and then you tried to kill her. But you didn't quite finish the job. What happened that night, Mr. Linton? Did you lose your nerve?"

Peter's face was red with rage. The chair shook in his trembling hands. "I won't lose my nerve with you," he said between clenched teeth as he took a step toward her.

Codella aimed the Glock's muzzle straight at his face. "Step back and put down the chair right now."

"Or what?" Sweat rolled down one side of his pallid face. "Go on. Shoot me."

"I will if I have to."

They were in a dressing room, she observed in her peripheral vision as she continued to train the gun on him. To her left were two racks of blue-and-white choir robes. To her right was a full-length mirror, several chairs, and a water cooler. On the far side of the room, behind Peter, was a second narrow staircase that she supposed must lead to the choir loft. Her swollen ankle throbbed inside her boot like a beating heart. She could still hear the loud echo of her bone cracking. She imagined the jagged edges of that splintered bone, and she knew she couldn't rise. *Don't think about it*, she told herself. "Put the chair down," she said again, but her words only intensified Peter's agitation.

"I've got two thousand dollars in the bank. That's it. That's all." His voice quivered. "I can't pay my mortgage. My credit cards are maxed. I can't keep things going anymore. He took away the one chance I had to get my hands on some cash. Either you kill me, Detective, or I'll kill you and eat your gun myself, because I'm not going to prison. I've seen inside prisons. I know what they're like." He clenched his jaw and shook the chair over her head. "Pull the fucking trigger!" He kicked her broken ankle.

The pain was so intense that tears rolled down her face, and although her gun was still raised, her arms shook, and she could barely see through the blur.

"All right," Peter said. "We'll do it the hard way."

She saw him raise the chair higher and prepare to bring it down on her. She aimed her gun at the biggest target—his torso. She was breathing in to squeeze off the round when someone yanked the chair out of his hands from behind, threw it across the room, and applied a chokehold. The arms did not let go until Peter stopped thrashing like a wild animal. Finally, his body relaxed, his eyes closed, and he slid to the floor unconscious.

Roger Sturgis stared down at her. "Are you all right, Detective?"

"Yeah, but the motherfucker broke my ankle."

Roger helped her stand. "You've got handcuffs? Give them to me."

Codella leaned on the wall and reached in her pocket. Roger fitted the cuffs around Peter's wrists. Then he supported Codella to the steps. She sat and took out her phone to call Haggerty. While she waited for him to arrive, Roger told her, "I wasn't lying about one thing, Detective. I never intended for Philip to die. I went out there to talk to him—to reason with him. I'm not even sure whether Peter meant to kill him, or me, or both of us. I'd never seen him like that before."

Although Roger had just saved her, Codella was in no mood to cut him any slack. "Who carried Emily Flounders to her car?"

"I can't say for sure, but I assume it was Peter. After he knocked Philip to the ground, I told him he was on his own. I went inside, and he stayed out there for at least another five minutes. When I came back out with Susan—after Rose found Philip's body—Emily wasn't where she'd fallen. I suppose Peter thought it would look as if the deaths weren't related and that someone from outside the church had attacked Philip."

"Then he shouldn't have hidden the shovel in the storage closet."

Roger smirked. "And he's a criminal defense attorney."

"You're not clean in this, Sturgis," she said. "You lied to police officers. You withheld evidence."

"Philip invaded my life, Detective. He violated my privacy. You didn't have a right to those details."

"We could charge you with obstruction of justice."

"Go ahead," Roger said. "But the bastard deserved what he got."

"Maybe so, but that's not the point."

Peter shifted on the ground behind them. They turned when he started to groan. Codella made sure he knew where he was and who she was, and then she recited his rights until he cut her off with, "I know, I know. I'm a lawyer, for God's sake."

Haggerty arrived minutes later. She filled him in, and then she said, "Get me up these steps. There's one more person I need to talk to."

CHAPTER 74

Todd Brookes finally unlocked the door after the uniformed officers warned him to stand back because they were going to break it down. "What the fuck do you think you're doing?"

Muñoz stepped forward. "Mr. Brookes, I'm arresting you on suspicion of criminal possession of computer-related materials."

"What?"

"And we have a warrant to search your cell phone and computer."

"I don't get it."

Muñoz slapped the warrant into his hands. "Here, read it."

Todd stared at the document until Muñoz signaled to a uniformed officer who moved behind Todd and placed handcuffs around his wrists. Muñoz read him his rights.

"I want my lawyer!"

"I'm afraid your *lawyer*'s indisposed," said Muñoz. "He's been arrested for murder."

"I don't know what you think you're going to find on my computer."

"Documents, Mr. Brookes. Documents that prove you were helping Philip Graves blackmail vestry members of St. Paul's." He was done talking to the snide asshole. He looked at the officer who'd handcuffed Todd. "Sit him in the living room, and don't let him move or speak."

Todd jerked away from the officer. The officer grabbed him by the arms and slammed him against the vestibule wall.

"You have no right!" cried Todd.

Muñoz stepped close to his face and smiled. "I have every right," he said, waving the warrant. "*You're* the one who had no right."

CHAPTER 75

Haggerty brought Susan Bentley into the Blue Lounge, and she sat on the couch across from Codella. "What happened to your leg?"

"Never mind my leg," Codella said. "I want the truth from you. What was your part in the murder of Philip Graves?"

"My part? What do you mean?"

"You know what I mean."

Susan looked away. The guilty always looked away.

"We've just arrested Peter Linton," Codella said.

"So Peter's the one." Susan covered her mouth with her palm.

"You knew?"

"I hoped it wasn't." She lowered her gaze. "But I was afraid it might be."

"What did you do, Doctor? Confess it right now, or I'll find out on my own, and I won't be happy about it."

Susan bent forward and hugged her knees. "I didn't know anyone was going to die that night. You have to believe that."

Codella watched her close her eyes and shake her head as if she could clear all the bad thoughts out of her brain. "Roger came to me while Philip was putting on his coat," she said. "He asked me to keep Mother Anna distracted for a couple of minutes."

"And you didn't bother to ask him why?"

"I didn't need to," she said. "He told me. He wanted to speak to Philip outside. He was afraid Mother Anna would rush out there and interrupt them."

"And you agreed."

Susan nodded. "Roger voted against the cemetery proposal too. As I told you yesterday, I assumed he was in the same predicament I was in—that Philip had compromised him the same way he'd threatened me. How could I say no? It never occurred to me that he would kill Philip."

Codella propped her swelling leg on the seat of a chair. "You're a very intelligent person, Doctor. You weigh consequences and make important decisions every day. Are you honestly going to sit there and tell me that when you flipped over the body and saw the face of Philip Graves that night in the garden, it didn't occur to you that Roger had killed him while you kept the rector distracted?"

"Of *course* it occurred to me," Bentley exclaimed. "I never intended to aid and abet a murder. You have to believe that. As soon as I saw Philip's face, I sent Rose back to the parish house for the defibrillator, and while she was gone, I asked Roger how he could have done this—taken a life, I mean—but he swore he hadn't, and something in his voice made me believe him. Maybe I just wanted and needed to believe him." She shrugged. "And then Rose came racing back to us, and Roger whispered, 'For your sake and mine, say nothing, Susan.' He promised to explain everything later. And that was the last opportunity we had to speak privately that night."

Susan gripped both sides of her head. "*I'm not proud of myself*, Detective, but self-preservation is a very compelling motive for silence."

Codella felt like telling the doctor that she was more disappointed in her than in anyone else. She, after all, had experienced the consequences of people's impulsive decisions more intimately than all the others in this case. She at least should have shown some character. But Codella didn't have to say these words. She knew Susan was already thinking them and that she would only be pouring salt into open wounds.

"I wish I'd had the courage to tell you the truth right away," Susan acknowledged, "but truth has been my enemy for so long. Philip used my worst vulnerability against me. He threatened to humiliate me in front of the whole world, to destroy the life I'd fought to build. He had no conscience. And when the EMTs peeled the electrodes off his chest and he was beyond a doubt dead, it wasn't at all hard for me to conclude—in the harshest Old Testament sense—that he got what he deserved that night."

CHAPTER 76

After Susan departed, Haggerty brought Anna Brookes into the Blue Lounge. She sat on the couch and stared at the bag of ice he'd placed on Codella's ankle. "What happened to you, Detective?"

Codella ignored the question. "It's over, Rector. We've arrested Peter Linton for the murder of Philip Graves."

"Then Todd didn't—" She paused. "He's innocent?"

"He didn't kill Philip, and he didn't attack Stephanie Lund," Codella told her. "But he's not innocent. You see, he was helping Philip blackmail Susan and Roger."

"Blackmail them?"

Codella quickly explained without revealing the details. "We have officers executing a search warrant at the rectory right now. They've found evidence on your husband's laptop that he supplied Philip with the information Philip used to blackmail them."

Anna lowered her head.

"We've arrested him for criminal possession of computer materials. There will probably be more charges to come."

Anna shook her head. "I could have prevented all of this."

"You're a priest. You're not God. You can't control people," Codella reminded her.

"I could have stood up at the vestry meeting and said no. None of this had to happen."

Codella shook her head. "You're not without fault, but you didn't make Peter pick up a shovel that night. You didn't give Philip Graves the idea to blackmail members of the vestry. And you certainly didn't make your husband have an affair or do Philip Graves's dirty work."

"I should have seen Philip for what he was."

"You're human," Codella said. "You don't have the power to see into everyone's soul. You were needy, and he used that to his advantage. That doesn't make you culpable. We all have weaknesses. We make mistakes. Some of us realize our limitations, but others think they can get away with terrible things. They convince themselves that they won't be the ones who have to pay the price—but everyone pays the price one way or another."

Anna wiped her eyes.

"If you believe you caused these deaths to happen, then you're playing God, and I know you don't want to do that."

"No," Anna agreed.

"Too many people have tried to use this church to further their own agendas. Someone needs to remind them why they're really here."

"I'm not fit for the task," said Anna. "I've proven that."

"I disagree," Codella replied. "I think you've been sorely tested, but everybody gets tested. Everybody falls. The strong people get up." Codella leaned forward. She thought of her own past, the trials she'd lived through. "Listen to me, Rector. St. Paul's isn't in trouble because of its financial difficulties. You'll solve those. You've got people who can help you do that. But you need to step up now. This is your time. You've got to make a difficult decision. Are you going to throw in the towel, or are you going to lead?"

Then Codella took a deep breath and spoke the words she knew would resonate most with Anna Brookes. "You're a person of faith. You know there are two paths you can go down—the path toward God or the path away from God. I admit, I'm not a religious person, but I know that your faith has deep meaning for you, and I think that you might not forgive yourself if you walked away from that faith. These people need you, and quite frankly, I think you need them."

She paused. Anna was sitting taller on the couch and listening intently.

"Vivian Wakefield is right about one thing," Codella continued. "St. Paul's has survived for more than two centuries. This is not its first crisis. Look at this tragedy as proof of the resilience and strength of your community. The night I walked into this church, the first thing I saw was the wall right outside of this room, covered with the portraits of past rectors who've served this congregation. Your photograph is up there, and now you need to decide what you want your legacy to be. Are you going to leave in the wake of tragedy, or will you make a long and lasting impression?"

CHAPTER 77

Codella wouldn't allow herself to be carried out of the church. She walked between Muñoz and Haggerty, her arms around their shoulders, careful not to put any weight on the ankle that was broken. Beyond the church gates were news vans and as many NYPD vehicles as there had been three nights ago. Several reporters stood behind a barricade, and Codella recognized the one who had interviewed Vivian Wakefield for New York One. Across the street, she spotted McGowan double-parked in an unmarked car. Their eyes met. "Take me over there," she told Haggerty and Muñoz as reporters called out their questions to her.

Codella slid into the front passenger seat of McGowan's car while Haggerty and Muñoz waited on the sidewalk for her.

"So you got your man," he said flatly.

She nodded.

He narrowed his eyes. "You never fuck up, do you, Codella?"

"Everybody fucks up, Lieutenant."

His hands pressed against the steering wheel as if he were pushing away a wall that was closing in on him. "Shit, Codella. I could send you back to a uniform, you know."

Codella shrugged.

"But I don't give a shit anymore. You're someone else's problem now. I gave my notice yesterday. I'm retiring."

She turned to look him in the eye. So that was it, she thought. He knew he couldn't beat the charges against him, and he was throwing in the towel. That's why he hadn't crucified her on the spot when she went over the line. That's why Fisk had called her instead.

"I admit, I'm not blameless," he said. "But she asked for it—Jane Young. She wanted it."

"I don't need to hear the details, Lieutenant." She didn't *want* to hear them. All that mattered was that his claws had been clipped, his fangs extracted, and his venom drained. He couldn't hold her back anymore. She thought of all the times he'd handed her insulting assignments below her grade and capability, refused her requests to lead investigations, and thrown roadblocks in her path. Her mind regurgitated all the protests, rebuttals, and condemnations she'd wanted to hurl at him over the past two years, but all she said now was, "Good luck, Lieutenant."

Then she pushed open the car door and stepped out on her one good leg. Haggerty and Muñoz supported her back to the church gate where reporters were waiting to descend upon her. Codella was in no mood to answer their questions. All she wanted to do was make a statement and get to the hospital for an X-ray—because the sooner she got her ankle in a cast, the sooner she'd get out of that cast. She held up her hand to get the reporters' attention.

"Homicides happen everywhere. We all know churches aren't exempt. It only takes one or two self-serving people to ruin the lives of many. But St. Paul's has stood on this little footprint of land for more than two hundred years, and it's not going anywhere soon. Many people, including Rector Brookes, will pick up the pieces and continue the important work this church has been doing in the community for many years. And Detective Haggerty, Detective Muñoz, and I will help ensure that the guilty receive the punishment they deserve. That's all I have to say right now."

TWO WEEKS LATER

CHAPTER 78

Codella stood on her crutches in the bathroom doorway and watched Haggerty. "How is it that you take more time in front of a mirror than I do?"

"I want to look good for you." He combed his hair, but it was so curly that the effort had little effect. "You do realize, don't you," he said, "that this is the first time we've been invited to someone's apartment as a couple?"

"It's just Muñoz," she said.

"Don't let him hear you say that. He's very excited for us to meet his boyfriend."

They went downstairs, and Haggerty flagged a taxi on the corner of Broadway. They'd perfected the taxi routine. She got in while he held the crutches, and then he slid them in across the back seat floor and got in on the other side. She was going to be taking a lot of cabs in the next six weeks, but she wasn't going to think about that now. Three screws in the ankle were nothing compared to cancer, and she had the satisfaction of knowing that Peter Linton would pay mightily for those screws—not to mention everything else he'd done.

As they sped down the West Side Highway, it occurred to her that in all her years on the NYPD, she'd never had dinner at another cop's apartment. She told Haggerty this.

"It's because you're all work and no play, but that's going to change with me in your life." He grinned.

304 | Carrie Smith

Codella rolled her eyes.

"Hey, be nice," he said. "Remember, you're a little dependent on me right now."

"I'm not amused," she said.

"Not even a little?"

"Who do you think will do the cooking?" She changed the subject.

"My money's on his boyfriend," Haggerty said. "Unless we're having vanilla milkshakes, since that seems to be Muñoz's staple."

Ten minutes later, Muñoz opened his apartment door. His head was only inches from the top of the doorframe. Another man peered around him and held out his hand. "I'm Michael."

"You're the one we really came to see," Haggerty said as he shook Michael's hand. "Please tell us you're doing the cooking and not him."

The dining room window looked out onto the High Line, and from her seat at the table, Codella could see a steady stream of pedestrians walking by on the narrow trestle tracks of the trains that once had run to and from the meat-packing district. As they finished their meal, Codella told Michael that his food was remarkable, and Muñoz said, "That's not his only talent. He can do so much more with a computer than hack into people's personal data. Michael stays up all night and makes games for people to play."

"Todd Brookes should have played some of those games," said Haggerty, "instead of doing Philip Graves's dirty work. Then he wouldn't be in so much trouble right now."

"What's going to happen to him?" asked Muñoz.

"Well, the DA's definitely going to take it to a grand jury," said Codella. "And meanwhile, he's moved out of the rectory. Anna isn't in a very forgiving mood. And who can blame her?"

"Linton's wife wasn't in a forgiving mood either, I guess," noted Muñoz. "I was glad she refused to post bail for her husband. I'm inclined to believe she didn't know he was siphoning off the cemetery profits, but she had to know about his drug use. She should have insisted that he get help instead of covering for him. People who snort their savings away don't just wake up one day and pull themselves together."

Codella took a sip of her sparkling water and thought of Stephanie Lund. When Stephanie's parents finally took her off the life-support systems a week after Haggerty found her unconscious, she'd died within an hour. She became the third homicide for which Peter Linton was charged. The DA had already made up his mind to charge Peter in the death of Emily Flounders. "He's going to have a long time to think about what he did. What gets me is how stupid he was through the whole thing—hiding the shovel in the closet, moving Emily Flounders's body, taking the vestry minutes home in his briefcase. He managed to wipe his prints off the shovel, but he didn't wipe them off Emily's minivan. And on top of everything else, he used a phone app to charge his taxi ride down to Houston Street, a block from Stephanie's apartment. He's a criminal defense lawyer, and he left a mountain of evidence for the prosecution. The only thing he's not guilty of is the defibrillator malfunction. That was purely coincidental. We got the manufacturer's test results this week. The unit had a defective battery."

"What about Roger Sturgis?" asked Muñoz. "What do you think will happen to him?"

"It's up to the DA," said Codella. "He could face obstruction of justice charges, but he came to my defense, and that'll count for something. He'll probably work out a deal and be a witness for the prosecution."

"And Susan Bentley and Vivian Wakefield?"

Codella sipped her water again. "They won't be charged. They'll just have to live with their consciences."

Codella recalled her final conversation with Susan Bentley, when the vestrywoman brought a bouquet of flowers to her room at the Hospital for Special Surgery the day after her ankle surgery. "I know I have no right to ask you this, Detective," she said, "but did you include my past in your report?"

"There was no need to do that, Doctor," Codella assured her. "Peter's guilt is beyond a doubt, and I'm not in the business of telling other people's secrets gratuitously."

Susan pulled up a chair next to Codella's hospital bed. "You're the only person I've told my secret to. May I tell you something else?" She didn't wait for Codella's answer. "I hate that I've lived with so many lies. Just before I married Daniel—my second husband—I came so close to telling him the truth, but I was too afraid he would walk away. And after our marriage, there were so many times when I almost told him but lost my nerve or talked myself out of it. And then, after lying for so many years, how could I tell the truth? It seemed cruel and unfair. He would think our whole life had meant nothing."

As Muñoz and Michael cleared the table, Codella recalled what Susan had said after Peter's arrest. *I'm not proud of myself, Detective, but self-preservation is a compelling motive for silence.* Self-preservation, it occurred to Codella now, had motivated everyone who lied at the vestry meeting on Wednesday night. They had all tried to preserve something precious and irreplaceable. Susan had hidden the true self she knew the world wouldn't understand or accept. Roger had concealed the lover who made him feel whole. And Vivian had protected the institution that embodied her cherished and precarious family history. But self-preservation had motivated far more than sins of omission. This basic human instinct had driven a man to commit three murders. And it was the instinct that compelled her to hunt down killers over and over, to prove to the world—or maybe just to herself—that she had nothing in common with her father.

She looked up when Muñoz returned to the table holding a bottle of wine. "Who needs a refill?"

Haggerty held up his glass.

"I saw a key lime pie in your kitchen," Codella said.

"An Edgar's Café key lime pie." Muñoz smiled. "Because I pay attention."

As they ate the pie, Muñoz and Michael told the story of how they'd met. And Haggerty told how he and Claire had gone from precinct partners to enemies to lovers. An hour later, they said their good-byes, and Haggerty hailed another taxi. The traffic on the West Side Highway was light, and the car sailed uptown. The sky was clear. The lights on the George Washington Bridge sparkled in the distance. Codella took Haggerty's hand and rested her head on his shoulder.

"Hey," he said, "who do you think will get married first? Them or us?"

"Don't be a wise guy," she said.

"I'm serious."

"So am I. I'm not in the mood to think about anything that involves a church."

"That's no problem." He hugged her tightly. "There's always City Hall."

ACKNOWLEDGMENTS

It takes a village to build and sustain a book series, and I would like to thank the people who have contributed in large and small ways to the Claire Codella mysteries.

Thank you to my editor at Crooked Lane Books, publisher Matt Martz, for his invaluable feedback and willingness to give Claire Codella time to find her audience. Thanks also to Sarah Poppe and Jenny Chen for all their hard work. And thanks to all my fellow Crooked Lane Books authors for their camaraderie.

I've been fortunate to have the brilliant novelist SJ Rozan as a teacher and mentor for the past four years. Thank you, SJ, for not letting me go astray—and for keeping that red toothbrush light out of chapter 1.

Kathy Green, my agent, was the first person to recognize the potential of Claire Codella. Thanks for your loyalty, Kathy, and for pushing me to go in new directions.

Writing can be lonely without a group of smart and supportive fellow writers willing to read and reread your drafts. Jackie Freimor, Ilaria Papini, Lorena Vivas, and Jane Young, thank you for your honesty, insight, and encouragement.

The mystery community is full of kind and generous people, and I am grateful to so many of them for welcoming me into the fold. A special thank you to Wendy Corsi Staub, Robin and James Agnew, and Hank Phillippi Ryan.

I would like to thank many others as well for their help, support, and friendship: my sister Constance Smith, Sue Foster, Sue Lund, Jean Bowdish, Judith Oney, Chris Reilly, Carol Christiansen, Elizabeth Avery, Warren Hecht, Kurt Anthony Krug, V. K. Powell, Ben Keller, Paul Willis, Adria Klein, Sera and Tom Reycraft, Gabe Salzman, Sunita Apté, Loren Mack, and *all* my friends and colleagues at Benchmark Education Company.

I could not do any of this without the love and support of my wife, Cynthia, and our children, Cammie and Mattie. We are a family that believes in pursuing dreams. Dreams, we know, are what sustain us all.

And last but not by any means least, thank you to every reader out there who has embraced Claire Codella. Without you, none of this would be possible.